Almost Final Curtain

"These books are tightly plotted and contain enough intrigue and action to satisfy any reader of paranormals." —CA Reviews

"*Almost Final Curtain* is a fast-paced tale of young love, emotional strength, and figuring out who you are—even if it's not exactly human." —Book Fetish

"An enjoyable, fast-paced adventure that will leave readers looking for more." —Monsters and Critics

"An exciting fantasy that kept me reading until the very last page. Tate Hallaway brilliantly brought together the ideas of forbidden love, attraction, and pure mystery." —A Novel Menagerie

Almost to Die For

"Hallaway's witty, fast-paced series starter cheerfully details the horrors of magical war and high school life."
—*Publishers Weekly* (starred review)

"Hallaway throws her expertise into the popular teen vampire genre with an original twist that adds witches and vampire servitude to the mix. . . . Fast moving, filled with fun, self-depreciating humor, this sparkling teen read features plenty of attitude."
—Monsters and Critics

"Put me under its spell and didn't let go! A great story and characters I can't wait to meet again."
—*New York Times* bestselling author Rachel Caine

continued . . .

"Ms. Hallaway deftly handles the life of a teenager and weaves in paranormal elements to make for an exciting story that'll captivate you. . . . *Almost to Die For* will hook you with its deft handling of teenage angst and supernatural problems, and leave you anticipating a sequel."   —Fresh Fiction

"Take *The Princess Diaries*, sprinkle on some *Charmed* and a dash of *Twilight*, and you're ready to enjoy *Almost to Die For.*"
                                                                     —*Justine*

"[It will] keep you turning the pages not because you want to get through it, but because you can't help yourself. . . . Hallaway gives readers young and old what they want from a YA romantic heroine."
                                                    —The Green Man Review

"Ana is a fighter and her story follows many twists and turns that I wasn't expecting. The dialogue is quick and the settings are vividly described. The anticipation of which guy she will choose and who is best for her is fun, and I am looking forward to the next book."
                                                                 —Page Turners

"Filled with plenty of teen angst and high school mishaps, this novel is on par with the many other vampire series out there . . . well written and fun to read."   —*Library Journal*

Praise for Other Novels
by Tate Hallaway

"A fast-paced, hilarious paranormal romance . . . the story captured this reader from the very first page, and is a must read for paranormal romance fans." —The Romance Readers Connection

"Well paced and lightly written, mixing magic, romance, and humor to good effect . . . perfect for lazy summer-afternoon reading."
                                                               —Love Vampires

"This paranormal romance overflows with danger, excitement, and mayhem; however, whenever things become too stressful, a healthy dose of irony or comedy shows up to ease the way. Tate Hallaway has an amazing talent for storytelling."

—Huntress Book Reviews

"A truly enjoyable read if you like a jaunt into the paranormal . . . and enjoy humor as well as the more serious side of life!"

—WritersAreReaders.com

"What's not to adore? . . . Tate Hallaway has a wonderful gift."

—MaryJanice Davidson, *New York Times* bestselling author of *Undead and Unfinished*

"Tate Hallaway kept me on the edge of my seat . . . a thoroughly enjoyable read!"

—Julie Kenner, *USA Today* bestselling author of *Demon Ex Machina*

"Will appeal to readers of Charlaine Harris's Sookie Stackhouse series." —*Booklist*

"[Hallaway's] concise writing style, vivid descriptions, and innovative plot all blend together to provide the reader with a great new look into the love life of witches, vampires, and the undead."

—Armchair Interviews

The Vampire Princess Novels by Tate Hallaway

Almost to Die For

Almost Final Curtain

Almost Everything

Almost Everything

A *V*AMPIRE PRINCESS NOVEL

TATE HALLAWAY

NEW AMERICAN LIBRARY

New American Library
Published by New American Library, a division of
Penguin Group (USA) Inc., 375 Hudson Street,
New York, New York 10014, USA
Penguin Group (Canada), 90 Eglinton Avenue East, Suite 700, Toronto,
Ontario M4P 2Y3, Canada (a division of Pearson Penguin Canada Inc.)
Penguin Books Ltd., 80 Strand, London WC2R 0RL, England
Penguin Ireland, 25 St. Stephen's Green, Dublin 2,
Ireland (a division of Penguin Books Ltd.)
Penguin Group (Australia), 250 Camberwell Road, Camberwell, Victoria 3124,
Australia (a division of Pearson Australia Group Pty. Ltd.)
Penguin Books India Pvt. Ltd., 11 Community Centre, Panchsheel Park,
New Delhi - 110 017, India
Penguin Group (NZ), 67 Apollo Drive, Rosedale, Auckland 0632,
New Zealand (a division of Pearson New Zealand Ltd.)
Penguin Books (South Africa) (Pty.) Ltd., 24 Sturdee Avenue,
Rosebank, Johannesburg 2196, South Africa

Penguin Books Ltd., Registered Offices:
80 Strand, London WC2R 0RL, England

First published by New American Library,
a division of Penguin Group (USA) Inc.

First Printing, February 2012
10 9 8 7 6 5 4 3 2 1

LIBRARY OF CONGRESS CATALOGING-IN-PUBLICATION DATA:

Hallaway, Tate.
Almost everything: a vampire princess novel/Tate Hallaway.
p. cm.—(Vampire princess; 3)
ISBN 978-0-451-23566-4 (pbk.)
1. Teenage girls—Fiction.   2. Vampires—Fiction.   3. Witches—Fiction.   I. Title.
PS3608.A54825A77 2012
813'.6—dc23   2011033388

Set in Minion
Designed by Alissa Amell

Printed in the United States of America

PUBLISHER'S NOTE
This is a work of fiction. Names, characters, places, and incidents either are the product of the author's imagination or are used fictitiously, and any resemblance to actual persons, living or dead, business establishments, events, or locales is entirely coincidental.
    The publisher does not have any control over and does not assume any responsibility for author or third-party Web sites or their content.

For Shawn and Mason, FTW

Acknowledgments

Thanks go to my fabulous and stalwart editor, Anne Sowards, and my awesome and tireless agent, Martha Millard. My poor writers' group, the Wyrdsmiths, sees less and less of my novels as my deadlines grow shorter and shorter, but I couldn't survive without their constant moral support. Particularly critical are the Wednesdays with the Women of Wyrdsmiths—Eleanor Arnason and Naomi Kritzer—at the Coffee Grounds in St. Paul that help keep body and soul together. Speaking of Naomi, thanks to her and to Sean M. Murphy for their usual, though no less amazing, oh-my-god-I'm-running-up-to-deadline critiques. The book would be much less than it is without them.

My family, too, deserves praise, especially my son, Mason, who cheers me deeply every time he reads out loud a sentence from one of my Ana books with shouts of joy, like he does with all his other favorite books. My partner, Shawn Rounds, I should tell you, is, in all honesty, mostly responsible for all the cool plot twists and revealing character moments. I just write the words down. She makes them sing.

*Almost
Everything*

Chapter One

You'd think one of the perks of being half vampire would be a resistance to weather. No such luck.

Or, considering that I, Anastasija Ramses Parker, am the vampire princess of St. Paul, you'd think a title like that would come with some supercute servant boys waving fans over my body and feeding me ice-cold bonbons.

Again, this doesn't seem to be happening.

Instead, I'm melting because my college professor mother doesn't believe in air-conditioning.

Minnesota summers are surprisingly hot and humid. I kind of forget how awful it can be until the first ninety-degree day with eighty-percent humidity hits St. Paul.

The oppressive stickiness in our house sent me out to the porch swing. At least there, with the brutal July sun finally sinking into brilliant orange and lavender streaks, there was a slight breeze.

It was too warm to even read. I pressed the sweating glass of lemonade into the hollow between my breasts and pushed a strand of hair from my eyes. Other girls complained about how the weather made their hair frizzy and unmanageable, but for me the problem was sticky flatness. This morning I'd tried to pull my past-the-shoulders deep black hair into one of those fancy French braids, but by this point in the day, bits kept slipping out and clinging to my neck and face.

A few gawker pedestrians strolled down the broad streets of my Cathedral Hill neighborhood, trying to act casual as they surreptitiously peered through the lighted windows into the Victorian-era mansions that lined our block. I guess our house, at least, suited my supernatural rank. With its ivy-covered brick and castlelike tower, it looked like the sort of place you might expect a vampire to live.

I just hoped no one I knew came by, since I was sprawled limply in my shortest shorts and last year's Hello Kitty tank top that had half the sequins missing.

A bicyclist whizzed by, the tires clicking, and I wondered what kind of health-crazed nut could work up the enthusiasm to exercise on a day like this. I would have given him the finger out of spite, but I couldn't muster the ambition to lift my hand. Even the flowers in the garden drooped. Tall stalks of lupine bent low, depressed by the humidity. Cicadas buzzed angrily in the trees as I pushed the swing with the tip of my toe to use as little energy as possible.

Okay, so maybe it wasn't the cicadas that were pissed off. I frowned darkly at the sunset.

Mom was inside, setting a table for "tea" in the sitting room. I could hear the good china clattering through the open window, and the noise set my teeth on edge. In about an hour, maybe less now that the sun was setting, Elias would rouse himself from a dead sleep, and the farce—I mean the *festivities*—would begin.

When I offered to let my ex-betrothed vampire boyfriend crash in the basement, I kind of expected it would be short-term. I really thought my mom would object, first of all. Mom is the Queen of Witches, and, even though I'm half vampire, witches and vampires don't get along. In fact, they usually hate each other.

A lot.

I shifted the glass to let the cool droplets of condensation run onto my skin. It was pale, like that of my vampire father's people. Even in the middle of summer, my legs stayed milky white. I didn't even get freckles. I was envious of the girls I saw at Lake Josephine with their golden bronze skin and Norwegian natural blond hair. The only benefit I derived from inheriting my dad's complexion seemed to be that I also rarely had to deal with acne.

Even before I realized my dad was a vampire, I knew I didn't look much like my mom. She was all hips and mousy blond curls, and she wore glasses. Despite my bookish bent, I'd never needed vision correction.

Dishes clanked through the open window, and I heard the sound of a mixer grinding. I shook my head. I would never have imagined it would be like this. Not only was Mom putting up with Elias; she was cooking for him.

For the past two months, I'd had to endure this increasingly bizarre evening ritual. Mom never used to cook for me. I mean, sure, she might open a can of this and mix in a can of that. On special occasions, like my birthday, she might pull out all the stops and make the one from-scratch meal she did well and burn me a cake, but lately it'd been like Rachael Ray around here, with food processors and clarifying butter. For instance, tonight she made some kind of freezer cheesecake that took her an hour and a half to prepare. And the result might actually be edible.

And did I mention that Elias is a vampire? He doesn't even need to eat. All this effort for a guy who doesn't even eat! How weird is that?

Wait—it gets stranger.

After Elias gets up every night, we all sit around and ... chat—in the nice room, with the good dishes and the straight-back chairs.

It's awful.

I guess I hadn't anticipated how much my mother needed the company of someone who could remember Kennedy's assassination and other ridiculously old, antiquated stuff.

I mean, at first, I was really happy that Mom seemed willing to sit down with a vampire at all. As I said, there's been a war going on between vampires and witches since the beginning of time. But then Mom and Elias started getting all nostalgic and friendly. Pretty soon, I found myself pushing cranberry sauce around my plate while listening to enthusiastic debates about the women's movement and economic busts and bubbles and other completely incomprehensible things that happened before I was born.

Worse, when I tried to change the subject to something vaguely twenty-first century, I got shushed. Shushed!

My mother and my kind-of boyfriend *shushed* me as if I were some kind of annoying toddler.

WTF!?

Running my palm over my forehead, I wiped again at the sweat and that damn uncooperative hair. A car drove by, snippets of *Prairie Home Companion* blaring through its open windows. I heard something about powder-milk biscuits as it turned the corner. Goddess, could this day get more irritating?

Especially given that two minutes ago, while letting me taste test the cheesecake, Mom admitted something I already suspected: she had a crush on Elias.

Okay, what she actually said was, "I'm working on a way to keep Elias around permanently. It's good having him here." But for my mom, the I-never-got-over-the-seventies, bra-burning feminist, that was pretty much a declaration of true love.

I so did not want to go back inside the sweltering house and pretend to enjoy cheesecake, knowing that my mom was trying to conceal googly eyes for my sort-of boyfriend. Not that Elias has been particularly boyfriendy lately.

Now that we aren't officially betrothed and he lives in the basement, we don't court. We used to have this wonderful weekly ritual where he'd come over and sit in the pine tree outside my window and we'd talk. Sometimes he'd bring flowers. Other times we might go up onto the roof and stare at the stars in companionable silence. He wrote me poetry.

Then my dad called off the betrothal and exiled both of

us for daring to stand up to him. You know those TV shows with all the crazy kings of England? That's kind of my dad. Of course, it goes both ways. I did nearly put his eye out with a white-hot magical talisman later, but he was trying to kill me—again.

My family totally puts the *dis* in dysfunctional.

I miss Elias's attention. Now I'm lucky if he gives me a wave before he settles in to American History 101 with Mom. I think maybe he's all broody because of the exile. But he should be over it by now. It's been months.

Jealous much?

Yeah, totally. I guess you always want the one you can't have, right? Because it's not that I'm hurting for boy attention. I have two other guys texting me on a regular basis, trying to get me to commit to a date.

First is my other ex, Nikolai Kirov. He's got those classically smoldering looks you get when you're half Russian, half Romany, and all rock star. Seriously, Nik's band, Ingress, has been getting tons of local radio play. Yet I went down that road before, and let me tell you, it's not easy being the dorky, high-school-age girlfriend of the lead singer in a popular college band. Talk about feeling shushed; only it's more like being shut out completely when the gaggle of groupies descends.

The ice in my glass clunked as it melted. The little air that stirred brought the sharp scent of lighter fuel burning on someone's barbecue grill. I sighed. If I was being honest, a lot of the problems I'd had with Nikolai's fame were my fault; I never felt cool enough to hang around with him. I felt most comfortable with people who made obscure references to Star Wars movies or Lord of the Rings novels, and people who got excited at the idea of new *Doctor Who* episodes and extra work in precalculus—in other words, nerds.

Nik was also the junior vampire slayer of the region, which gets messy given my title—you know, vampire princess.

Yeah, me, a *princess*—lying here in my ragged, sweat-soaked clothes. You can see it, right? Glamour, thy name is Anastasija Parker.

Anyway, trust me as far as me and Nik—it's too complicated by far. Romeo and Juliet had it easier.

Speaking of theater, the other guy vying for my attention is Matthew Thompson, former hockey star turned lead actor. See, ever since we did the spring play together, Thompson has been trying to get me to date him. He's nice enough, I guess, though we come from different cliques at school. He's a popular jock—the homecoming king type—and I'm . . . well, I'm a theater geek with two differently colored eyes and a reputation as a spooky witch, and I'm an honor student.

Different worlds.

Especially since Thompson is a mundane. If I told him I couldn't bring him over to the house because a vampire lives in the basement and Mom practices True Magic, he'd think I was kidding. That made social situations kind of dicey. Oh, yeah, and when I was discovering I was the vampire princess, I kind of licked blood off his face after a floor hockey accident in gym—in front of everyone.

Awkward.

You wouldn't think Thompson would be all that interested in me, given that particular moment in our history, but, thanks to the forget-me spell Bea had cast, he remembered it as a kiss. He thought I'd been so sorry to see him hurt that I'd risked crossing our social cliques to peck him gently on the cheek.

I still knew the truth, though.

So, as far as I was concerned, my options were limited. And the least complicated one would rather talk ancient history with my mom.

It sucks to be me.

"Elias! Good to see you. Come sit." I heard Mom's singsong greeting through the window. Then she shouted to me, "Anastasija Ramses Parker, stop sulking! Time for tea!"

The full-name treatment, eh? Just for that, I'd sit here for a few extra minutes.

I crossed my arms in front of my chest and stared down the street. Three people were out walking, heading in my direction. I probably wouldn't have given them any notice except that one of them was wearing a cloak.

Did I mention it was ninety degrees in the shade?

I sat up and watched the approaching trio with new interest. Was there a vampiric jaunt to their step? Who else would be so impervious to the weather? Because, even though I wasn't, *full* vamps were.

Draining the watery lemonade in a gulp, I set the empty glass underneath the porch swing. With the sun setting behind them, they presented only a shadowy silhouette. The cloak-wearing figure was shorter, and I thought there was something protective and Praetorian Guard–like about the way the other two flanked him. Yes, they definitely trailed one precise step behind, their heads swiveling every so often to scan the area for threats.

The streetlamps lining the boulevard flickered on.

They were less than half a block away now, and I could make out more details. Dark, unruly curls framed the shockingly pale face of the leader. Despite the whiteness of his skin, his features suggested to me that he might be Latino. The guard on the left was black, though his flesh had that strangely drained hue of a vampire. A gold earring flashed in one ear, and he had thick, puffy hair and muttonchop sideburns that reminded me of Samuel L. Jackson in *Pulp Fiction*, that Quentin Tarantino movie. His partner was the palest of all three of them. His long straight hair was tied back neatly at the nape of his neck, but otherwise he bore no resemblance to John Travolta's character in the same movie. In the artificial light, his auburn hair glowed almost bloodred, and his sharp, cruel expression reminded me of a gentleman pirate . . . or something much worse. I found myself the most wary of him. I stood up.

"Ana, I'm about to cut the cake!" my mom shouted through the open window. I jumped. I'd been completely absorbed watching the strangers, who were now standing at the gate looking directly at me. "Are you coming in?"

"In a minute," I answered distractedly. I heard my mother clucking her tongue and making excuses for "moody teenagers" to Elias.

I moved to the edge of the porch steps and peered nervously

around a column at the men at the end of our sidewalk. The leader had his hands on the gate, but he didn't push it open. I could see now that he looked to be close to my age or younger. There was the hint of stubble on his chin, but his cheeks still retained a lot of baby fat—in a cute way. In fact, when he smiled at me, he looked downright charming. "Anastasija Ramses Parker?"

Wow, I'd heard my full name twice in ten minutes.

But why did I get the feeling that hearing it now meant I was in a whole lot of trouble?

"Yes, that's me," I agreed cautiously. "Who are you?"

It was the mean-looking guard who answered. Even his silken, Cajun-accented voice gave me the creeping chills. "I present His Royal Highness, Luis David Montezuma, prince of the Southern Region."

A vampire prince? Oh crap.

"Ana?" The screen door squeaked, and Elias stepped out onto the porch. "Your mother wants . . ." He stopped the moment he saw Prince Luis and his entourage at the end of the walk. I felt a breeze and, in a blink, Elias stood protectively in front of me.

His movement made the redhead snicker.

The prince shot his guard a dark look. To me, he put on that smile I'd found so charming a moment ago. However, now it seemed more like a politician's—a bit oily and forced. "We have traveled some distance, Princess."

I got the hint, but I wasn't sure I wanted to invite Luis and his goons in. Besides, why was he here with me and not in the underground cave courts of my father? I tried to catch Elias's eye so I could ask him what to do, but he was busy staring menacingly at his counterparts.

"For Goddess' sake, what is going on out there?" my mother shouted. "Come in and have tea!"

I knew that the stalemate had been broken with Elias's soft curse and the chuckle of the goons, who reached around the gate to let themselves in.

"Don't mind if we do," said Luis with a grin.

Chapter Two

A nd I thought tea was awkward before.

Mom fumed over having accidentally invited three new vampires into her house. She'd tried to kick them out right away, but Elias had pulled her aside and whispered something about royalty and duty. It hadn't calmed her much. She flounced off to the kitchen to get a few more plates and cups for tea. I could hear her angry mutterings about upping the wards as we directed the prince and his entourage into the sitting room.

Luis swept the cloak off his shoulders and tucked it under his arm. The shirt he wore was a rich indigo color and clearly pure silk. His pants, more correctly classified as slacks, had been tailored to a perfect fit. Everything from his ivory-studded cufflinks to his polished black shoes smelled of old money.

Meanwhile, I was acutely aware of the tiny holes in the threadbare, too-tight fabric of my tank top that, no doubt, showed off my contrasting-color sports bra. The tiny hairs I hadn't shaved off my armpits this morning prickled in the heat. I bet Princess Kate never had days like this. She'd at least have some kind of awesome hat.

Thank the Goddess for Elias. He swept in, took coats, and made everyone take places around the table. He pulled out my chair for me, which was nice, but it made me feel especially grubby. If I'd known visiting dignitaries would be dropping by, I'd at least have put on a better shirt. Or pants! At least no one would see my naked legs under the table.

We now sat in the stuffy, dusty room staring silently at one another.

I should probably have said something dignified and welcoming here, but all I could think of was that most of my "gilty pleasure" bronze nail polish was half-chipped and missing. So I took the opportunity to look around at anything other than Prince Luis and his looming goons.

The room, at least, suited the prince. It was expansive, with oak flooring and pressed tin on the high ceiling. Unlike the rest of the house, this room was sparsely decorated and neat. It was like that because we almost never used it. Mom and I had inherited our house from my grandparents, and it was much too large for the two of us. Before the tea ritual with Elias started, we kept this room shuttered. It still had lace doilies and pale blue painted dishes on the plate rails that were vestiges of my grandparents' lives. Odder still, there were no books anywhere in the room, not even a half-finished paperback tucked into the windowsill or resting open, spine-bent on a coffee table. That was damn near unnatural for a house with two word nerds like

Mom and me. I always felt like a guest in this part of my own house.

Having made their tour, my eyes returned to Luis, who was smiling patiently at me. Expensive cologne hung in the air, and I had to hold back the urge to sniff my underarms. I couldn't even exchange glances with Elias since he refused to leave my side, even to sit. He stood behind my chair like a sentry. Though my back was to him, I could picture the formidable image Elias presented. Even in his simple black T-shirt and jeans, he was lean, hard, and infinitely dangerous—even among his own kind. If he was angry or spoiling for a fight, his eyes would turn yellow and catlike, and his fangs would drop. Otherwise, he'd measure them with ice-cold, utterly ruthless gray eyes. His black hair was cropped short, his face clean shaven, and everything about him was perfectly crisp and precise.

The Samuel L. Jackson clone and red-haired guy likewise stood at attention behind Luis. Their eyes watched for any movement from Elias. The tension was thick.

Mom, meanwhile, paced around like a caged animal, ostensibly setting cups and forks in front of the new guests' places.

I desperately wanted to know what Luis expected from me, but we seemed to be following some kind of protocol I didn't know. Perhaps we would start talking when Mom finished fussing. Not knowing what else to do, I folded my hands in my lap and tried to think princesslike thoughts.

That was hard since I was sweating in a very unladylike fashion. My hair had stuck to my face again, despite the fan's humming from its perch on the windowsill. Occasionally, I'd feel a bit of night air on my forehead, but it disappeared too quickly to offer much relief.

"Who are you, again?" Mom asked bluntly, plunking an extra plate down in front of the vampire prince and glaring at the two goons standing in her way. Mom, like me, wore as little as possible because of the heat. She had on a white spaghetti-strap top and cutoff jeans. "And why are you in my house?"

"You invited them in," Elias said quietly, though unnecessarily.

Mom cast him a dark, angry look. "Well, I didn't know they were out there, did I?"

Luis raised his hand with a gentle smile. "It's quite all right. The Queen Mother has every right to be properly introduced. My name is Luis Montezuma, and I am the prince of the Southern Region. I've come seeking restitution for a grave loss." At this, Luis turned to stare pointedly at me, as if I should have some clue as to what he meant.

Only I didn't.

Plus, I found myself struck dumb by the sudden revelation, in the low glow of the electric lamplight, that Luis had one green eye and one brown.

He had two differently colored eyes.

Just like me.

Did that mean we were the same in other ways? I'd never met another half vampire. Were his differently colored eyes accidental or an indication that he was a dhampyr too?

Luis cocked his eyebrow at my confusion. "Did you not release Khan from her betrothal, Your Highness?"

Oh, um, who? Had I? I shook away my questions about Luis's eye color and tried to remember. A vague memory surfaced of a vampire sneaking into my school last year and asking me to cancel her betrothness or whatever, and Elias and my dad telling me there'd be serious fallout for what seemed like such a common-sense decision. Come to think of it, her name *was* Khan. "Uh, yeah," I admitted hurriedly; I had a bigger question on my mind. "Hey, like, are you a dhampyr?"

Everyone on Luis's side of the table looked shocked, as if maybe I'd used some kind of racist slur. Luis's cheeks colored. Since I couldn't catch Elias's eye, I shot a look at Mom. She shrugged. "Dhampyr" was the only word we knew for what I was: half vampire/half witch.

"About Khan . . . ," Luis prompted quietly. It was clear I was supposed to drop the subject.

So I did. I guessed being a dhampyr wasn't something to be proud of in the Southern Region, if, in fact, that was what he was. I could feel myself blushing now too, but I managed to stammer out something I remembered about Khan. "She was in love with some other guy. What else was I supposed to say?"

Luis gave me a highly skeptical look. "What does love have to do with confarreatio?"

"I don't know what that is."

Everyone on that side of the table looked completely stunned. Even the two otherwise immobile guards actually exchanged a look. I tried to look at Elias, but his gaze and expression remained unchanged.

"What do you think betrothal ends in?" Luis asked.

"Marriage?" Didn't that seem like the obvious answer?

"Oh, I see why you released Khan. You're one of the modernists."

My mom snorted and started cutting the cheesecake. "We're full of those up here. After our confarreatio, I made Ramses marry me in front of a judge." She handed me the biggest slice with a wink.

Luis shook his head, frowning deeply at my mother for a moment. Then he shook his head as if dismissing her from his thoughts. To me, he said, "Your foolishly romantic action has caused a great deal of strife for my captain here." He indicated the mean-looking vampire—Captain Creepy, apparently. I suddenly understood Khan's hesitation at the idea of hooking up with this guy. "The dissolution of the contract leaves the fate of our empires unresolved. Without the bond, peace cannot be guaranteed, you understand."

"Not really," I admitted.

Luis blinked at me. I don't think he was used to someone admitting this much stupidity in one meeting, but, seriously, I still had no real idea what he was talking about.

"Let me put it simply," he said. "There needs to be a marriage treaty, a confarreatio. You must provide a replacement suitor or there will be war."

"Marriage treaties are archaic, misogynist crap," Mom said, plopping a very slender bit of cheesecake in front of Luis. "My daughter was right to deny you."

I rolled my eyes. Way to bring up the "patriarchy," Mom. Goddess, sometimes it was so embarrassing having a women's studies professor for a mother. More to the point, the only reason I existed was because Mom had agreed to an arranged marriage, though I'd never heard it described as a "confarreatio" before.

Mom put her hands on her ample hips and stared down at the prince over the bridge of her nose. The look was ruined only a bit by the sheen of sweat on her forehead. I thought Mom seemed especially defensive, as if maybe she was attacking him to make up for the embarrassment of my potential gaff with the whole dhampyr thing. I could feel her magic swelling, like an undercurrent tugging at the edges of my consciousness. She was gearing up for a fight—possibly even a magical attack.

I had to stop it.

The only thing to do was blurt. "Why is this my problem, anyway? Why aren't you down in the underground kingdom talking to Dad? He's the regional ruler and, like, he probably totally agrees with you. Plus, he knows all the vampires in town." I gave Captain Scary Pants a glance. "The only person I could recommend is Elias." I gestured where Elias still stood ramrod straight behind me.

"Elias Constantine? You would offer your captain of the guard?" Luis looked at Elias, as if for the first time, and as if he suddenly realized he was in the presence of a celebrity. "Yes, this is more than acceptable." Luis stood up and held out his hand for me to shake. "I didn't expect to come to an agreement so quickly, or that you would be so generous with your military assets. The papers will be drawn. Congratulations."

"Wait, what?"

I stared at his hand, still extended across the table.

He smiled, gesturing for me to seal the deal. "You offer. I accept. That's how negotiations usually work, Princess."

"But—but, Elias is a guy." My mouth hung so far open, I was having trouble forming words.

"Indeed," Luis said with a little chuckle. "In fact, if his reputation is even half deserved, he's quite the man."

"No, that's just . . . wrong. What I mean is . . . your captain is a guy too."

"We are vampires, Your Highness; not men. I would think you would already know that some of the greatest alliances in history have been between male vampires." Luis finally withdrew his hand. "Given what happened with Khan, I'm afraid I must insist that the ceremony be performed before we return to Mississippi. We can do something simple here, now, or you can send your captain off with style. But we leave within the fortnight."

"No . . . this isn't happening. I didn't agree to this," I sputtered, finally finding my feet.

"Are you stupid?" Mom asked belligerently. "She was obviously joking."

"She had better not have been," Luis said sharply to Mom. As he turned to me, I noticed how captivatingly strange his intense gaze was. Did people look at me like that, wondering which eye to focus on? "Do I need to remind you that this is a matter of regional security? If you renege, the war resumes here. Now."

Elias looked at the three of them with the confidence of a man who felt he was evenly matched. "Your army is at hand?"

A smile cracked Luis's hard look. "You are certainly bold, Captain Constantine. But, yes, we camp in Hudson, awaiting my word that all is well."

I turned to Elias and grabbed his hand. He didn't look at me; in fact, he stared straight ahead, over my head, his expression completely blank. "You don't want this, do you?"

"We may not have much choice." With a sigh, he dropped his eyes to our hands. His voice was low. "Of course not. I was once happily betrothed to you."

But did that still mean what I thought it did? Didn't Luis just imply that all betrothals ended in this cold, political contract they called confarreatio?

Not that it mattered anymore; my stupid father had dissolved our bond in a fit of pique—which reminded me that we were supposedly in exile from Dad's court. "Hey," I said, dropping Elias's hand and turning toward Luis, who seemed to be getting ready to leave. "Wait. What if Elias weren't the captain of the guard anymore, huh? I mean, I probably don't even have the authority to make a treaty or whatever. We're banished."

Luis, who had been slapping the back of Captain Creepy, stopped dead. He turned around slowly. Standing in the foyer, he looked between Elias and me for several beats. The humidity stuck in my throat. "Is this the truth?"

"Check with my dad if you don't believe me," I said.

"Are you calling my daughter a liar?" Mom added, waving the pie slicer menacingly. I shot her a you're-not-helping glare.

Luis looked around me to Elias, who nodded and said, "Yes, Your Highness. It's true."

"I see," Luis said slowly. His eyes roamed up and down Elias, as if looking for hidden solutions in every angle of his form. "I must consult my advisers," he said at last. Finally, as he looked at me, his eyes were dark with disappointment. "Your offer honors me, and I wish to accept it with all my heart. But, if Constantine is truly rogue and has no allegiance, there is little value in such an alliance. I came to make a treaty with the Northern Region, not with one man, a prize though he may be."

In that dramatic way that only vampires seem to pull off, the entourage swept out the door and was gone.

When the door shut, Mom let out a loud sigh. "Can we have a normal tea now?"

I snorted. When were they ever normal? The freezer cheesecake continued to melt where it sat on the table. Mom moved to sit, but Elias frowned at the door, his eyes darkly intense. I brushed the back of his hand with my fingertips. "Are you okay?"

He shrugged, pulling away from me. The fan clicked as it swiveled from side to side, punctuating his silence.

"I didn't mean to offer you up like that, you know," I said desperately, following him as he made his way to the table to take his customary seat. "I had no idea Luis would just pounce. That was totally creepy, right? I mean, yikes. He acted as if you were some kind of prime steak or something."

"I didn't like him," Mom agreed, taking a big bite of the dessert. "Any of them."

"It would have been an acceptable pairing," Elias said, picking up his fork.

"Seriously?" I asked. "Did you not see Captain Creepy?"

He glanced up briefly, catching me with those silver smoke eyes. He quickly turned his attention to pushing around bits of the cake. "Captain Valois has a formidable reputation, it's true. But then, so do I." He took a small taste. "Or at least I did."

Oh, not this again. Ever since my dad exiled Elias, he'd been moping around, acting all man-without-a-country. I could guess now why he was all gloomy. "If I hadn't brought the exile up, you could be married to some dude right now. Would you really prefer that?"

"You shouldn't confuse vampire confarreatio for modern marriage or even the ancient Roman version," Mom said, her voice taking on that professorial tone she used when she lectured. "I'm pretty sure the whole idea of a wedding cake came from this practice, but we're talking about a property exchange, the building of a household—or a kingdom. . . ."

I ignored her and watched Elias's face.

His jaw twitched, but he didn't look at me. Abruptly, he stood. The chair made a moan as it slid across the maple floorboards. "Excuse me; I must go."

"What? Where?"

"That might be good," my mom muttered. I was surprised at the sudden irritation in her voice, but I focused on Elias.

"Your father should be warned that Prince Montezuma has come seeking restitution," Elias said, starting for the door.

My flip-flops lay in a pile of discarded footwear by the Parsons bench. I hurried to slip into them. "Then I'm coming too," I told Elias.

He was already outside, on the porch. The screen door snapped shut in my face.

I wrenched it open and ran after him. My mom yelled something about not staying up too late because I had driver's ed in the morning, and that she'd be changing the wards, so I should be careful when I came back.

"Wait for me," I shouted after Elias's shadowy form as he disappeared down the mulberry-lined walk. In the warm evening air the seeds I crushed underfoot smelled slightly fermented. "You can't just waltz in there as if nothing's happened, you know."

Elias's purposeful stride hitched as though my words had literally tripped him. In the darkness, his voice echoed softly. "How could I forget?"

Did I mention Elias was taking this exile thing kind of hard? Elias used to be my dad's right-hand man. He was the king's sword, his Praetorian Guard, his confidant—the big effing deal. He did not like being *just* some vampire who lived in my basement. I wondered if he enjoyed tea with my mom so much because it was all about the past, a place he really preferred over the present these days.

I managed to catch up with him when he stopped to lift the latch of the wrought-iron gate. "I'm not sure you remember how mad my dad was." For my part, I sometimes woke up in a cold sweat in the middle of the night with the image still reverberating in my mind of Elias having been chained in my father's court and whipped like an animal. "I really don't think it's smart to go back."

"I must warn my king."

I wished he could just call, you know? But my dad's underground kingdom was literally under a ton of rock and dirt—no cell phone reception, even if vampires carried cell phones, which they didn't for some stupid reason. I guess they all preferred living in a time before modern conveniences. At least Elias had a car.

"He's not your king anymore," I told him bluntly.

"He was my lord and liege for more than two hundred years."

"And he threw you away in a minute because he was feeling petulant. I don't think you owe him anything," I said. "Besides, what makes you think he doesn't already know Luis is in town? There's apparently some kind of troop of vampires camped along the banks of the St. Croix. I mean, you're really awesome and everything, but I'll bet Dad has a couple of other scouts who might have noticed *an entire army.*"

Elias let out a little chuckle, though, as he set the latch back in place, he only grudgingly agreed with me. "Perhaps," he said.

The streetlamp painted the edge of the glossy, pointy leaves of the mulberry in an artificial yellowish glow. Elias didn't move out onto the main sidewalk, but he didn't seem ready to turn back yet. His eyes looked over the rooftops in the direction of downtown. A crescent moon rose low on the horizon.

"If I came to him with this news . . . ," Elias started, but ended with a heavy sigh.

I shook my head because I knew why he stopped—if Elias came with news of the Second Coming, Dad still wouldn't forgive him. My dad was nothing if not stubborn. I'm not even sure my father really meant to exile us that day, but he'd said it in front of his whole court and, by Goddess, he was going to stick to it.

Elias's eyes found mine. "I know it's difficult for you to understand, Ana, but I would have gladly accepted betrothal to the Southern captain because then, at least, I would belong to a kingdom again. I would be a knight of the realm. I could . . ." Without finishing that last thought, he shook his head sadly.

"Yeah, but that guy freaked me out."

He laughed. "Me too."

It surprised me to hear that. I didn't think anyone could spook Elias. "You've got a pretty serious reputation, huh? The guys in the South sure think you're something else."

The crinkle in his eye showed he knew I was fishing. Thing was, Elias's past was a mystery. Thanks to Mom's evening tea sessions, I knew all about his opinion on human politics for the last forty years, but I didn't know anything about who he was as a vampire. Heck, I didn't know much about vampires at all, despite being the princess of some of them.

He didn't look as though he planned to enlighten me, so I poked him in the ribs lightly. "Cough it up, Constantine. Tell me why those Southern boys want you so bad."

Leaning on the gate, he regarded me with a slight frown. The crickets, which had hushed with our approach, started to chirp softly. "If you had a former gladiator as a slave, what would you do with him?"

"Have him clean my room?" I joked. "Take out the garbage?"

"He's not known for his cleaning skills, my lady," Elias said seriously.

A mosquito buzzed my ear, and I swatted at it. "I didn't think it mattered very much what you were before . . . as a human," I said carefully.

Elias and I had never really talked about what I'd learned last spring about the way vampires were made, and I didn't want to offend him. Vampires came from a place "beyond the Veil," an otherworld that people might confuse with hell, though it was much, much older. But they didn't just step out, like walking out of a closet. What they were became bonded with a human host, irreparably destroying the former person's soul, but not killing the body.

"Physical memories remain," he said quietly, as if lost in a thought. "Consider the alternative. If our bodies didn't remember how to walk or speak, what use would we be?"

That made a certain kind of sense, and I could see how witches might use that to their advantage. "So sometimes host bodies were chosen because they had specific physical skills?"

"Yes, now you see."

I started to ask what he *was* good at, when the moonlight reflected the intense ice of Elias's eyes. "Oh."

"'Oh,' indeed," he said.

"So you were . . ." What did I say here? A killer? An assassin? How about if I just left that blank? I dropped my gaze and continued on. "For the witches?"

"I did as my masters commanded."

Except they were mostly "mistresses," being witches. Vampires had been brought from this other dimension by the First Witch, who bound their will to hers with a talisman, a statuette in the shape of her snake-headed goddess.

A couple of hundred years ago, Elias managed to get his hands on that talisman, even though he was a slave at the time. He lost it, but without the talisman, the witches' power over their slaves diminished. There was a big war. The vampires call it the secret war, and many vampires were freed. Some stayed with their old families, but the rest broke up into underground kingdoms, like the one my dad ruled.

The statue had been rediscovered last year. Nikolai, my ex-boyfriend, had stolen it from a traveling Smithsonian exhibit. I destroyed it. I still had a small scar on my hand, actually. As it turned out, blowing up the talisman put an end to the witches' ability not only to control vampires, but also to make new ones, because, as an extra-special bonus, the path to that other place was forever closed with a big, old bang.

I must have been looking at the tiny white line on my wrist with the memory, because Elias took my hand into his. "When the talisman was lost, I was free to be who I wished, but by then my path was already laid. There was a war; I was a warrior."

"Wait—are you saying you were a killer for my dad too?"

I hadn't meant to say that word, or to jerk my hand away so forcefully, but I did. From the stricken look in Elias's eye, I knew it was too late to take it back.

"I did as my king demanded."

"Well, that sounds like a cop-out. When are you going to do what *you* want? Maybe this exile is a blessing. Maybe you can finally stop doing everything people tell you to."

That was apparently not the thing Elias wanted to hear. His eyes narrowed dangerously, and I saw the hint of fang in his snarl. In one deft leap, he cleared the garden gate and stalked down the sidewalk.

This time I let him go. I figured he just needed to clear his head. I'd see him later tonight.

Mom was nothing if not a fast worker. When my foot hit the porch stairs, I could feel the house vibrating with energy. Thanks to being half vampire, I can't actually work True Magic, but I didn't know that for years because I've always been extra sensitive to it.

As I took another step, my foot started to prickle. Even through the flip-flops, I got the sensation of pins and needles. On the porch, the house really started to resist me. My feet dragged with numbness, and my stomach soured. I thought I was going to barf. A feeling that was amplified as my head began to spin with vertigo. I lurched toward the doorknob like a drunk. It took all my strength to pull and then heave myself through the screen door.

And I lived here.

"I think the wards are a bit high, Mom," I shouted from where I stood, doubled over and panting on the welcome mat.

"You got through them. They're fine," she insisted.

"Are you freaking kidding me?"

Mom was sitting at the table, eating a second piece of freezer cheesecake. She looked up guiltily when I came in and hastily pushed the plate aside. She cleared her throat. "Accidentally or not, I managed to invite three strange vampires into our house. Vampires who are apparently at war with your father's kingdom, or will be when they confirm your proposal of alliance was a sham. You're just going to have to deal."

"Will Elias be able to get back through?"

"It'll probably be a bit harder for him, but he's a big boy . . . and apparently some kind of superstar vampire. I'm sure he'll be fine." She sounded a touch angry, as if upset by how little she knew about him after all this time as well. She picked up her fork and then put it down. Looking over my shoulder, she asked, "Where is he, anyway? I thought he'd come back with you."

I shrugged. "He's off brooding, I guess." I didn't want to tell my mom that we'd had a kind of falling-out over the whole killer thing, because I felt so awful about it.

Worse, I'd forgotten to ask Elias about our betrothal. Had it just been a political thing for him? Was that why we'd never kissed?

"Situation normal, eh?" She looked wistfully at the remains of the dessert but wiped her mouth with a cloth napkin instead. "Weird night."

"Yeah," I agreed, slipping into my spot. I examined my own abandoned slice, but I couldn't muster any interest in eating it. It reminded me too much of the whole disastrous meeting with Luis. "Did you know that Elias was a gladiator . . . um, before?"

My mom's eyes widened; I guess she didn't. "I suppose I

should have," she said. "Constantine was a Roman emperor. Elias must have been one of the last ones. When Constantine adopted Christianity, he was under a lot of pressure to stop the games."

Vampires took the surname of whoever was ruling at the time and place of their bringing over. My dad, for instance, was named after an Egyptian pharaoh.

I didn't mention the other bit of information I'd learned about Elias. I wasn't sure my mom would continue to let Elias stay here if she knew he used to be an assassin. It was one thing to be a bloodsucker, but vampires needed to kill only once every human generation to live.

When I looked up, Mom was smiling. "What's so funny?" I asked.

"I keep trying to see Elias as Russell Crowe in that movie. You know, in a funny little skirt and sandals," she said.

My mind rebelled at the image, but I had seen vampires bring scimitars and katanas to a fight. I could easily picture how deadly Elias would be with a Roman short sword. I swallowed hard, thinking what it must have been like to see him coming down some dark alley on the orders of his witch masters.

My stomach twisted, and I pushed away the plate I hadn't touched. "Yeah, that reminds me—I should . . . uh, do my summer reading." Great Goddess, that was a lame lie, especially since I'd finished it ages ago. Still, I knew Mom would never protest the idea of my doing schoolwork. I got up from the table and headed to my room before Mom could ask anything that might blow my cover, as it were.

My room was one of three upstairs bedrooms. It was one of the smaller ones, but I liked it because it had a dormer, a cubbyhole-like section with a low, slanted triangular ceiling that followed where a window jutted out. It was big enough that I wedged a desk in there against one wall, and a makeshift bookcase against the other. Manga, graphic novels, and books of all sorts were piled everywhere. The rest of the room was occupied by my bed and more overflowing bookshelves.

I'd left the top of one case bare. It was the only section of the room not smothered in reading material. It was my altar. I hadn't changed it since the dark moon meditation I'd done a couple of weeks ago. It was still covered in a simple square of black cloth. Two silver candleholders held one black and one white candle. A round mirror from one of my compacts lay faceup between them. I'd forgotten to put away my athame, a black-handled ritual dagger, and it sat next to the mirror. There used to be a snake-headed Nile goddess figurine in a place of honor on the altar, until I discovered, last year, that the talisman was in the same shape. Now it was stored in the bottom of my desk drawer, collecting dust.

After I closed the door, I grabbed my cell phone from where it was charging on my desk. I intended to distract myself by checking in with my sometimes BFF, Bea, but discovered a dozen or so texts waiting. Lying down on the bed, I scrolled through them.

Thompson wanted to know if we were going to try out for

Renaissance Festival together tomorrow. I sent him a quick reply that he could pick me up after driver's ed. I also warned him that from what I'd heard from Lane, one of our other theater friends, the whole audition was improvisation—not something either Thompson or I was any good at. One of the reasons I loved theater so much was that it came with a script— something I found lacking in real life. Improv was all about making stuff up on the fly. As weird as it might sound from a longtime theater geek like me, I really didn't like all the pressure of people staring at me while I tried to be clever.

Bea had left a couple of messages about this big midsummer picnic that was supposed to go down this weekend. Our coven—actually, since I failed Initiation, it was really more *Bea's* coven—had this "open house" every summer where the Inner and Outer Circle were invited to a potluck at Como Park. You could even bring mundanes, non–True Magic people, and Bea wanted to know if I was bringing Thompson as a date.

"Ha-ha," I texted back. None of my friends could deal with the fact that he and I were just theater buddies. Heck, I still thought of him as Thompson, despite his constant insistence that I call him Matt.

Plus, I think everyone, "Matt" included, really liked the idea of the star-crossed lovers: the jock and the class weirdo. I wasn't completely opposed to the idea—Thompson had that he-man appeal of the high school hockey star—but, it didn't seem right that I couldn't talk to him about the most important stuff in my life. What kind of relationship could we really have? It was not as if I could tell him about my dad being a vampire or that my mom was the Queen of Witches.

Bea wrote back. "Come on. It would be fun. T. would totally freak."

Even though no one ever used Real Magic or brought along their vampire butler, the potluck did bring out some of our stranger members. There were all sorts of people in the Outer Circle, for instance, that Thompson would consider "woo-woo." Even Nikolai's mom, who was an actual Romany, aka Gypsy, might give Thompson a heart attack.

Nikolai.

If I went to the potluck, it would be almost impossible to avoid my ex; as both an initiated witch and a vampire hunter, he was part of the inner Inner Circle. I wanted to ask Bea if she'd heard whether Nik was bringing anyone, but part of me didn't want to know. What could I say? I still wasn't over him. It didn't help that his band kept getting more and more radio time. I couldn't listen to Cities 97 without hearing about whatever venue Ingress would be playing at next.

I looked at the last text he'd sent me. I had it saved in my in-box. He'd sent it last week. "Thinking of u." I hadn't replied, because I didn't know what I was supposed to do with that. I thought about him all the time too, but we were supposed to be trying to move on, weren't we?

"What r u wearing?" Bea asked.

"Not sure I'm going," I typed.

My thumb had barely pressed Send when her response chirped. "What? U can't not go!"

"What about Nik?" I wrote.

"Forget him. Bring T. He'll be jealous."

Well, that was the best argument for bringing Thompson I'd heard so far. I was kind of curious if Nikolai would care if I showed up with another boy, and it wasn't as if I could bring Elias—too much sun and too many witches. "Maybe."

I almost dropped the phone when it rang. The display said it was Bea. I answered. "You must really want me to go."

"You have to. I can't go by myself."

"Aren't you going to bring Malcolm?" Bea had recently started dating another one of our theater pals. Actually, he'd hounded her for months until she finally caved in.

"I can't really gossip with him." She had the same problem with Malcolm that I did with Thompson. He was normal. She couldn't talk to him about all the witchy and vampire stuff.

Which reminded me, I totally wanted to get her take on Luis. "Hey, guess what? I got a visit from another vampire prince today."

"Seriously?"

I told her all about what happened, including the near betrothal.

"Wow," she said. "Who knew vampires were so liberal about gay marriage?"

I'd been thinking about that aspect, because my brain really went tilt if I thought about Elias kissing Captain Creepy. "It's not marriage," I said. "They have another word for it. The whole thing seems so political. Luis even said love had nothing to do with it."

"Do you really think Luis is a dhampyr?"

"I don't know. I kind of think he is, because he reacted so

strongly to the word but didn't deny it. I guess I feel like if he wasn't and it was such an awful thing to be, he'd just say something, you know?"

"Yeah," she said. "I suppose it is kind of . . . different."

That was an understatement. Silence hung in the air between us for a moment, and I remembered how horrified everyone had been when my true nature had come out at my non-Initiation. For a while, I hadn't thought my friendship with Bea would survive the revelation. And we've been tight since kindergarten.

"Anyway, promise me you'll come tomorrow?" she asked. "If you bring Thompson, I'll bring Malcolm."

For a moment I could still feel all those judging, disgusted eyes on me. "I have to think about it."

"Well, don't think too hard. My mom's bringing her famous pastries."

"Oh, well, that changes everything," I said in all seriousness. I would never miss Bea's mom's food. Bea's mom was a failed Initiate like me, but she made the best treats the coven ever tasted. "I'll be there."

We spent a few more minutes talking about the latest reality show Bea had been following and other inconsequential things. Bea wouldn't let me off the phone, however, until I absolutely solemnly swore I'd be going to the potluck tomorrow after Festival tryouts.

Elias didn't come home until after three a.m. I'd been waiting for him, just to make sure things were okay, and passed the time streaming old episodes of *Firefly* on Netflix. I heard the screen door snap shut downstairs and looked at the alarm clock by my bed. He'd certainly had a long brood. I was considering going down to talk to him, when glass shattered in the kitchen.

I jumped to my feet and raced down to see what had happened. Of course, the downstairs was completely dark; Elias didn't need the lights. I flipped the switch. The harsh overhead light flicked on.

Elias lay, sprawled facedown on the linoleum. I couldn't tell if he was breathing, but there was no obvious pool of blood. The decorative bowl that usually sat on the table was in tiny pieces. Oranges, apples, and kiwi littered the floor.

Heedless of the broken porcelain, I knelt beside him. "Elias!"

There was no response.

Chapter Three

Elias's face was always pale, but I thought there was something particularly sickly in the stark contrast of his dark curls against his brow. I shook his shoulder anxiously. "Elias!"

He groaned.

I nearly fell over from relief. He was alive, at least.

Behind me, Mom shuffled into the doorway in slippers. A sleepy mutter of, "What's going on?" turned into an ear-piercing shriek.

The noise made Elias's eyelids flutter—another good sign, I hoped.

"I think he's alive," I told her.

"Think?" Her hand was over her heart. She wore her plain white nightshirt. She started to step into the kitchen but stopped when she saw the broken bowl. "What happened?"

"I have no idea." I couldn't imagine that he'd been hungry for a kiwi, since he hardly ever ate human food that wasn't set in front of him, so the only thing I could think of was that he'd passed out. On the way down, he must have hit the table and caused the fruit bowl to drop somehow. "Maybe it was the wards."

"He wouldn't have made it this far," she insisted. But when I shot her a doubting look, she added, "Listen—I don't always like him, but I accept that he lives here. I didn't make them lethal to Elias. I marked him as friend."

If friend was more painful than family, it still might have hurt him. "What else could be wrong with him?"

"I have no idea," Mom said. "I wish we could call a doctor."

I couldn't have agreed more, but could you imagine? What would a doctor make of his fangs? But, he was mostly human. Maybe some of the same sorts of things would apply. But what? One of the only things I remembered from CPR class was that you weren't supposed to move people if you didn't know what was wrong with them. But, it didn't seem right to leave him facedown. He might be hiding some major injury. "Maybe we could roll him over? See if there's something obvious?"

Mom must not have heard the question in my words, because she got down on her knees right away to help me try to heave him onto his back. He was heavy, but the two of us got him over quickly. I pushed the bigger bits of bowl out of the way with my forearm before we gently set his head down.

Mom put her cheek to his lips. "I can't feel much breath," she said. We gave each other worried looks, but she added the same thing I'd been thinking, "Not that that means anything. Does he normally breathe?"

"He does, but I don't know that he *has* to, you know?"

She nodded, taking his wrist into her hand. "Of course, there's no pulse that I can detect. But I can barely find my own without help." She sat back on her heels. "We might have to call Victor."

Victor Kirov was Nikolai's dad, and the local vampire hunter. "Mom! You can't be serious."

"He's the only one of us who has ever seen a vampire die. He might have a clue as to what's wrong with Elias."

He was also the sort who would just stake Elias out of spite. "You'd have to reveal that Elias is living here. Wouldn't that hurt your reputation?"

"I informed the council immediately after he moved in," she sniffed.

"You did?" I couldn't imagine it. My mother had admitted to letting a vampire stay under our roof freely? There was more to this, I thought, but I couldn't cope with it right now. I returned my attention to Elias.

I began frantically looking for some clue as to what was wrong with him. I'd assumed an attack of some kind, but there were no cuts or blood or even a bruise anywhere on his body that I could detect. His T-shirt was black and untorn, and there were no obvious scuff marks on his jeans.

I was beginning to think he hadn't been in a fight, after all. What could be wrong with him?

Mom glanced over to where our landline telephone sat in the butler's pantry, gathering dust. "I'm going to call Victor."

"It's not a good idea, Mom."

We were spared further useless argument by Elias's sudden, deep intake of breath. His eyes popped open.

His eyes darted about, taking in the scene and our worried expressions. Then, after a moment, he laid his head back and shut his eyes again, almost as if too embarrassed to look at us.

"Are you okay?" we demanded in unison.

"I'm fine," he said unconvincingly in a hoarse voice. He calmly folded his hands on his chest and opened his eyes to stare at the speckled plaster of the ceiling. "Strong wards, Amelia."

It was the cause of his distress I was expecting, but something rang false. I couldn't put my finger on it, but the resigned way he reacted when he awoke made me ask: "This has totally happened before, hasn't it?" I shifted so that my face was in his field of vision. "What's wrong? Are you sick?"

With a grunt, he pulled himself up into a sitting position. He leaned heavily on shaking arms. "As I said, I'm fine."

"And you ended up on the floor . . . ?" my mom asked.

"I slipped."

I pressed him: "And, what, passed out? Because that's perfectly normal."

He didn't answer.

I watched his muscles tremble until I couldn't take it anymore. I put my arm around his shoulder to support him. I'd never seen Elias like this. "You're shaking."

"Stop lying to us," Mom said, taking his hand. Together we helped him into the nearest kitchen chair. "Something's wrong, Elias. Tell us what it is. Maybe we can help you."

"It's your wards."

"They're not that strong," my mother insisted. "Not for a healthy vampire marked as a friend. Ana got through."

I was a bit shocked to be lumped in with "healthy vampires," but I was too worried about Elias at the moment to protest. "I'll agree they're strong," I said, giving Mom a bit of the stink eye. "But you passed out, Elias. That's bad."

He sat with his head in his hands. Mom stood beside him. I stayed on my spot on the floor but pulled my legs out into a more comfortable position. His face was obscured by his hands, but I could tell he was struggling with something. Finally, he lifted his head.

"I'm starving," he said.

For a second, I didn't get it and nearly offered to pop a frozen pizza into the oven; then the true meaning hit me. He wasn't talking about a craving for a midnight snack. He meant blood.

Mom let out an exasperated sigh. "Oh, for heaven's sake, then go get . . . something. I don't approve, but I can't have you starving to death either. Just do your business somewhere far away from here."

Mom didn't really get the full implications either.

Elias looked to me, and it was my turn to shift my gaze away. "It's bigger than that, Mom," I explained, feigning a sudden interest in collecting shards of porcelain. "He's talking about the hunt."

There was a reason that "bloodsuckers" was a pejorative term for vampires. They didn't survive on blood. Blood was really important; don't get me wrong. I knew from personal experience that the first taste awakened all our special super-powers and could revive us if we were injured, but, believe it or not, we couldn't live on it—not forever. The thing that truly sustained vampires was . . . well, it was death—magical, ritualized murder. It was a thing Dad called the sacred hunt. Traditionally, it was performed once every human generation, about twenty years or so.

The reason I couldn't look at Elias right now was that he and I both knew that if he died of starvation, it was completely my fault.

I'd stopped the hunt not once, but twice.

"I'm not the only one who suffers," Elias said.

Like, I didn't suspect that. As if I needed that kind of responsibility. I so needed to hear that there were hundreds of vampires who were slowly dying, thanks to me. My cheeks burned as I gathered up all the big pieces of bowl and tossed them into the garbage. I got the broom from where it rested behind the pantry shelf.

But I'd had good reason to stop the hunt. Last time, it had been Mom in the crosshairs. I couldn't have let her be the victim, could I?

"So, you see, the Southern prince and his army are double the threat." Elias's voice was quiet, not at all accusatory, and he looked at my mother as he spoke, but still his words cut me. I focused on sweeping the floor and gathering up the bruised fruit.

Mom pursed her lips. "You worry too much about Ramses' problems. You should focus on taking care of yourself. Go find a . . . friend. You'll feel better."

"Mom!" I was utterly grossed out by what Mom seemed to be implying.

"What? Blood has to help him, doesn't it?"

I started to speak, but Elias cut me off.

"Where do you think I was? Nothing does much good. I can't get enough. Not without killing," he said. As he crossed his arms in front of his stomach, his eyes flashed cold. "I could do it. I have . . . wanted to. But, if I kill outside of the hunt, alone, that makes me nosferatu. No turning back. Not ever."

My mouth hung open; so did Mom's. I didn't know what "nosferatu" meant in this context, but the dark look on Mom's face made me think that maybe she did.

Elias didn't seem fazed by our reaction. "And if I cross that line, I would lose more than my place in the ranks of the kingdom. I would lose my mind. Over time, nosferatu are reduced to unthinking, soulless animals. That's why their name is synonymous with zombielike vampires."

It sounded as though he had some personal experience with one of those nosferatu. Our eyes met, and he nodded solemnly as if he'd heard my unspoken question.

He continued. "It was once part of my duties to hunt down and destroy escaped slaves who had become nosferatu."

No wonder his reputation preceded him. Elias wasn't just any old assassin; he was a *vampire* killer.

Mom chewed her lip and adjusted her glasses. "And you say you were tempted to cross this line . . . recently?"

Elias nodded. "I understand your concern, Amelia," he said, hanging his head again. "It's no longer safe for you to harbor me. If I could tarry but one last day, to gather my things and make alternate arrangements?"

"That wasn't what I was thinking about, but, yeah, that sounds like a really good idea. You should go," Mom said plainly. I wanted to protest, but she continued before I could form any words. "But what I wanted to know was, if you're tempted, how are the others faring? I mean, everyone says you're such a noble gentleman, as if that's something unusual. Is there going to be a nosferatu problem?"

Even though she stood in her nightshirt and slippers, there was something in the tone of her voice that made it very clear she was asking as the Queen of Witches.

Elias lifted his head defiantly. "I am in exile, and, as such, at much greater risk. The prince will surely call a hunt, and the kingdom will feed, if it has not already."

"Oh, I think we'd know if it had." There was that royal "we" Mom used only in her Queen of Witches role. "We need to talk to some people, if you'll excuse us."

Elias nodded briefly, as if only grudgingly acknowledging her sovereignty.

As I stood leaning against the broom, I suddenly felt exhausted. The clock on the wall ticked hollowly. Elias frowned, watching my mother head upstairs.

"Why didn't you tell me you were sick?" I asked, feeling an old hurt. We talked so little these days; yet I couldn't believe he'd kept something so important from me.

He gestured with his chin in the direction Mom had disappeared. "Her Majesty," he said, his voice dripping with disdain.

"I haven't had a chance to have a private conversation with you the entire time I've been her guest. Do you think that wasn't intentional?"

I'd thought he just wasn't that into me anymore. I didn't want to say that, though. To cover my expression, I took the opportunity to put the broom back in its place. "I had kind of noticed, honestly," I said.

"She's been desperate for just this sort of information. At least I will no longer have to endure the interrogation she called 'tea' when I leave."

OMG. Elias hated tea too? This news was almost as shocking as finding out that he was a vampire slayer. But I felt as if he and I had been attending a completely different event all these months. "Are you saying she was pumping you for information this whole time?"

He looked a bit surprised I hadn't guessed. "Subtly, but, yes. I know this sounds a bit paranoid, but I think she was putting potions in my tea."

"I doubt that," I said quickly. I mean, my mom a poisoner? We didn't always get along, but I couldn't go that far. "I seriously thought you guys were talking about American history."

"Sometimes we were, but more often it was barely veiled attempts to get me to give over information about the kingdom and what we have been doing since the secret war."

"Oh." Wow, I felt stupid. How did I manage to miss all that subtext?

"And now she has something she can use at last. Damn it all. Damn my weakness."

Gripping the edge of the table, Elias pulled himself up on wobbly knees.

"We must see your father," he said. "He may have a war on two fronts now."

"With witches? And Luis?" He nodded. I could hardly deny the urgency in Elias's face. "But how are you going to get in? They'll kill you. Didn't we already have this discussion? Don't you remember last time?"

"I surrendered before because I mistakenly trusted in my prince's mercy. I will not go so unarmed this time."

I wanted to believe the fierce flash in his eye, but his face looked so stark and pale. "You're sick, Elias. You can't fight. You can barely walk."

"Then you have to go."

"Me?"

"Your father wouldn't dare harm his own blood heir."

I wasn't nearly so sure. My loving father had no problem calling a hunt on Mom, a woman he was still officially married to, or sending his vampire minions to attack me when I had the talisman. Still, Elias was in no shape to do it. "I guess I can go. You think I should try to go tonight?"

"I do," he said. A creak in the wood floors upstairs had him lower his voice conspiratorially. "If the others suffer as I do, they'll be even weaker now that the dawn is soon upon us."

"So, what you're saying is that now is a good time because I won't get eaten before I can reach Dad?" I asked. He didn't deny it and had the decency to look a bit chagrined. I sighed. "Fabulous."

Have I mentioned how much I hated going to see my dad?

First of all, thanks to their sun allergy, the vampires have to live underground—literally. In fact, St. Paul was the vampire capital of the Midwest because of its extensive sandstone tunnels, underground rivers, and warrens of natural and manmade caves. And, while that might sound kind of cool, trust me, it's not. Sandstone always seems to smell kind of like dog piss, and, every time I go, I end up finding gross grit in my hair and clothes for weeks.

The other reason I loathed going to my father's court was because the dress code freaked me out, in that they didn't have one. Vampires will tell you that they are "natural" creatures, more like elves than demons. For this reason, they liked to cavort in the buff. Buck naked. Nude. Completely in the altogether.

I swear I put twenty bucks in my future-therapy fund every time I saw my dad in his birthday suit.

Being out at four in the morning is always kind of eerie, but in St. Paul it's doubly so, because the streets are entirely empty. To be fair, downtown kind of shuts down early in my hometown, so much so that people joke that we roll up the streets after five p.m.

Since the buses stopped running just after midnight and time was of the essence, Elias dropped me off just a few blocks away from the railroad tunnel entrance that led to the kingdom.

He pulled into an unpaved driveway, the kind that always

seemed mysteriously useless but was probably for rail crews of some sort. Elias put his hand on my arm when I reached for the door. "You won't let me accompany you, my lady?"

I shook my head. It wasn't as if I wanted to go alone, but I really didn't see much choice in the matter. "It's nearly dawn. You should hurry home. If you were overcome by torpor at court, there's no way I could drag you somewhere safely by myself, and Dad would probably command some Igor to stab you in your sleep."

He grimaced. "A vivid image."

"It's also pretty accurate," I said, opening the door and stepping out onto the scrub grass and gravel. The air felt heavy and humid after the air-conditioning of Elias's car. I sort of regretted changing into jeans, but I couldn't exactly go crawling around in tunnels in cotton shorts. I should really invest in decent hiking boots if I was going to keep making this trip on a regular basis. Glancing over my shoulder, I sighed. I should really get going, but I had one more question before I left. "Can you make it in past the wards?"

"Your mother promised to let me in when she saw me coming."

I hoped she would keep her word. With all the queenly posturing she did before she left, I had my doubts. But I trusted Elias to be resourceful even if Mom didn't play fair. "You have an Igor in the neighborhood, right? A backup hidey-hole?"

Vampires attracted a strange assortment of human groupies that acted as assistants during the daylight hours. Everyone referred to them as "Igors"; it was kind of a dis, but I'd heard worse, especially from Nikolai. But I had no idea what else they called themselves, if anything.

Elias's cheeks reddened as if I'd just suggested he was up to something naughty by being prepared. But he admitted, "I do."

"Good," I said. "We'll talk tomorrow night, okay?"

"Be careful," he said.

I nodded that I would and clicked the door shut. "You too," I said, though I wasn't sure he heard me with the windows rolled up. I watched him drive away, up the steep streets into Lowertown. The skyscrapers of St. Paul seemed to look reproachfully over one another's shoulders at me as they rose up along the river valley basin. With a sigh, I turned away and headed along the tracks toward my father's kingdom.

Court was winding down for the night by the time I'd wormed my way under the fence, deep into the abandoned tunnel, and through the narrow, natural canyon. The Igor sentry at the cave's mouth almost didn't let me in, but, in my very best (and loudest) regal tone, I told him to announce that the exiled princess Anastasija Ramses Parker requested an audience. Curious vampires peeped around the cave wall, and the sentry shrugged and let me pass.

Quartz flecks glittered where dim candlelight flickered against the cave walls. The temperature underground was quite a bit cooler than outside. An underground river gurgled through the center of the vast space, and, where it dropped in a miniature waterfall, it sprayed mist into the already-damp air. Vampires, pale naked forms, clustered together on the natural shelves along the walls. My father sat on a throne of stone near where the waterfall disappeared into a hole in the floor that I'd always expected led to an underground lake. Brown bats were returning from their night forages, and they clung to the ceiling in clusters like tiny shivering, living chandeliers.

I wanted to hide my face in my hands. This place was so danged creepy.

But it seemed emptier than usual . . . and quieter too. Most of the times I'd visited, there were crowds of vampires milling around, talking, doing whatever it was they did when they visited royal court. Where was everyone?

My dad, meanwhile, looked as if he could use a serious jolt of caffeine. He seemed to be having trouble staying awake. There were deep bags under his eyes, and his usually ageless face seemed ragged and worn. I could see the burn marks on his otherwise handsome face from where I'd blasted him with the talisman's magic.

Outside of how awful he looked, I was struck as always by how much alike we looked. His hair was silken, black, and straight as a board. He had crystal blue eyes, like one of mine, and his body was lean and long. Frankly, it would have been nice if I'd inherited my mom's curls or at least some of her curves.

He glanced blearily in my general direction. "What brings you here, exiled princess?"

Other eyes seemed to find me now. Those that had first watched me with curiosity now seemed to have a hint of something else. Was it hunger? Mom was right. Dad had not yet called a hunt, which meant *all* the vampires were starving just like Elias.

I suddenly did not like the odds, even without the usual complement of vampires at court. What would happen if they all decided to pounce? My cell phone did not get reception this far underground. Besides, I didn't think 911 would take seriously the call for help from a vampire attack.

"Um . . ." What had I come here to tell him, again? I found myself backing toward the door with every word. "Prince Luis wants a bride, or a groom, or whatever you call a partner in that marriage treaty thing. Confarreatio? Anyway, he brought his army to Wisconsin, and my mom is planning something also . . . uh, maybe."

Wow. All that had somehow seemed so much more critical when Elias had suggested I had to come here. Now it seemed kind of stupid, and with all the eyes on me, I really wished I hadn't agreed to this, especially given my dad's reaction—

He laughed.

And, frankly, his laugh didn't sound very sane either. It was the sort of cackle a movie supervillain might utter, only scarier. The sound startled a few bats who took to the air with a screech.

Worse, whenever I turned my attention back to the courtiers, they seemed to have sneaked closer by an inch or two, like cats stalking prey.

"It was very kind of you to come with this news, child," my father said, though it didn't sound as if he meant a word of it. In fact, he didn't even seem interested. He brushed an imaginary speck from his naked shoulder, as if brushing off the collar of a coat.

What was wrong with him? So we hadn't exactly been best friends since the whole exile scene, and, okay, I totally smacked him down when I destroyed the talisman, but he was behaving really unhinged. When he first appeared on my doorstep, he seemed totally normal—like a proper dad. I still kind of held out a sliver of hope that we might, you know, get to know each other better and be less estranged. But now he acted just plain strange.

His eyes, in particular, seemed focused on something just out of reach. Was the hunger hitting him worse than the others?

I glanced over my shoulder. The vampires were definitely closing in, forming a circle around me.

"Perhaps you would like to stay for dinner?"

I shook my head. I took a step back, and nearly collided with a female vamp. I ducked before she could seize my shoulders. "You don't mean that," I said, scanning the closing ranks, desperately looking for an opening. My heart pounded with fear. I felt my body beginning to change, just as I saw the vampires around me doing the same. First, my fangs elongated. They stretched through my gums with a familiar ache. My perception shifted as my pupils went cat-slit. All around me I saw the reflective glitter of gold and green irises.

"Please, Ana, don't go," my dad said somewhere behind me. My eyes stayed glued to the closer threats. "We're dying to have you."

Chapter Four

Dying to have me? Seriously? That old joke? Hunger must make Dad not only mean but also stupid.

"Are you trying to be funny? Are you seriously calling the hunt on me?"

He snorted, as if I'd suggested something ridiculous. "Don't be silly—we don't eat our own kind. We might tear you limb from limb for a light snack, perhaps, though. . . ."

"You are really, really sick, Dad," I said, not bothering to look at him. Instead, I continued to search for an out.

When I spotted a vampire I thought I could take, I didn't wait for Dad's response. I rushed forward with a wild shout. The vampire in question instinctively moved out of the way to avoid my aggressive move. I'd picked him because his expression hadn't seemed nearly as inhumanly hungry as the rest, and, well, he just looked like he might dodge instead of counterattack. It seemed I'd gambled right for once.

I found myself on the back side of the circle. Luckily, they'd all moved in tightly, so there was room to dash for the door. But could I make it? I mentally steeled myself as I ran by, pretending this whole moment had already been blocked out on the stage and we were all just doing our bit in some grand play.

I tried not to feel hands grabbing for me. I could see the mouth of the cave. Just a few more steps . . .

And I'd have to deal with the sentry. Having heard the commotion inside, he was ready for me. Using a broken broomstick as a weapon, he smacked me expertly across the shoulder. I let the force of the blow knock me down, and I rolled into the narrow stream. I was going to be bruised tomorrow and my jeans were completely soaked, but for the moment I was more afraid of what would happen if I were caught.

I stumbled a bit recovering from the roll, but I mostly kept my momentum. The dumbstruck sentry, however, was a perfect obstacle for the vampires spilling out of the cave. In fact, from the sounds behind me, some of them seemed to have decided he made a fine substitute for a meal.

Resisting the temptation to look behind me, I kept running. It had been a lot slower going in because my eyes had to adjust to the dim-to-no light. With my body in vampire mode, I could run without hesitation. Rats scurried along the wall, squealing their protest, but I outpaced them easily.

My heart pounded in fear more than in exertion. Transformed, I could run for miles without breaking a sweat. But I could run only so fast. My now more sensitive ears picked up the sounds of fleet footfalls gaining on me. *Don't look,* I told myself. Seeing how close they were would only make me stumble. Focus on feet. Move. Hadn't Elias said they'd be in a weakened state? How far to the entrance?

I hoped that the sun was rising and that it was the bright, clear, hot day the meteorologist promised on the news last night. I actually didn't know exactly what happened to vampires in the sunlight, but I knew Elias couldn't stand it.

The ground leveled out when I reached the railroad tunnel, and I was able to pick up a little speed. Unfortunately, my advantage was also the vampires'. I swore I could feel breath on my neck, and the hem of my jeans snagged on something. Hands? Teeth? I didn't want to know, nor was I going to check. I kept my eyes on the prize, which was, literally, the light at the end of the tunnel.

I was almost there. The biggest hurdle now was the fence, which I had had to shimmy under to get in. Dropping down to wiggle through seemed like a recipe for getting grabbed. How was I going to do this fast? Was there another way?

I could feel myself slowing down as I anticipated the problem. Someone got a hold of my ankle. My foot slipped through the grasp, but it was too late. I could feel myself falling. I wasn't quite close enough to slide underneath, baseball-style, but I did manage to hurl myself close enough that I was able to grab the links of the chain and hold on tight. Hands closed around my legs and started to pull. I heaved myself in the other direction with all the strength of desperation.

Teeth grazed my jeans, and I started kicking. Someone grunted in pain as my sneaker connected to a jaw or teeth; I wasn't sure which. But I took advantage of the moment and dragged myself under. Of course, to do this while still holding on to the fence, I had to twist around. For the first time since I started running, I was face-to-face with the seething mass of pale flesh grasping hungrily at me. I was glad I hadn't given in to my earlier impulses, because the shocking sight of the naked, twisting forms just about caused me to lose my stranglehold on the fence. I screamed despite myself.

When one of the vamps managed to puncture the cloth of my Converses, I realized that giving in to that panic had cost me precious time and breath. I redoubled my efforts to pull myself the rest of the way through the fence. My shoe came loose. I pulled myself upright and then scampered with one stocking foot for the shaft of sunlight that had slanted into the tunnel.

I'd been *so* smart up to this point that I can't quite tell you why, but when I reached the outside, I stopped and turned around. Maybe I just felt as if I'd made it to gool, base, safe. Or perhaps I was just curious to see the effect of sun on vampires. I leaned against the mouth of the tunnel to catch my breath and watch.

I think I was hoping for something spectacular—bodies bursting into flame or instantly crumbling to dust. At the very least, I thought they'd . . . stop.

To be fair, most of them did halt just at the edge of where light cut the darkness. But many more than I would have liked barreled right out into the morning sun. A woman managed to tackle me before I could get over my surprise enough to make an escape. I landed hard on the tracks with her full weight on top of me.

The wind was knocked from my lungs, and, as I gasped for breath, I had a close-up view of her face. The sun definitely had an effect on her.

She looked like a corpse.

I mean, technically, that was what they all were—sort of. As I'd said, a vampire had explained the process to me, and it involved human sacrifices who were taken over by the entity— the vampire—brought by the witches' talisman from beyond the Veil. The original human body didn't die, but that person was gone, overcome, emptied.

I could see the truth of that with the daylight on her face. Her eyes looked glassy and dead. There was a gray cast to her skin.

The sight shocked me so much that, at first, I forgot to fight. In those few precious seconds, the other vampires who had ventured out came to her aid. She leaped off my chest and grabbed the waist of my jeans, clearly intending to haul me back inside the lip of the cave. Someone had my feet again. My head bumped on the ties and gravel as I was being inched closer to the hungry horde waiting in the shadows.

I started flailing and screaming. My fingers scrabbled painfully as I grasped for the steel rail or anything. Where were the police when you needed them? Or even a helpful passerby?

But it turned out I didn't need either. Without warning, the woman let go. She clutched her own stomach instead. Her body was shaking violently, and then she lost it.

She puked all over.

And what came up was blood.

It splashed my one remaining shoe, my socks, and everything. I jumped back, suddenly able to find my feet because the other vampires either rushed to help her or were similarly afflicted.

Blood was everywhere.

I stumbled and slid in the gore, but I managed to get to my feet. Then I ran. Oh my God, I ran. The sunlight had sapped all of my vampire superpowers, but I didn't need them. Horror compelled me forward. I just wanted to get away—very, very far.

My own stomach threatened to rebel at the odor that seemed to cling to me. The copper tang of blood was heavy and everywhere, but there was also something in the stink that smelled rotten and spoiled, like meat left out too long.

My sock squelched on the pavement, leaving a bloody footprint. I hazarded a glance over my shoulder. There were no vampire pursuers or pukers. . . .

I slowed to a trot and looked back at the cave. There was no sign of anyone, only a dark stain on the tracks that was easy to mistake for an oil spill. Hunching over, I breathed hard. Adrenaline pumped through my veins. Tears stung my eyes. My dad nearly had me killed. Holy crap. I hardly knew what to think of all that. He said they wouldn't eat their own kind, but I wasn't sure he had much control of his people anymore.

Despite the heat, shivers racked my body.

This was awful. I had to fix this somehow. Even though they'd acted like beasts, these weren't total strangers. I'd never really made friends with any vampire other than Elias, but I felt a certain kinship with them—you know, like the people at school you pass in the hall.

At least I hadn't recognized anyone at court tonight. But what if that meant those vampires had broken from the hunger, left the kingdom, and become nosferatu?

My stomach lurched again, and I clutched at it. Clenching my teeth, I willed myself not to barf. How could my dad let this happen? Was he truly insane?

Though it was still early, a few cars sped by, heading into downtown offices. How was I going to get home? I couldn't take the bus looking like this. Besides, I was sure there was a "no shoes," or in my case, single shoe, "no service" policy. And, of course, everything below the knee of my jeans was covered in blood—not exactly inconspicuous.

It was moments like these that I wished I had a regular boyfriend. It would be really nice if I could call someone who would ride to my rescue.

I supposed I could try to wake up Bea. She'd come, no hesitation. But I would have to endure a barrage of questions I wasn't sure I wanted to answer, not the least of which was, "Why the heck even go there in the first place?"

My stomach twisted at the thought of recounting the scene I'd just endured. Bea already fell firmly in the witch camp. I doubted her impression of vampires would improve after I explained the chasing and barfing.

Right now I really needed someone who would understand how I felt, even though I myself wasn't entirely sure what that was. I was extremely mad at my father, but I was scared for him too. I couldn't believe he could turn on his own daughter. At the same time, it had seemed clear to me that the hunger had screwed him over something fierce. I couldn't blame him—not entirely.

I pulled out my phone and looked at the time. It was just a few minutes past five. My fingers punched the area code for Bea's house, but then they stopped. Snapping the phone shut, I crammed it back into my filthy jeans.

She would just tell me I'd been naive and that I should expect animalistic behavior from vampires. She might even say something stupid about how much better off we'd all be if I hadn't destroyed the talisman and the vampires were under witch control and slaves again. Then I'd have to hate her. Plus, I had to start considering future car karma too. I'd owe Bea one seriously inconvenient ride at a ridiculously early hour. I sighed. It wouldn't take me that long to hoof it, or limp it, as the case might be. I should just cowboy-up and walk, even though it was uphill the whole way.

Besides, I told myself that I was really enjoying the fresh air after the dank of the cave. Sure, my heart wasn't racing a mile a minute, and my stomach wasn't still churning with bile. This was lovely. Yeah, I believed that.

The bottom of my bloody sock started to collect sidewalk grit. I stopped to lean against a lamppost to pull it off. While I was at it, I stripped off my Converse and sock from the other foot. First garbage can I found, I was going to toss them in.

Barefoot was a bit better, though this close to the tracks I'd have to watch for broken glass and other garbage. At least it was early enough in the day that I wouldn't have to worry about scorching the bottom of my feet on hot asphalt.

I looked at the mess of socks and shoe, and shuddered. Was that what would happen to Elias in the sunlight? Would he look like that—so . . . dead?

I didn't want to think about it—none of it. Instead, I tried to ignore the wet ick in my hands and watched seagulls circling a barge in the Mississippi. A few wisps of clouds promised the possibility of a cooling rainstorm in a couple of days. Bugs chirped and bees buzzed in the tangle of sandburs, white clover, and yellow alfalfa on the boulevard.

Yeah, I'd almost convinced myself it was a pleasant day.

Except at some point I was going to have to deal with the fact that my dad had slipped a mental gear and was utterly insane.

What I didn't get was, if things were this bad, why hadn't my dad done something about it? As the king, he had the authority to call a hunt at any time. It wasn't as if he had to wait for a blue moon or eclipse or something.

Of course, if he called one, it would mean one of the True Witches would be the victim. Somebody I knew would have to sacrifice his life, which is why I'd fought so hard to stop the hunt before.

Hmm, so maybe I could see his problem.

Except he couldn't really be scared of me, could he? He'd just tried to have me lunched.

Maybe he was waiting for something, but what? Surely, if he didn't do something soon, his entire kingdom would be in disarray. They'd all go rogue or nosferatu or whatever.

Perhaps he was hoping for another solution. I know I was.

There must be some other way to satisfy the vampires' hunger. If there wasn't, my dad and all the local vampires, even Elias, would die.

But what to do? I had to do something.

I couldn't believe no one had had to deal with this problem before. Someone must know the answer. Vampires had been around since the Stone Age—literally.

Yeah, but, as I was sure Bea would point out, they'd had someone else taking care of them for most of that time. I tended to forget that vampires had been slaves until only about two hundred years ago. They probably didn't have much practice figuring this out on their own.

I'd learned another bit of grisly history last spring. In the past, witches not only condoned the hunt; they also supported it. They gave up coven members to the vampires. As much as I didn't like to imagine it, I could see a certain Machiavellian advantage to that strategy. The hunt became the ultimate boogeyman. If you didn't play by the queen's rules, off with your head—or neck, as the case might be—in the next hunt. I supposed if they had some real troublemaker, they wouldn't need to wait. You could feed the vampires anytime you had someone to dispose of.

I suspected that after the secret war, vampires used the hunt as revenge on old masters. Some bastard used to mistreat you? Nom, nom, nom: no more bastard.

Maybe Mom could help. I mean, normally her solution to any vampire problem was on par with "kill them, kill them all," but she liked Elias now, right? She'd been making plans to keep him around. That was what she'd said.

Surely, if there was an ancient witchy spell or solution, she'd share. Witches had made vampires. They must know how to feed them without killing someone, mustn't they?

Why would the First Witch have made that part of the spell, anyway? The only answer that made any sense was that it had been an accident, something unforeseen.

One of the first things my instructors tried to teach me when I was learning magic was that you needed to be careful about how you worded requests. Asking the Goddess for things was a bit like talking to that genie in a bottle. If you asked for eternal life, you had to be sure to ask for perfect health as well, or you might find yourself feeling every day of your ten thousand years, you know?

Similarly, we were cautioned off hexes. Not that Bea tended to worry overly much about that, but I remembered her aunt Diane telling us that spells bind people together—whether for good or bad. So, if you cursed a bully, you were actually binding your fates together, in a way, on the spiritual plane.

Maybe that was something the First Witch hadn't known about. Perhaps when she tore open the heavens and dragged through that first vampire slave, she didn't realize she'd tied herself to hell.

Traffic was starting to pick up a little, though the Caribou Coffee I passed by was still shuttered. I sighed wistfully. I could do with a strong, hot mocha right about now. At least I was able to dump my shoe and stuff into the public garbage can on the corner. I wiped my hand on the thigh of my jeans and wondered what the city would think if they found those. Would they go all *CSI* and trace them back to me? And whose blood was on my clothes anyway? Was it the vamp's or that of someone they'd eaten, as it were? Would I get the blame for an attack? Or even a murder?

I told myself I had enough problems without worrying about something that might not even happen, not in this era of budget cuts. St. Paul didn't have enough people power to deal with the bad guys as it was. A couple of bloody socks probably wouldn't raise much alarm.

It would probably also help if I didn't stand around looking guilty.

I moved up the block, past the Children's Museum and Mickey's Diner. Mickey's was open. I could smell the bacon and grease through the vents of the trolley car–shaped restaurant. Frying green peppers made my stomach growl. I felt for the ten I had wadded in my pocket. But, after a moment's consideration, I put it back. They got a lot of strange characters in Mickey's, but I still figured my bloody jeans and bare feet would cause a stir. I hurried on.

A city worker blasted the baskets of petunias hung from the streetlights with a hose connected to a tanker truck with WASTE WATER printed on its sides. She didn't even notice me as she moved methodically to the next lamp.

A few blocks down, a couple of homeless guys with heavy-looking army green backpacks called out to me from the court-yard of Catholic Charities across the street. I thought maybe they were harassing me for change or something. When I looked more closely, they were smiling and waving me over, as if they'd noticed the state of my clothes and considered me kin. God, I must have looked worse than I thought. I smiled back at them but kept walking.

The sunlight glinted on the golden cross on top of the cathedral. I was not too far now from home. The steepness of Kellogg Avenue made my knees ache. Some commuter on a bicycle whizzed by, going downhill.

Boulevard trees started to change from scraggly young ginkgo twigs to majestic, ancient maples. I could smell summer here—freshly cut grass, blooming roses and daisies, warm cobblestone dust. A mourning dove hooted, its low, sad song mingling with the chirps and cackles of the other birds hidden in the canopy of leaves.

I was so tired and emotionally drained by the time I got home that at first I didn't register the figure sitting on the porch steps. It wasn't until I'd stooped down to pick up the *Star Tribune* from in front of the gate that I thought I saw a pair of cowboy boots. Blinking, I looked up at Prince Luis.

I probably should have been more polite, but the first thing out of my mouth was, "Oh no, not you again."

Chapter Five

Prince Luis was the last person I wanted to see right now. In fact, the only thing I wanted to see at the moment was a bubble bath. At least today he'd forgone the cloak. Instead, he wore a T-shirt under a suit coat and jeans. It looked kind of *Miami Vice*, especially with his dark curls, but at least it was a fashion out of this century.

My eyes were gritty with lack of sleep and tears. I almost told him to come back later, until I noticed that the hand stretched out to me held a paper coffee container. The sleeve displayed the logo of my favorite shop too.

"The barista told me this was your 'usual,'" Luis said. The coffee bobbed in his hand as he waited for me to take the peace offering.

My mom must have been true to her word and significantly turned down the wards for Elias, because my feet only tingled slightly when I came up to stand beside where Prince Luis sat on our stoop. A little skeptical but too desperate to resist, I snatched the coffee container.

As I took a deep draft of the chocolaty caffeine goodness, Luis glanced at my feet and jeans. "What happened to you?" he asked.

I didn't think Elias would be happy if I told an "enemy" prince that the kingdom was completely falling apart because my dad was crazy with hunger and I'd nearly been eaten by a zombie horde of his subjects. Besides, I didn't think I was up to it, emotionally, so I shrugged and changed the topic of conversation. "Look at you, out in the sun. What are you doing here, anyway? Don't you have an army to, I don't know, command, or something?"

"I don't suffer from the allergy," he said. He squinted in the sun to look at my pants legs again. "Do you?"

"No, the blood isn't mine. Someone else yakked on me."

"Is everyone okay?"

Of course he'd worry about the vampires! It was strangely refreshing since so many of my friends were witches. "I don't know. I was too busy—" I was going to say trying to survive, so I took another irritated sip of my espresso drink. My head was far too fuzzy to keep from spilling the beans much longer. All I could think about was the bath I wasn't taking. "Why are you here?"

He stood up, stretching. Joints popped as he cracked his knuckles. The sound made me want to yawn. I barely held it in check. He said, "I've spoken to my advisers."

Somehow I doubted he'd waited on my doorstep with a mocha if what he had to say was a declaration of war. "And?"

"Captain Constantine is so well associated with the Northern Kingdom that he still makes an acceptable bargain. The other kingdoms will see ours as linked, which is all we need this union to provide politically. Also, my spymaster tells me that she has heard no whispers of his exile anywhere." He gave me a sidelong glance that lingered on the bloody calves of my jeans. "She also assures me that we negotiated with the correct Ramses."

I sipped my mocha, hoping that with enough caffeine, I'd follow all the politics a bit better. I had the feeling my dad had just been insulted or dismissed, but I wasn't sure how I was supposed to respond to that. I mean, there really *wasn't* any talking to Dad right now. I didn't like the idea that Luis's people knew how little control my dad had. Did he know what the hunger was doing to everyone?

I squinted at him questioningly but held my tongue.

Standing next to Luis, I noticed he wasn't that much taller than I was. I was fairly tall for a girl, but he was noticeably shorter than most of the boys I hung out with. The breeze rippled the leaves of the maple beside the house, and shards of sunlight danced in the gaps.

"Just to be one hundred percent clear," I said, taking another swallow of the warm drink, "you want Elias."

Luis nodded. "Yes. I accept the exiled Captain Constantine in exchange for Lieutenant Khan. Once the ceremony takes place, we will leave your people in peace."

I didn't fancy the idea of Elias's marrying someone else, even if it was this strange loveless confarreatio thing. I mean, I'd never thought we'd make good on our betrothal by actually walking down some aisle, but I liked him. If he married Captain Creepy, he'd leave. I might never see him again.

Weirdly, Elias would probably be okay with it. He'd be part of a kingdom again, back in service, with a purpose and all that. Plus, he'd probably get regular "meals" again.

"What do you guys do about the hunt?" I asked abruptly.

"The witch queen sacrifices herself every generation. Isn't that how it's always done?"

"What, you mean, she goes voluntarily?"

"How else would you do it? It's an honorable tradition, going back thousands of years."

"Sure, before the secret war, but—still?"

"Yes, still. Always." Luis seemed very baffled by this string of questions and my reaction. For the first time since I met him, I heard the barest trace of a Southern accent in his voice. "What else would you do? Draw lots? A queen has a duty to keep the peace."

His certainty surprised me. I was having a hard time wrapping my head around this scenario. I'd made up all sorts of reasons why covens might decide to give up one of their own, but give up their queen? And, if they sacrificed once a generation, they must run out of queens pretty quickly. Unless they waited for the queen to produce an heir before killing her—but that was just too sad and horrible to even consider.

The whole thing seemed opposite of human nature. If you have power, you fight to keep it, right? I couldn't imagine being so certain of my duty to my people that I'd be willing to die for it. It seemed antiquated, more like King Arthur than Machiavelli.

And from what I'd seen of my fellow witches, their tables were anything but round. We always seemed on the verge of some war or another either with the vampires or ourselves. "So you're all still friendly with witches?"

"My father is a witch," he said, then gave a guilty little shrug before adding, "as you already guessed."

"But he's not the King of Witches," I said.

"Good Heavens, no! Whoever heard of such a thing? A witch king! A man couldn't rule witches. Anyway, how could there be peace if I had to lose a parent to the hunt?"

Yeah, how, indeed. I was beginning to think my dad's people were the only ones without some kind of hunt plan in place. "Okay, one more time, with feeling," I muttered, through sips of mocha. "I'm having trouble really understanding this, so let me see if I've got it. In the Southern Region, the witch queen ritually sacrifices herself to the vampire hunt."

I was getting tired of standing, so I sat down on the cool concrete of the steps. Luis sat down next to me, and, when I looked at him to make sure I'd understood correctly, he nodded in agreement.

"But why?" I continued. "I mean, why would she do that? Aren't vampires and witches enemies where you come from?"

He put a hand on his chest. "Do you think I would exist if they were?"

"I do," I said, exasperated. "I exist. And my mom is the Queen of Witches, and my dad is the vampire king."

"Oh, that's not good," Luis said. "What will you do when it's time for the hunt?"

"Stop it, is what I did," I said grimly.

"You stopped the hunt? That's impossible. There is no stopping the hunt, only postponing it."

"Yeah, I'm kind of getting that," I said with a sigh.

"Your mother will have to pick a substitute," he said pragmatically. "But she will have to choose carefully. Everyone eventually resents a lottery, but unless someone volunteers, it may be the only way."

I glared at him over the rim of my cup. "I'm actually looking for a way where nobody has to die."

"And how do you expect to manage that miracle?"

"Magic?"

He didn't look very impressed. "Let me know how that goes."

Damn. I'd been really hoping he'd tell me all about some ancient spell he'd heard about or some fragment of myth or legend that I could go on. His flat-out disbelief made me lose hope. "I'm screwed, aren't I?"

A bold sparrow fluttered down to peck at the squashed mulberries that stained the sidewalk.

Luis's eyes crinkled like a kindly old man talking to a deluded teen. "Don't you think if the witches had a secret, magical alternative to blood sacrifice, they'd use it?"

Maybe it was the caffeine kicking in or his slightly patronizing tone, but I sat up a bit straighter. "It's possible no one's considered it before, you know. Tradition, tradition!" I half sang. "Vampires and witches aren't exactly big on change. All you ever hear is 'It's been done this way for thousands of years.'

My dad doesn't even own a cell phone or have cable TV. What the hell does he know of possibilities?"

Luis nodded, as if considering. Then he smiled. "Maybe there's an app for that, eh?"

"Ha."

He stood up and brushed his palms on his pants. "Listen, Ana. I don't mean to be rude, but I couldn't care less what you do about your hunt problem as long as this wedding goes off. It sounds as if you may be having some kind of internal crisis right now with your people, so I won't expect you to cover the cost of the wedding or provide a dowry beyond the captain's reputation and whatever goods and services he brings to the table. We can just take him home with us as soon as you release him."

A dowry? Was he being serious? I tilted my head to look up at him. Prince Luis, as always, had a serious expression. I wondered if he ever smiled when he wasn't trying to soften someone up for a deal.

I sighed and nudged at a mulberry stain with my bare toe. I couldn't believe it was coming to this. Elias married? And to some vampire dude? It was too weird.

"He's not really mine to give away," I said dejectedly. I didn't really want Elias to leave, but if he wanted to, how could I stop him? I frowned at my cup. "Why is this marriage so important?"

"Confarreatio," he corrected. Then he said, "You have your problems; we have ours."

"And this confarreatio thingie is going to fix your problems?"

"Partly," he said. He studied me for a long moment, and then for whatever reason, seemed to decide that it was okay to tell me more. "Constantine will help a lot, honestly. We lost so much in the hurricane. My people are scattered, some gone forever, and we need to regroup. The East is spoiling for another war, and we won't survive it without a strong military presence. Having someone like Constantine on our side will help tip the balance."

"Because he's a vampire killer?"

Luis's eyebrows jumped in surprise, but his voice betrayed none of it. "Just so."

"I don't want him to go," I admitted.

"I understand it must be difficult," Luis said. "But don't misunderstand me, Princess. This is serious business. If you try to back out, we will fight. We will have to."

"Even though—," I started, but he cut me off.

"Yes, even though," he said. "Because if my people can't have a wedding, they will want a fight—a cause to unite us."

I figured Luis would use that vague threat as an opportunity to leave.

Instead, he stood over me, frowning. "You care for Constantine, don't you?"

"Duh." What can I say? It was rude. I was exhausted, emotionally and physically.

"At first I thought he was your mother's lover. Now I see he is yours."

Lovers? I shook my head at the old-fashioned word. "Not really like that." I felt the need to explain. "We used to be betrothed, but that was because I bit him once, during a fight . . . uh, not with him, but, anyway, my dad dissolved all that."

"You're blood-bonded?"

I leaned back on my elbows to look up at Luis's shocked expression. Why did I get the feeling that he was about to tell me something else about vampire culture I should have known? "I don't know what that means."

Sunlight reflected in his bright green eye, making it flash silver. "Did he give his blood freely, or did you take it?"

I tried to remember. I was pretty sure I'd asked before I bit him. "Freely . . . ?"

"Crap." With that pronouncement, Luis sat down next to me again with a thump. He cradled his head in his hands as if he were the one with the sudden headache. Then he actually said, "Ai-yi-yi."

"What? Is that bad?"

He peeked at me in disbelief through interlocked fingers. Lifting his head, he said, "A confarreatio isn't going to last very long if you're blood-bonded to someone else, is it?"

"I have no idea," I said in all honesty. "I mean, I thought love had nothing to do with it."

"It doesn't, but the only thing more impossible to dissolve than a confarreatio is a blood bond." His head dropped back into his hands. "This sucks."

A smile twitched on my lips. I quickly hid it behind my cup. It was kind of awesome that every time I thought Elias was gone for good, another roadblock popped up.

But why hadn't anyone mentioned this blood-bond thing? I'd only bitten Elias in front of a zillion witnesses during a fight between my parents and their various minions at the farmers' market. I used to think that Dad kept things from me out of neglect or disinterest. Now I suspected it was intentional.

The gunk on my jeans had congealed, cold and stiff. "Does that mean the wedding is off again?"

Luis pulled his head up quickly. "No. I'm sure there's some historical precedent. The alliance doesn't need to be jeopardized just because of a romantic mistake."

He seemed to be trying to convince himself more than anyone else. "Okay, but what about Captain Cre—I mean, your captain? What if he finds out?"

"He won't, will he?" Luis gave me a meaningful, threatening look. "Not until after the contract is settled. Then it's between the two of them what happens next."

"I hate to tell you this, but it happened in public."

"If no one objects at the ceremony, it will be fine. You just have to make sure no one objects."

So it was my responsibility to keep everyone hushed? Awesome, considering I didn't really want Elias stuck in this weird political marriage. But if I didn't, we'd have war. Given the state of my dad's kingdom, that would be little more than a complete massacre.

I sneered at my nearly empty coffee container. "So you don't really care what happens after the wedding, so long as the confarreatio goes through, huh?"

"I don't. As prince, I'm obligated only to make arrangements and perform the ceremony. After that . . ." He shrugged.

I wondered what the ceremony would be like. Mom said

something about cake, so was it like a regular wedding? Did the priest ask the groom to bite the bride—or the other groom? I was guessing not, since this whole blood-bond thing seemed super-special. "Did you say you're performing the ceremony?" I asked.

Luis gave me a look as if I must be the stupidest vampire princess on the planet. "Of course. Your father must have done them when he was . . . feeling better. Surely you've had confarreatio here in the north?"

Hell, I'd never even heard the term before now. I shook my head. My back prickled with the growing heat and the constant pressure from the wards. My mocha was nearly empty. I swirled the remainder around the container.

Luis was shaking his head as if arguing with himself silently. Maybe he was trying to figure out how we survived up here in the north with a princess as dumb as me in charge. I might as well complete his assessment of me, by asking one last question: "Why are you embarrassed about being a dhampyr—or half vampire or whatever the polite term is?" I asked.

"I am a vampire," he said, stiffly. "Dhampyr is the term for someone like us who hasn't chosen a path."

"Oh, you mean like me."

Again, I seemed to have shocked him on some very deep, profound level. He actually jerked away slightly, as though I had announced I had the plague and he was afraid he'd catch it.

"How old are you?" he demanded.

"Sixteen, almost seventeen," I said, confused by the sudden line of questioning.

"Your sixteenth birthday has already passed?"

"That's what going on seventeen usually means," I agreed, kind of perversely enjoying watching his face contort.

"You decided to be a witch," he decided suddenly.

"No," I corrected. "I decided to be neither, or, maybe, both."

"It's unheard of," he said, and he made some gesture with his hands. Was he making a vampiric sign against the evil eye or something? "You have two animuses?"

What the hell was that? It sounded like "hippopatomuses" or some other ridiculous made-up word. "What are you talking about? Why are you so freaked out? It's actually kind of cool. I get all the vampire superpowers, plus I can still practice a bit of magic, though I need blood to do it."

"You're an abomination."

Well, okay then. That sort of ended the constructive part of the conversation. I'd have been hurt if I'd actually cared what he thought of me. I stood up and made a show of straightening my shirt. "Thanks for that lovely assessment, but I have things to do, people to see, so you can go screw yourself. 'Kay? Bye-bye now."

Even though the wards stung like a slap, I walked to the door without hesitation and let myself in. I left him staring, openmouthed at my back. What a jerk. I couldn't believe I wasted all that time talking to him when I could have been napping, especially since we ended up where we started with Elias. I hadn't resolved the stupid confarreatio problem, nor was I any closer to figuring out how to deal with the hunt, my dad's madness, or any of it. I could just cry.

I braced myself against the wall near the open staircase and took a breath. It came in jagged, and I felt my muscles start to shake. I'd managed to suppress my emotions long enough to try to get information out of Luis, but, now that he was gone, everything started to surface again. If I thought about it too hard, I thought I might break. Instead, I concentrated on breathing and emptied my mind. It was the only way I was going to stay focused, and I needed to stay on target. I couldn't let myself break down.

As far as I knew, Elias and I might be the only fully functional vampires right now. And he wasn't doing that great either. In this case, maybe being exiled actually helped him. But who knew how long he could hold out? It might be down to me.

Once I felt more in control, I dashed up the stairs to the bathroom. I started the water and stripped out of my pants. At least the stuff no longer looked like blood. Dust and road grit had covered all the spatters, and it appeared as if I'd been rolling in mud more than gore.

Still, the jeans were a disaster. I didn't think even a power wash would save them. At least they weren't favorites. I wadded them up and stuffed them into the garbage can.

Hot steam filled the room. Exhaustion swept over me. I felt so worn down, I wanted to sob. When I looked in the mirror, the feeling doubled. I had a big blue bruise on my shoulder where the Igor had hit me with the broomstick. My cheek was scratched. I looked like I'd been in some kind of crazy fight and lost—big-time.

The tub was nearly filled, so I stripped out of the rest of my clothes. I lowered myself in gingerly, the heat reminding me of all the other injuries I'd sustained.

What was I going to do about my dad? I wanted to just ignore the whole thing and focus on figuring out how to stop Elias's wedding, but Elias was starving too. . . . He wouldn't even make it to the ceremony if I didn't solve the problem of the hunt first.

I pulled myself out of the water and leaned over to where the radio sat on the far shelf. I flicked it on. The robotic voice of the National Weather Service told me today's high was expected to be eighty-seven, with ninety-percent humidity. Blurgh. I rolled the dial over to the music station and nudged the volume up a little. I knew Mom was still asleep, but I was kind of hoping to wake her. I had a lot I needed to talk to someone, *anyone* magical about. Mom was rarely my first choice as a sounding board, but, well, she might actually know something about the hunt and what exactly the vampires needed from it. Despite Luis's nay-saying, I still held out hope of some magic spell that might satisfy their need to kill.

I was forced to sing along with several songs—very loudly— before I heard my mother stir.

"Why can't you sleep in like most teenagers!?" A pillow smacked the door of her room, and I had to chuckle. She sounded like the petulant kid in our relationship. I was draining the tub and had put on a terry cloth robe when she knocked on the bathroom door.

She squinted at me with bleary eyes. "Seriously, when I was your age I slept in until noon during the summer."

"If it's any consolation, I haven't been to bed yet."

She grunted. "A little."

I got out of her way and went to my room to get dressed. I didn't think I'd be spelunking through any vampire caves anytime soon, so I opted for cutoffs and a tank top. The bruise on my shoulder looked purple under the white strap, so I grabbed a loose, cotton shirt. I hoped if I left it open and unbuttoned, I wouldn't get too hot.

I had to dig deep into my closet to find a replacement pair of Converses. The ones I found I'd rejected as too "girly" shortly after I bought them. My feet were small, and so sometimes I impulsively bought kids' sizes. These were hot pink with rhinestone butterflies on the side of the ankles. My toes were a bit squished, but they'd have to do until I could get to the shoe store. I never did like sandals, so I didn't have many other options . . . unless I wanted to teeter around in high heels. I checked out the look in the full-length mirror on my armoire. I decided they looked kind of good with the outfit. After I brushed out my hair and put on a touch of makeup that mostly hid the scratches, I headed down to find some breakfast.

Mom was still grumbling under her breath when we met at the kitchen table over our respective bowls of sugary cereal.

"Can I pick your brain about something?"

Mom said something that sounded like, "Murph. Brains," but then the coffeemaker made a happy percolating sound from the counter, and the strong scent of roasted beans seemed to revive her a bit. "Do you think Elias will be okay?" she asked, getting up to retrieve a cup.

"Well, not long term," I said. "In fact, I kind of want to talk about that."

"I'm worried about this nosferatu thing," she said, as if she didn't hear me. She pulled down a mug that one of her students had made. It had been shaped like a Venus of Willendorf—a headless, naked woman with big breasts and a round belly. She filled it up and sat down across from me. Adjusting her glasses, she blinked sleepily, like an owl. Her eyes widened, and then she nearly choked on her first sip. "What happened to your face? Who did that to you?"

My hand jumped up to cover the scratch.

Mom's power spiked. Magic welled up so quickly that I would have sworn the ground shook slightly, like some freak micro-earthquake. "I can't believe I let you go off with a hungry vampire! If Elias touched you, I will kill him."

"It wasn't Elias! It was Dad's minions."

"What? What is Ramses playing at?" Mom's power continued to grow and consolidate. She sat up straighter, but to my mind, she grew and spread out like a solid oak.

Meanwhile, I felt myself sinking in my seat. "I think they're starving, like crazy starving."

"He sent vampires after you? Here?"

"Uh, I kind of went to see him." I thought she'd known we were off last night, although maybe Elias had neglected to tell her where. Given her slowly purpling face, I could completely understand that.

"What?" she sputtered. "Why?"

This wasn't what I wanted to talk about, especially since it seemed so stupid in retrospect. How had I gotten so far off track? "I didn't know it would be like that, okay? I thought . . . I thought Dad would have things more under control. I assumed he'd take care of this before it got crazy. But things are really bad, Mom." My voice shook with the memory. "Really bad. We've got to do something. Do you know if there's some work-around to the hunt? What I mean is, I don't want anyone to have to die. There must be some kind of magic, right? We brought them over."

Mom sipped her coffee and gave me a very hard stare. Her power settled around her, like a heavy shroud. "You're right, honey. They're ultimately our responsibility. Frankly, it's stupid that we still have to feed them when they don't even belong to us anymore. We should have let them starve years ago."

I coughed up a Cheerio. "You don't mean that."

"Actually, I do. It was one thing to pay the price when it bought their servitude. But now? Now they're just parasites. Dangerous parasites."

I pushed away from the table. I didn't have to sit there and take that. When I stood up, however, I was hit by a wave of nausea that pushed me right back down. I gripped the table and concentrated on breathing.

Mom came over to see what was the matter. She put her arm around me, and I smelled her earthy, human scent.

My stomach growled.

Holy shit. I was hungry too, and and not for more cereal. My mom must have sensed it too, because her eyes went wide. Like tendrils, I felt her magic begin to twist toward me. I didn't know what her spell intended, but I had to get out of there. I pushed out from under her arms and ran for the door.

Chapter Six

I got as far as the curb and stopped, trying to calm my beating heart. I couldn't believe my own mother was going to entrap me in some kind of magical net, if that was what I'd sensed—not that she hadn't done it before. She'd once put me under a zombie spell just to keep me placid and at home. And the way she talked about vampires!

"Ana? Come back here. We need to talk!"

I bolted down the street, sending scurrying a group of cottontails foraging for clover on the boulevard. A flock of starlings took to the air as well. I ran all the way to the end of the block before I slowed.

I wanted to see Bea. Talking to Mom had been more than a bust, but Bea had something no other witch did. She had an ancient grimoire that we'd stolen from the Elders of the coven. The book had the spell that made vampires. The words were useless without the talisman, of course. But if it contained a spell that powerful, who knew what else it had?

I checked over my shoulder, but no one was coming after me. Maybe I'd imagined Mom's attack. Even though my sense of magic had never failed me before, it was better than thinking that both my parents had tried to do me harm within the same day.

Shit.

How was I going to get to Bea's? I'd stuffed my emergency money and bus pass into this pair of jeans when I'd changed, but the city bus could be such a pain. Bea lived in a neighborhood that required several transfers. I could sneak around to the back and "borrow" Mom's MINI. It would serve her right if I took off with it. But I had only a learner's permit. I was getting pretty good, but I was super nervous about being busted by some cop or getting in an accident. My luck hadn't been that awesome lately.

I did find myself turning down the alley, though.

St. Paulies can be so strange. Our block was one of those that had gotten into the recent fad of competitive alley scapes. People spent an inordinate amount of time and money on plantings to make the little scrap bits of yard in the alley into showpieces. The first one I passed had a gorgeous spray of deep indigo clematis climbing along a cedar plank fence. They'd also added clay pots full of white tea roses.

It was stunning.

Of course, everyone was gearing up for the annual Tea and Garden Stroll charity event. Lawn mowers had been running nonstop since this Saturday was the day when houses would open up their backyards to show off million-dollar landscaping and offer genteel cups of tea and other goodies to troupes of paying tourists.

Our own alley looked sad compared to the others. We had an asphalt slab next to the carriage house where Mom parked the MINI. A thick bunch of ferns had taken over the untended area near the drainpipe. Mom's mountain bike was propped, unlocked, against the carriage house door.

I might not feel right taking off with the car, but the bike seemed a fine substitution. Not much of an eff-you, but I still felt a surge of rebellion as I pedaled off.

Twenty minutes later I felt more sore than rebellious. My shins ached, and my hair was a plaster of sweat underneath the helmet. I'd mostly stuck to side streets with low traffic, but by the time I had to venture across University Avenue's constant construction, I thought I was going to die. How could my mom do this for fun? She must be crazier than I thought.

I smiled grimly to myself. That kind of you-baffle-me insanity would be a pleasant change, honestly. If I came up with a solution to the hunt, I might have to start being grateful for the normal kind of crazy my folks drove me.

Finally, I turned down Bea's street.

Even though they were older, the houses on the block looked remarkably similar. They were all in the Tudor style, with brown beams and white stucco. Each was about a story and a half, and they all sat right in the middle of identically manicured lawns. It was kind of Stepford, but the uniformity also made me feel weirdly . . . safe.

I coasted onto the sidewalk. Hopping off, I let the bike drop to the kind of springy, stiff grass that only existed at other people's houses. Our own was part clover with a dash of creeping Charlie, but mostly dandelions. I'd say Bea's dad had worked some kind of green magic, but all the other houses managed the same trick. I hardly saw a single yellow or fuzzy ball on the entire block.

Before ringing the bell, I checked the time. My cell told me it was nearly eight. Though not exactly a "decent" hour to wake someone during summer vacation, it wasn't ridiculously early either. I punched up Bea's number and called.

"Mmmr," she answered.

"I woke you. Sorry," I said. "Can I come in?"

"In?" I heard rustling. I looked up in time to see her part the curtain of her bedroom window and look down. I waved. The curtain shut. "This had better be an emergency."

My speaker picked up the sound of her huffing down the stairs, so I hung up. She opened the door a second later. Bea stood blinking at me in sweatpants and an oversized T-shirt showing a cartoon fluffy cat holding a garden spade and a potted flower. The words underneath said HAIRY POTTER. Her brown hair, streaked with pink, was flattened on one side, and her face was bare of makeup. I tried not to notice the zit forming just under her chin. At least she'd managed to get a little color this summer, and a spray of freckles dotted either side of her button nose. Normally, I considered Bea was the cuter one of the two of us, since she had that hourglass shape all the boys craved. But, at the moment, she looked ready to bite my head off.

She glared at me for another second, then turned and stalked off to the kitchen. I followed her inside, shutting the door quietly behind me.

The interior of Bea's house was a lot like the exterior. There were crisp, clean lines and carpeting so white I always felt as if I must be tracking filth on it even after I kicked off my shoes and left them in the pile by the door. Air-conditioning kept the temperature almost chilly, but the house never felt stuffy or closed up. In fact, it always kind of smelled freshly polished. There were no dust bunnies lurking in the corners, or cobwebs filling cracks in the crown molding.

I found Bea in the gleaming chrome kitchen, pressing buttons on a fancy coffeemaker. A sound like a buzz saw made me jump, as fresh beans were processed into grounds. Bea leaned against a sink completely empty of dishes and rubbed her face. "Spill."

Where to start?

Might as well get right to the point. "Remember that book I asked you to hide? I need it."

Bea gave me a suspicious look as the water in the coffeemaker sputtered and hissed. "You told me never to tell you where it was. Ever." ·

I stood awkwardly in the archway. There were tons of chairs and stools to choose from, but they seemed so artfully placed, like something out of a magazine, that I wasn't sure I was actually supposed to sit on any of them. "I'm getting hungry," I admitted.

"Huh? Oh, well, we've got cereal you can have," Bea said, turning to a cupboard.

"That's not what I mean," I said quickly. *"Hungry."* I emphasized the word, watching her half-lidded eyes for comprehension. "You know, as in the hunt."

Her expression widened a little, but she shook her head in confusion. "That's bad," she agreed, rubbing her face heavily. "But what does that have to do with the book?"

I explained my hopes that the grimoire might contain a spell that could substitute for the hunt. Bea took it all in slowly. When the chime rang on the coffeemaker, she poured herself a big cup and added a ton of milk and sugar. I joined her at the polished oak table in the breakfast nook.

The room was a new addition, though it fit in seamlessly with the rest of the remodeled kitchen. Windows covered all four walls. Bea sat, sipping, for several minutes. I didn't think I'd laid such a difficult proposal in front of her, but, well, I knew she wasn't a morning person. I waited as patiently as I could, but this was getting ridiculous.

Finally, I broke. "Look—are you going to help me or not?"

"It's not that." She waved her hand dismissively. "Of course I'll get the book for you, even though I don't think you're going to find anything in it. I'm trying to decide if I should tell you something."

"You know you should! We're supposed to be best friends." Except, we weren't always. We'd fought about pretty much everything at some point or another, and, of course, there was the whole witch versus vampire thing.

Bea must have decided I was right, because she leaned across the table. "There was a secret coven meeting called last night for the Elders," she said, her voice dropping, even though we were very likely the only people awake in the house. "We discussed the vampire problem. Seems your mom already knows about the hunger that's spreading through the kingdom, and, well, some people think this could be a 'final solution,' if you know what I mean."

There was so much about what she just said that made my brain strip its gears, but I'd gotten stuck early. "'We'? Since when are *you* an Elder?"

Color rose on Bea's cheeks. "Keep your voice down!" she hissed. Looking around as if expecting spies, she leaned even closer. "My dad named me as successor, okay? That makes me a kind of an apprentice Elder. I'm not allowed to vote or anything. I just have to take notes like a secretary or an aide-de-camp. When he retires, I'll take his place on the council."

I couldn't decide if I was mad, jealous, or both. Even though my mom was queen, Bea's family had always been much better connected to the witch scene than mine. So I shouldn't have been so surprised that Bea, who'd passed her Initiation with great success in contrast to my monumental failure, was invited to participate in high muckety-muck meetings. Yet I felt totally betrayed, as if she'd left me behind on purpose. Plus, I couldn't help thinking that if I hadn't been such a loser at the Initiation, we'd be doing this stuff together, as a team.

Bea must have seen it all in my eyes, because she sighed. "I knew you'd be like this. Try to listen to what I'm saying, though, would you? There's a really large contingent of Elders who think the best course of action is to do nothing—to let all the vampires starve themselves to death."

"That includes me!"

"Yeah, I don't think your mom was counting on that."

"Wait, are you saying that mass genocide was Mom's idea?"

Bea tsked. "No, of course not. I just think she was more willing to entertain the idea when she thought it was, you know, just *them*."

"I can't believe that. I thought she was really starting to like Elias. God, how could I have been so wrong?" Of course, it seemed I'd generally put far too much trust in my parents lately.

Pursing her lips, Bea took a sip of coffee before answering. "I don't know. Anyway, I thought she said something about his leaving to get married off in some political ceremony."

That made a little more sense, at least. Mom was counting on Elias's being away before letting the local vamps devour themselves, or whatever they thought would happen if they denied them the hunt forever.

Bea was giving me a funny look. "So it's true?" she asked.

"Yeah, remember, I told you about this last night? Well, that prince wants Elias to marry his captain. Well, I guess 'marry' isn't the right term. They'd enter a confarreatio."

"Whatever," she said. "Isn't that just what they call vampire marriage?"

"No," I said. "This seems like a completely different thing.

My mom said she insisted on getting a real marriage to my dad on top of a confarreatio."

"But it still binds two people, right?"

"Seems to," I agreed.

"Well, I thought you and Elias were together."

I had no idea what to say about that. I mean, I'd thought Dad had broken us up, but now Luis suggested we were forever bound by some kind of "trust blood bond." So I just shrugged.

"Is he really going to marry a dude? I didn't know he was bi."

Wow, my mom must have told the council everything. I guessed Bea just needed me to confirm it. "I don't know if he's bi. We never talked about that. I have to say that the confarreatio seems very arranged and political, not so much on the romantic side. I'm beginning to think vampires don't marry for love, only politics. I mean, it's not as if they're going to have kids together."

"You've got a point there," Bea agreed. But she really didn't want to let the subject of Elias's sexuality go. "So you've never asked him? He's been alive forever, and you're not even curious if he ever kissed a boy in all that time? I mean, Constantine, right? That's Greek, or Roman—whatever. I watched *Spartacus*. There was a whole lot of sex with dudes in those days."

"Oh, would you stop it? Don't we have bigger things to worry about than whether Elias has kissed a boy?"

She gave me a serious, measuring look. Setting her cup down, she declared, "You don't like the idea, do you?"

"Well, would you? Would you want to know if your boyfriend had boyfriends?"

Bea smiled lasciviously. "I'd think it was kind of hot."

"You are so weird."

"Oh, come on! You don't think the idea of two Roman dudes together is kind of sexy?" she continued. "The point is, that's like total *yaoi* fantasy." Bea referred to a subset of Manga written for girls that features boys in love. We'd both gone through a phase when we read a lot of it, though apparently it had made a much bigger impression on Bea.

"Yeah, but see, that's just it, isn't it? It's fantasy. Elias is my *real* boyfriend."

Bea cocked her head. "So you *are* still together. Does Thompson know?"

I was seriously getting frustrated with this conversation. It had spun away from me—and from the point. "For the hundredth time, I'm not dating Thompson."

"I don't know if he knows that."

Crossing my arms in front of my chest, I sat back. "Can we just go look at the book?"

Bea laughed. "You know what? No. Not until you promise on your witch honor that you will ask Elias about his past relationship with men."

"Seriously? You are such a pervert."

"I know I am, but what are you?" she said in that singsong tone we used when we were kids. Bea got up and put her coffee cup in the dishwasher. "Just ask. I'm curious, okay? I just told you a whole bunch of stuff I wasn't supposed to, and that could get me in a whole shitload of trouble. You could at least do this for me."

I raised my hands in defeat. "Okay, okay. You win!"

"Good. Now let's go fetch the grimoire."

When I told Bea to hide the book, I'd had visions of secret caves or, at the very least, a wall safe with multiple combinations. She pulled a cardboard box out from under her bed.

"This is where you hid the grimoire?"

"Don't act so horrified," she said. At least she'd put a few decoy papers on top. As she shifted them to the side, I thought they looked like old school papers. Bea sat in a clear spot on the floor of her room. "No one knew I had it. It was as safe here as anywhere else."

The walls of Bea's room were covered in movie posters and pencil sketches of celebrities. In a corner she had a wooden drawing table and a stool, which I perched on. There were art supplies everywhere. Magazines and books littered the floor and all other flat surfaces. Discarded clothes draped over everything else. Bea was a slob; I felt completely at home.

She handed me the book. It was leather bound and smelled of red rot. The pages were brittle and so thin as to be nearly transparent. Spidery, cursive handwriting and illustrations filled all the spaces. Here and there pressed flowers, which had been pasted to the paper, crumbled into the book's gutter.

I looked at the words for a clue, and I discovered I couldn't read it.

"Is this English?" I asked.

"Kind of. It's Old English," Bea said. When I gave her a how-did-you-know-that look, she shrugged. "I looked it up on Wiki-pedia."

"Can you read it?"

"If I work at it, but I never even really learned cursive, did you?"

Actually, I had. I'd suffered through hours and hours of rote practice because my mother, being a college professor, said she would be damned if a child of hers couldn't read historical documents such as the Constitution because no one in the St. Paul public school system could be bothered to teach it. Still, it wasn't something I used every day. "A little," I admitted.

I joined Bea over on her bed, and we sounded out the titles to most of the entries. There were effective poultices for the treatment of gout and other ailments, botanical lists, and even a spell for the "discoverie of a familiar" that both Bea and I kind of wanted to try.

Outside of that and the one very important spell for the "creation of the vampyr," nothing in the book seemed terribly outside of what you might find in a modern grimoire. I copied down everything written on vampires, all three pages of it, but it seemed everyone had called this one: the grimoire wasn't going to be much help.

At least not in any obvious way.

Resting my back against the headboard, I felt defeated. Bea sat beside me adding sketches of the symbols and other illustrations to my notes. She hummed to herself as she drew. Under the surface of reality, I could feel another vibration, not unlike when Bea worked magic. Her fingers dashed lightly over the paper, and I was amazed, and, as always, just a little surprised at how good she really was.

"Are you going to apply to MCAD?" I asked. Minneapolis College of Art and Design would be a perfect fit for a college for Bea. They even taught courses on graphic novels and animation.

She shook her head lightly, not breaking the deep concentration she always entered when drawing. "My dad won't pay for it. He thinks art is a fine hobby, but I should get a real education to support my 'dabbling.'"

"Your dad's an asshole," I noted, leaning over her shoulder to watch as she transformed the blank section of the notepaper into a work of art. "You'd be wasted as a computer programmer."

That was what Bea's dad was, and, consequently, he thought all this artsy-fartsy stuff such as theater and drawing were trivial distractions from the real world. Bea's mom was a little more supportive, but she was in the same camp when it came down to the importance of a decent job and financial security.

Heck, neither of Bea's parents had much respect for my mom's work. I'd heard them at parties tell her half jokingly, half seriously that it was time for her to grow up and move out of the dorm. It was true that my mom worked long hours, but that was because she wasn't tenured. To make up for that, she taught as an adjunct professor at several different colleges and universities in the area.

At least I knew my mom wouldn't turn up her nose if I applied to a theater program somewhere. She figured all college degrees were valuable, even the most liberal of the liberal arts. But I would have a fight if I decided not to go to college, or,

Goddess forbid, a technical or community college. In fact, I'd better pick a school with a good reputation or I'd never hear the end of it. She would probably rather die than tell her colleagues her daughter was off at some kind of party school, like the University of Florida–Gainesville.

"You're missing driver's ed," Bea noted when she looked up long enough to stretch her neck. Pointing to the candy red analog alarm clock, complete with big brass bells, she said, "It's after ten."

"I know," I said. Speaking of things Mom would be mad about, I'd begged and begged her to get me into a driver's education program that wouldn't interfere too much with my summer plans or my vampire princess duties. To spite me, I swear, she got me into a class that started at eight in the morning. This would be the third class I'd missed. I'd slept through the other two. "I'm never going to get my license."

"You don't need to drive. You could get an Igor as a chauffeur," Bea pointed out.

I made a face. "Only if he's not one of the smelly ones." A lot of the Igors I'd met had a dubious sense of hygiene. They hung out in too many caves, I guessed.

My cell beeped. I checked the text. It was Thompson, wanting to know if I was up for meeting him for lunch before tryouts for the Renaissance Festival. Sounded like a date to me, so I turned to Bea. "Want to go to lunch with me and Thompson?"

"I don't want to be a third wheel," she teased.

"Gah! We are not dating!" I said, though I was beginning to wonder if I *had* missed that particular memo. Anyway, I was already telling him that he could pick us up at Bea's house because she was coming along. Having done this with theater people before, I added, "We should decide now where we want to go. I hate all that 'I dunno, where do you want to go' stuff."

"Jimmy John's," Bea suggested.

I had enough money for that, so I texted Thompson. Then I sent another one telling him to bring his truck because I needed to throw my bike in the back.

He replied, "Bike? Bet u look like W. Witch."

Bea, who read it over my shoulder, chuckled. "He thinks you're cute."

"How do you get that? The Wicked Witch was green."

"You know that's not how he meant it," Bea said, her grin widening. "I don't know why you're so resistant. He's cute and sweet on you, and now he's a theater guy. That's all win, girl."

"If you ignore our terrifying history." I grimaced. When Bea had the audacity to look confused, I explained. "He used to bully us, Bea. All the time. Don't you remember putting a spell on him when it looked like he was going to punch us? The rude words on my locker? The licking incident? Hello, that was only last year."

Bea frowned briefly and then dismissed all that with a little shrug. "We were in a show together. That forgives everything."

I wasn't sure I agreed. Sure, doing the updated version of *My Fair Lady* opposite Thompson was pretty amazing. He seemed like a completely different person during the run of the show. Maybe that was part of it. I just didn't trust the change to last.

I had to admit it was nice to be worrying about boys instead of vampires for the moment. I wondered, however, if Bea intentionally distracted me. She'd dropped a pretty big bomb at the breakfast table—that the Elders were seriously considering letting everyone in the kingdom die from neglect, as it were. I wasn't even sure that would work. I got the impression from Elias that they would become nosferatu before that. Mom had found that out last night too. Hadn't she brought that up to the Elders at their secret meeting?

I wanted to ask Bea but was afraid that if she didn't know, she'd tell. I didn't want the Elders to have any more of a head start than they already had.

Knees bent up and ankles crossed, she lay on her bed, putting the finishing touches on her drawing. The grimoire sat open beside her. She looked so comfortable with the book that I got the feeling she'd done this many times before. She claimed she couldn't read the writing, but I'd have bet it wouldn't take her artist's eye long to parse out the letters if she put any effort into it at all. She'd known it was in Old English.

Bea was craftier than I gave her credit for.

Putting her pencil down, she noticed me staring at her and smiled broadly. "Hey, what do you think I should wear to tryouts?"

And she hopped up to drag me into the furious business of fashion decisions. I didn't surface until we heard the beep of Thompson pulling up to the house.

Matt Thompson arrived in the kind of truck you'd expect to have a gun rack in the back and, in the proper season, a dead deer in the bed. He was a hockey player and had the kind of dark curly hair that made cheerleaders swoon. His jeans were dusty and grass-stained, and he had a body that looked as if he actually used it for something.

I dare say I noticed that body thanks to a nicely fitting T-shirt that clung in all the right places.

We stood on the stoop as he walked up the sidewalk. Bea leaned into me and quietly said, "Yum."

"You should date him," I told her, even though I couldn't have agreed more about his appeal.

"He's not even looking at me, girlfriend."

It was true. Bea could have been invisible for all that he seemed to notice her. And I'd helped her pick out her cutest outfit too. She wore a sparkly belly-shirt that showed off a tiny bit of skin and low-slung, curve-hugging jeans. We'd learned from experience that it helped to show off your, uh, assets when auditioning. It usually worked even with gay-guy directors. But Thompson was apparently immune.

"Hey," he said to me, stopping just short of the steps. Standing as I was at the top, we were almost eye to eye. For the first time, I noticed that Thompson's eyes were blue—a soft, sort of denim color. Like the jeans he wore, they seemed faded but lived-in.

Bea broke the spell by clucking her tongue disapprovingly. "You look as if you've been rolling in the grass," Bea said, pointing to the flecks of clippings that clung to his cuffs. "Where've you been?"

"Work," Thompson said, his gaze finally leaving me for a brief glance in her direction. "I didn't have time to change."

Thompson worked for his dad's landscaping company during

the summer. I hadn't told him, but I'd actually seen him earlier in the week. His crew woke me up at nine o'clock when their gigantic mowing machines trimmed the neighbor's lawn. Surreptitiously through the lace curtains, I'd watched Thompson clip the hedges that I'd crashed into last year when I attempted a vampire-ninja jump off my carriage house roof. I probably should have gone out to say hello, but, honestly, I was kind of worried I might embarrass him.

"You look fine," I said quickly.

But Bea already started in, saying, "You can't wear that to an audition. They're not doing *Oklahoma!*"

"You really think it matters?" Thompson looked down at the dusty T-shirt that fit him oh so well and frowned.

"No," I said honestly. It was a classic double standard, but the truth was that usually shows were so hurting for male bodies that directors would take any boy, even if he came dressed in a gunny sack. I wouldn't have thought a few grass stains would matter.

Bea shot me a look. "Of course it does. There are going to be a ton of other guys there. This is Festival, not some high school play. We should skip lunch and get you some better duds. Do you live close?"

He looked around at the large perfect houses in Bea's neighborhood and shook his head as if she must be kidding. "I live in Phalen."

I watched Bea struggle not to make some kind of derogatory comment or look down her nose. "Oh. Well then, we'd better hurry."

If Thompson noticed, he didn't say anything. He just went

over to where I'd tossed my bike on the ground, and picked it up. We trailed behind. I scrunched my face at Bea. She lifted her shoulders and opened her palms, as if to ask what I was so cranky about. Bea could be so insensitive. Ever since we were in *My Fair Lady* together, I knew how much Thompson struggled to feel a part of our theater clique. He might not be my boyfriend, but I didn't like to see him hurt.

I hurried to stand beside him as he lowered the tailgate. "You know, if this is awkward, I honestly don't think it's absolutely necessary. Like I told you before, I heard the audition is all improv. I don't think they're really going to care if we're dressed up. I mean, I'm going in this."

After moving aside a toolbox and a case of Diet Pepsi, he carefully set my bike down. He wiped his hands on his jeans and straightened up. He looked me over. "Yeah, but you look good in anything," he said with a smile. Then he looked down at his broad, manly chest, clearly seeing something I didn't, because he looked disappointed. "Bea's right. I should probably clean up a little. If I'm going to be a knight in shining armor, I probably shouldn't be sweaty."

Actually, standing as close as we were, I wanted to tell him that the scent of freshly cut grass and musk smelled damn good on him. But Bea pulled at the car handle impatiently. "Are we going or what?"

A brief flash of irritation flickered across Thompson's face. "Yeah, let's go."

I should *date him*, I thought. He and my best friend already hate each other.

The drive to Thompson's house continued the awkward mood.

Bea insisted I sit in the middle. The cab wasn't really meant for three. My thighs pressed against Bea on one side and Thompson on the other. Every time he used the stick shift, Thompson's arm grazed my breast. Worse, I was kind of tippy because my butt straddled a raised section of the slippery upholstery. Each corner we took brought me much closer to either of them than I would have liked.

Actually, I think Thompson and I would have been fine. Each time gravity threw me at him, we shared a secret, amused smile.

Bea, however, was complainy and seemed determined to start a fight. "You don't have an MP3 player?" she asked, though the answer was pretty clear, especially given that she was pointing at the simple dashboard radio.

"You can listen to music if you want to," Thompson said, reaching past me to flick the knob. Heavy metal blasted from the speakers.

Even though Thompson clearly knew the song as he bobbed his head along with the rhythm, Bea knocked into me as she grabbed for the tuner. I scrunched up against Thompson's shoulder as she spun the dial. She settled on an alt-rock station . . . which just happened to be playing Ingress, my ex-boyfriend's band.

Bea gave a squeal of delight. "Hey, Ana! It's Nik!"

Did she really think any of us in the truck needed the identification, or the reminder that I used to be romantically attached to a rock star?

Beside me, I felt Thompson's body stiffen. To his credit, he tried to act mildly interested. "I heard they've got some kind of record deal."

I'd heard that too, but even so, something weird twinged in my chest. Jealousy?

"Columbia," Bea agreed. "The big league."

The twinge suddenly felt more like a punch in the gut. She knew *details*? Was Nik still talking to Bea? She once wanted to date him, but she was with Malcolm now, wasn't she? I opened my mouth to ask her when she last talked to Nik, but she shushed me to sing along.

To a song, I wanted to point out, that he wrote for *me*.

Chapter Seven

I had a hard time concentrating on anything else for the rest of the trip. Memories and emotions roiled around in my head to the point that I didn't even notice when we'd turned up Johnson and sped past the lake Thompson's neighborhood was named after.

Apparently sharing gossip about Ingress constituted some kind of truce between Bea and Thompson, because they chatted amiably about the upcoming audition. I didn't really pay the conversation any mind until Thompson's admission: "My dad thinks I'm at a job fair."

"You lied?" Bea was horrified, although she herself rarely told her folks anything; I couldn't even remember the last time she had.

"I had to," Thompson said, turning down a narrow street lined with brick apartments. Kids playing kick ball in the street moved out of the truck's way. "My dad would never give me time off to go to an audition."

Remembering that his dad never came to see him star in the show, I gave his leg a sympathetic squeeze. He tried to smile at my gesture, but his expression looked sadder than anything else.

"What are you going to tell him if you get in?" Bea wanted to know.

"It's on the weekends. It won't interfere with work," he said with a defiant lift of his shoulder. "Besides, there's a paycheck. It's like a second job. He has to respect that."

He seemed to be trying to convince himself. But it was true that the Renaissance Festival paid. It wasn't much; in fact, the amount was laughable for first-year rookies, which we would be, but it *was* money.

"Your dad sounds like mine," Bea said.

Thompson grunted. I wasn't sure if it was in disbelief or sympathy. Directing his question to me, he asked, "What about your dad, Ana? What does he think of your theater stuff?"

"My dad?" I remembered the crazy haze that clouded his eyes before he suggested that his hungry subjects devour me, and I shivered. "I don't know, and I don't care. We don't really talk."

Bea was gesturing over my head when I looked up, and I thought I saw her mouth "separated," which I guessed was technically true.

"It's cool," Thompson said. "My parents are divorced too. My mom moved back to Ohio, and we lost touch. I heard she might finally be in rehab, though." He trailed off then, as if he suddenly realized he'd said just a bit too much. His announcement, "Here we are," spared us the opportunity to completely mess up a thoughtful response. He pulled the truck up to a curb. There were no sidewalks in this part of town, and the houses were one-story squares in various states of repair. The one I guessed to be Thompson's had the nicest, greenest lawn, and the framing around the front door had recently been replaced, as the wood was bare and unpainted.

Bea started to open the door, but Thompson reached across me to put a hand on her shoulder. "I'm just going to be a minute. Why don't you girls wait here?"

"Aw, come on." Bea pouted. "I totally want to see your house."

"There it is, four two one," he said, gesturing toward the house. His face was closed, and I could tell he would resist any argument. "Just wait here."

I gave Bea the don't-push-it glare, and, for once, she listened to me. "Fine, but I'll expect a full tour sometime!" she called after him as he dashed up the asphalt drive.

"Yeah, maybe next Garden Stroll," he shouted back, referencing the fancy tea and garden charity event in my neighborhood. I blushed.

"Check out this place," Bea said gleefully, once Thompson had slipped inside. "Oh my God."

I couldn't see what her problem was. Okay, so these weren't hundred-year-old mansions with sprawling, palatial lots, but they seemed homey and mostly well cared for. There was that one house in the middle of the block that had a dirt-packed yard full of filthy children's toys and other detritus, but Thompson couldn't control who his neighbors were any more than I could.

I was just about to tell her to be nicer when I noticed a woman coming out of Thompson's house. Thin to the point of being scrawny, she wore a bikini that left little to the imagination. She tottered toward us in high-heeled sandals. She waved at us. I returned her greeting halfheartedly and gave Bea a questioning look. Bea's eyes nearly bulged out of her head.

The woman leaned into the open window on the driver's side. She had bleach blond hair and smoked a cigarette. She blew the blue smoke off to the side and then smiled at us. I couldn't determine her age. If Thompson hadn't said his mother was in Ohio, I might have assumed this was his mom.

"Hi, girls," she said. Her skin was tanned, but it had that sort of leathery look of someone who's spent too much time exposed to the elements. "Which one of you lucky ladies is dating Matt?"

I couldn't find words for a reply, so, of course, Bea chimed in. "Ana," she said with a helpful point at me.

"I'm not dating Thompson," I said for the fifteenth time that day, but my voice was very small.

She didn't hear, anyway, because she talked right over me, "Oh, Ana! I've heard so much about you. Matthew says you're so smart, and some kind of actress?"

"I guess," I admitted, since the last part seemed to be a question of some sort.

She gave me an appraising look and seemed to decide something. "Most of his exes are total sluts. You almost look respectable."

"Almost?" Bea gasped.

"Don't talk to my friends, Sheila." Thompson's voice boomed out from behind the woman.

She started in surprise and nearly bonked her head on the window frame. She turned in fury to face him. He'd changed into a clean pair of jeans and a white button-down. She scowled at him. "Matt, honey, what is wrong with you? I'm just saying hello."

"Just . . . don't." Thompson's eyes narrowed threateningly as he spoke, and he took a menacing step toward the door she blocked. I held my breath. I thought there was going to be a fight. He just kept coming, and she got out of his way, though not happily.

"You're a bully just like your father," she shouted as he started the engine. "You should show some respect. I'm your stepmother."

"You're nothing except trouble," he growled.

Thompson hit the gas so hard the wheels squealed.

Nobody said anything for a long time. Finally, Thompson muttered, "I'm sorry. I thought she'd stay in the house. Why didn't she stay in the house?"

"She seemed nice," I offered, even though she'd completely insulted all his exes and me in the same breath.

He snorted and rolled his eyes at me. "That's because you don't live with her."

"Honestly, I thought she was a bitch," Bea muttered out the window.

"No shit," Thompson snarled.

I had no comment on that, though I felt I probably should have either agreed or consoled him. Once again, the more socially adept Bea came to our rescue. "I'm starving," she said. "Can we drive through somewhere?"

We ate our burgers in the cab, parked outside the building marked LITTLE THEATER on the Augsburg College campus. It looked more like a rickety house than the sort of theaters I was used to. It had wide, plank siding and a strange sort of scalloped top, which reminded me of something out of the Old West. There were other early arrivals, sitting on concrete block stairs underneath the theater's triangularly shaped awning. More sat in the shade of the trees in the large, flat grassy quad across the street. We'd found a spot on the curb next to the wooden noise barrier that separated the campus from the highway.

None of us mentioned the scene at Thompson's house. Instead, we talked about the upcoming audition and our impressions of what it might be like to work at the event. I'd been to the Renaissance Festival once or twice with Mom when I was much younger. It was a long drive from St. Paul, almost a half hour out. I had the strongest memory of a gigantic parking lot filled with row after row of cars. As you got closer to the main gates, the signs marking rows took you back in time by a decade or more—2000, 1990, and so on all the way back to 1500. It was pretty clever, honestly. The whole thing was built like a walled city, and there were permanent shop buildings, stages, an arena for falconers, and a jousting contest.

"I don't even remember anybody out there except Puke and Snot," Thompson admitted. "And Snot died a couple of years ago."

I didn't even have very strong memories of that because the crowd around the stage was so thick that I couldn't even see what was happening, much less hear it. I remembered that the stage had been decked out to look like a pirate ship, though, and I thought that was cool.

"I know what you mean," Bea agreed, around a mouthful of cheeseburger. "I think I might have been accosted by one person who made a big fuss about my having to use the 'privy,' and a bunch of people yelled out anytime I spent a twenty-dollar bill. But I don't remember a lot of free-range actors. And yet they say they employ more than a thousand people."

"We don't have to have some kind of act or anything, do we?" I got nervous at the thought. I wasn't ready for anything that serious.

"No, they audition those people separately." Thompson was the one who'd originally heard about this, so I trusted him. "In fact, if I don't make the cut, I have a lead on a job with the guys who do the jousting."

"Seriously?" I was impressed. Those guys seemed crazy, but in a kind of awesome way. They wore real armor and knocked themselves off horses.

Bea made a strangled, excited sound and shoved the remains of her food into her mouth while gesturing wildly with her hands. I looked where she was pointing. They were opening the doors.

We emerged an hour later, having played a lot of games. I spent most of the time convinced that everyone else was much better at improvisation than I was, especially since some people's antics made me laugh out loud. Still, I always felt it was encouraging when I'd had fun. Thompson and I sat on the stoop, enjoying the hot sun and quiet after the cool darkness and chaos of the theater. Bea was still inside, flirting outrageously with one of the funnier boys. I wondered if *her* alternative plan to getting into Festival was being snuck in the back as someone's girlfriend.

Frankly I didn't think there was much hope for the three of us. The director was a stern, gaunt man whose face seemed perpetually stuck in a scowl of distaste. He never even cracked a smile when the rest of the house was rolling in the aisles with laughter. He just scribbled something down on his clipboard and yelled, "Next!" in that booming directorial voice that made even the laziest slacker hop to.

"I'm going to call that jousting organization," Thompson said. He pulled himself upright with a sigh and wandered a short distance down the block to dial the numbers on his cell.

I probably should have told him that he'd done fine and not to worry, but Thompson was even worse at improvisation than I was, and he knew it. I'd cringed in my seat while I watched his stiff performances. I could sympathize. He and I were much better with scripts. If they'd had an opening for a singer, though, he would have rocked the house. That was how he'd gotten the male lead in *My Fair Lady*, after all.

The double doors behind me swung open, and Bea flounced out, accompanied by not one, but a whole troupe of boys. I'd have been irritated or jealous, but this was standard operating procedure for Bea. She had those curls and curves, and boys had no choice but to fall into her gravitational field. Even gay boys liked her.

She plopped down beside me, and the guys took up positions around us, enclosing us in a circle of testosterone. She waved her hand in various introductions, and I shook hands, desperately trying to hang on to names I could feel myself already forgetting. Part of my difficulty was that they had a kind of similarity despite all their differences. They were loud, boisterous, made a lot of obscure cultural references, and clearly found themselves deeply amusing. Still, for the most part, I found them charming—and cute.

I particularly liked the ponytail dude, who had been so good at coming up with puns and other hilarious bits during the improv games. He was a touch on the pudgy side, but I thought it made him seem even more approachable and friendly.

"Hey," Thompson said with the kind of tone you might expect from someone who had come back to find his spot inhabited by a whole gang of theater boys.

Bea jumped in with a repeat of names, but I was too busy watching everyone to catch them this time either. It was funny the way the males reacted to the sudden appearance of another set of clearly more alpha XY chromosomes. They squared their shoulders as if they hoped that fluffing themselves up might add the inches they'd need to look Thompson in the eye. You could almost hear knuckles cracking as they exchanged manly handshakes.

A rival had clearly crashed their party, though you could see a few sneers forming instantly. In their obvious list making of attributes, they remembered Thompson's poor showing on stage. I knew what was going to happen next. Jokes would become more biting, references more obtuse, and there would be this subtle play among the theater people that would serve to highlight Thompson's weaknesses.

So I got up and took Thompson by the hand. He looked down in shock for a moment at our clasped palms, but he let me lead him away from the pack of boys. "How'd it go with the jousters?"

"Pretty good," he said. "They were impressed that I'm a brown belt in kuk sool wan. Apparently, it's really important to know how to fall properly and not kill yourself. They said I could come in for an interview."

"That's great," I told him sincerely. We'd crossed the street and were strolling along a dirt path that had been worn into the quad. I felt I should probably let go of his hand, but I found I didn't entirely want to. I asked, "What the heck is kuk whatever?"

"It's a Korean mixed martial art."

"And you have a brown belt?"

He nodded. "I got into it by accident. It's not really my normal kind of sport, but my parents were looking for something to channel my energy when I was little, you know? I think they were hoping it would make me less . . ." He shrugged, searching for the right word. "Hyperactive? Anyway, I ended up sticking with it. There's actually a bunch of Festival guys at my dojang. That's how I heard about this jousting company and the tryouts."

"You never fail to surprise me," I told him honestly.

He stopped and used my momentum to swing me around to face him. His voice was low and intimate. "Is that a good thing?"

His face was very close. I could smell his aftershave, and the sunlight played along the strong line of his jaw. If I wanted to kiss him, I'd have to go up on tiptoes. But, if I did that, I'd have to finally admit that we *were* dating.

"Of course it's good, silly." I twirled away, but didn't let go of his hand. I tugged him forward. "Let's go exploring!"

I'd never been to the Augsburg campus, and it didn't look as though it would take very long to see the whole thing.

We crossed the street again, dodging through tightly packed cars. Apparently, there were a lot of students around on the weekend. We saw people coming in and out of a building clearly marked STUDENT CENTER, and I stopped to check out a wooden kiosk in front of it. There were all sorts of notices tacked up for student organizations and prayer groups. It took me a second of scanning the posters to suss out that Augsburg was a Lutheran college. I probably wouldn't be going there. I wondered what they'd do if I marked "witch" on the application.

I turned to Thompson. He was staring at our hands, as if trying to divine something from the way our fingers curled around one another. I ignored that. "You're Catholic, right? I remember you telling me something about being an altar boy."

"I sing in the choir," he said distractedly, as if I'd awakened him from a daydream. "I haven't been an altar boy since I was nine or ten."

Catholic! His family would probably consider me some kind of devil worshipper—another reason "us" could never work. I loosened my grip on his hand, but he sensed my movement and held me tighter.

"Ana, there's something I need to ask you," Thompson said. Instead of waiting for a reply, he blurted out, "Will you go out with me?"

Why do boys always ruin things!?

I couldn't believe Thompson had just asked me directly if I would date him. Now I was going to have to say something, and every moment I hesitated was going to complicate whatever answer I chose. If he'd just let things go on the way they had been, we could have stayed in this happily ambiguous place!

Luckily, he decided to keep talking. "I like you a lot. I think we could have fun. Everybody already thinks we're dating, even my evil stepmother. But I want to, you know, take you places—movies, dancing, dinner—all that traditional stuff."

Thompson would take me out to dinner? And dancing? *Dancing?* Seriously? I don't think I've ever had the kind of boyfriend who actually made dates for a movie. Usually, we were too busy fighting off vampire hordes or dealing with some evil plot of my mother's coven. "I'd kind of like that," I admitted.

I'd never seen anyone look so relieved. I wanted to tell him that while it sounded good in theory, I had my doubts about the logistics of reality. But when I opened my mouth, I found his lips pressed against mine. He swept me up in his arms and held me tightly against his chest. His tongue worked its way into my mouth. Somehow I'd let go of his hand and was grasping his shoulders, pulling him closer. I guess my body had a clearer idea of what I wanted than my brain did.

Time didn't stop. No sparks exploded. But it was a damn fine kiss.

I ran my fingertips along the short hairs at the back of his neck. The sensation reminded me of Elias's militaristic cut. Guilt tugged me away from Thompson's kiss.

When he opened his eyes, he frowned at me. He seemed to be able to tell that I had someone else on my mind.

Before he could ask a question I didn't want to answer, I asked, "Will you really take me dancing?"

He brightened. "They have dances in the Wabasha Caves; did you know?"

Caves! I wondered how many vampires trolled that scene. "Uh, I don't really like going underground."

It was mostly true, but I would have happily lied and said I was claustrophobic. Could you imagine what my dad would say if he saw Thompson and me together? The skeptical way Thompson looked at me made me wonder again if our kiss had given him psychic powers.

"I thought the caves would be your sort of scene," he said, chewing on the edge of his lip. We stood face-to-face, arms still encircling each other. I felt every muscle of his body move against mine. "Sometimes they do big band nights where people dress up in 1940s styles."

"It sounds cool," I admitted. A big part of me seriously wanted to see Thompson decked out as some kind of retro GI. "I can't do caves. At all."

He still seemed to be scanning my face for evidence of falsehoods. "Okay. What kind of music do you like? I mean, there's a folk dancing group in town. We could go to one of their public events."

"Folk dancing?" Now the image of Thompson in lederhosen jumped into my mind, and I giggled. "I guess I was thinking we'd go out to a club or something."

Thompson considered this very seriously. "Do we like the same bands?"

I remembered the music the radio had blasted. "Probably not."

He nodded and then sighed almost wistfully. "I suppose we should go rescue Bea."

I agreed. When we broke our intimate contact, I kind of felt "it," you know? All that stuff people tell you you're supposed to feel when you're with a boy shimmied along my nerve endings. I might even have gasped. I grabbed his hand suddenly, as if I needed his touch to survive.

Gah. How hopeless did that sound?

Still, I found myself leaning into his shoulder as we walked. This was so unexpected. In fact, my brain still rebelled. Thompson!? I mean, he was the last person I thought I'd date. Plus, I was going to have to actually start calling him Matthew or Matt or something other than his surname.

Bea was going to tease me mercilessly.

———

I thought for sure she'd be able to tell something was different when we walked up to the theater steps. Bea, instead, hardly even noticed our approach. She and the lone survivor of her admirers' club were head-to-head over something on his iPhone. I was glad to see it was the pun guy. Erik? Nathan? Rupert? I had no idea, and I wondered if I needed to remember, given that she was supposed to be dating Malcolm.

Thompson cleared his throat. "Ready?"

Bea blinked as if coming out of a dream. "Oh!" She grabbed the pun guy's phone and messed around on it, as though she owned it, and then made more noises of concern. "Ana! We're going to be late to the potluck. Malcolm is picking me up at my place in ten minutes."

The pun guy's eyebrows twitched at the mention of another boy's name. He grabbed for his iPhone petulantly, but Bea handed it back without protest. She was up and moving to the truck, leaving us to apologize and say an awkward good-bye to her jilted paramour.

We followed after her, shaking our heads at her frantic dialing and constant stream of inventive curses. She let out a blue streak when she apparently connected to Malcolm's voice mail. "Hey, hon," she said, in a voice as sweet as her expletives had been strong. "Tryouts ran late. You'll have to meet us at the park." She proceeded to give directions to the band shelter at Como Park.

"Where are we taking her?" Thompson wanted to know.

"Oh, um, do you have plans?" I asked, and when he didn't immediately jump in, I continued. "Bea and I have a potluck for this, uh, group we belong to. Anyway, it's kind of a big deal. Bea always calls it the social event of the season. Want to come?"

Thompson looked a bit unsure.

"As our first date," I added to sweeten the deal.

So many witches attended the Midsummer Gathering that Thompson had to park his truck two blocks from the pavilion. "Wow," he said as we started the long walk through the park. "What is this? Some kind of charity event?"

"Sort of," Bea said snidely, and then went back to her phone.

I shot her a glare, but she didn't see it. She was busy trying to figure out how to meet up with Malcolm. Their conversation had been going on for more than five minutes. I was beginning to think he'd gone to the wrong part of the park. Como was huge.

"Sort of?" Thompson asked.

"Bea's just being a jerk," I said. What she meant was that the Midsummer Gathering was one of the few events where non-Initiates, or failed ones, like me, got the "privilege" of hanging out with the Inner Circle and the Elders. "It's just a party for our coven."

"Wait." Thompson, who had been holding my hand again, jerked back. "You guys really are witches?"

"Duh," Bea said before going back to berating Malcolm for going around Como Lake instead of coming over to the zoo side.

"I'm not really," I said. "I didn't make the tryout."

"You have to audition?" he asked incredulously.

"In a way," I said. I was under a strict oath not to reveal too much about the nature of True Magic, but I hated lying. If Thompson and I were going to try to date, I needed to be able to tell him something about all this, didn't I? "Think of it like cheerleading squad or hockey, right? There are some things you have to be good at. If you are, you make the team. If not . . ." I shrugged.

Thompson looked ready to ask more questions, but the reverberation from an electric guitar cut him off. We stepped under the band shelter just as my ex-boyfriend took the stage.

Chapter Eight

knew I'd see Nikolai there, but I wasn't really prepared for it to be like this. Spotlights always adored him, and he was in his element on stage with a guitar slung over his shoulders. He looked incredible. His long, silken black hair hung like a mysterious veil in front of his eyes. In tight leather pants and a poet shirt that would have looked dorky on anyone else, he captured everyone's attention.

He opened his mouth and began to sing. Wouldn't you know it? It was the song he wrote for me, the one we'd just heard on the radio. Somehow, through some awful luck, he spotted me and swept me into the intensity of his gaze.

I flushed bright red under his scrutiny. Even though I knew it was impossible, I felt certain Nikolai could tell I'd kissed Thompson.

Just as quickly as he pinned me under his gaze, he seemed

to remember he was performing for other people, and I was released.

Even if Nikolai couldn't read my mind, I was beginning to think Thompson could, because he was watching me curiously. "It must have been nice dating a musician, huh?" he said lightly, but I could hear the jealousy in his tone.

Actually, it kind of sucked. But no one believed that when I told them. They thought it was all VIP parties and backstage passes. The reality was that Nik was always either busy practicing or in the spotlight being adored by legions of fans way hotter than I. But, even if I told Thompson that, he'd take it the wrong way. I sighed. "I'm going to get a drink. Do you want water or something?"

"I'll go with you," he insisted. "It's too loud here, anyway."

Thompson followed me as I went in search of a cooler. When we stepped out from under the shade of the shelter, the music seemed farther away. The sudden sunlight stunned my eyes.

The crowd was thick with bangles, beads, and other accoutrements of the groovy. A lot of the people in the Outer Circle compensated for not being True Witches by adopting the costumes and customs of the pretenders. Others didn't know any better. Thompson and I threaded our way past a group of long-haired, gray-bearded drummers pounding out a meditative yet danceable beat, oblivious to the competing throb of the bass a few feet away. Women of all ages and sizes swirled around nearby, mirrored silk skirts and scarves winking in the sun. Under the shade of a sprawling maple tree, a heavyset woman with a spike of short dreadlocks held court, reading palms. All the exposed skin sported tats of images familiar to me—ankhs, runes, Celtic knot work, dragons, faeries, and, of course, classic goddess images, like the snake-headed Nile statuette, which had been the talisman. Fashion ran the gamut from the faux gypsy belly dancers, classic Goth, punk, and everything in between.

In among all the woo-woo, there were hints of normal: booths promoting witch-friendly financial services, pediatricians, and law firms. There was even a bloodmobile taking donations. I smiled at the irony, given the current vampire problem, but it was just one of a dozen civic-minded volunteer opportunities.

Thompson's eyes grew wider the deeper into the crowd we moved. He looked a bit gob-smacked. He'd forgotten all about Nikolai. "All these people are witches?"

"Yep," I said.

"I had no idea there were so many," he said.

"Minnesota has one of the largest pagan communities in the United States. Some people call this 'Paganistan.'"

He nodded, but I didn't think he'd heard. We'd just walked into a row of vendors, and his eyes were darting from witch-related T-shirts and clothes to jewelry and magical tools. We slowed as he admired some handcrafted staffs with dragons' heads carved into the top. I figured he'd spasm when he saw the "athames." But he breezed right past those and stopped dead in front of a silk-draped caravan tent that looked like something straight out of some mundane's wet dream of a gypsy camp.

"Wow, check this out! A tarot reader!"

Thompson was desperate for me to try it. I wanted to tell him I'd had Bea read my cards a dozen times, and her readings were spookily accurate because she had a divination talent. But since he was so excited and already had money in his hands, I let the lady pull me into her tent. Thompson followed behind.

I didn't recognize the reader from the coven, but that didn't mean anything. A lot of people who didn't make the Initiation had real talent. Nikolai's mom, for instance, was Romany. Though most of the people who were true sensitives didn't bother with all the flimflam this lady seemed to be into—she had lit a stick of incense and was going through elaborate motions to banish the negative energy or whatever from the room. Thompson ate it up. His eyes were wide with fascination. I waited patiently in the metallic folding chair set out on the flattened grass. It was a bit tippy because the ground was hard packed and uneven.

When she sat across from me, I realized she wasn't that much older than I was. Her face was heart-shaped. She had a lot of piercings in—one stud glittered like a faux mole over the left edge of her black-painted lips. She had a ring through her nose and in her eyebrow. Her hair was so black, I suspected she dyed it.

Henna dotted the hands that shuffled the cards. In a low voice, she asked me to cut them. When she handed them to me, she reminded me to "concentrate on the question you want the cards to answer."

Even if this woman had no particular divination skill, I had a healthy respect for tarot. Even though Real Magic didn't work for me, I'd found that some things worked for everyone. Tarot was one of those things. Even working alone, I could get pretty good readings. Of course, tarot, like many divinations, worked partly on intuition, which lots of mundanes could tap.

So I thought about the hunt and my dad. I really, really wanted the cards to tell me there was a solution out there. I wanted a hint as to where I could find it, especially since the grimoire had been a dead end. I wanted reassurance that all this wasn't going to end in massive bloodshed. My mind started to wander to Elias and his potential upcoming nuptials, so I quickly handed the cards over to the reader.

She did some more drama. Closing her eyes, she held the cards meaningfully in front of her. She set them on the table and waved her hands over them. Thompson was silent in anticipation. At least he was getting a good show for his ten bucks.

Just when I wondered if she'd fallen asleep, she separated the deck into three piles facedown. She opened her eyes with a start. She flipped the top card of the first pile over so fast that the cardboard hit the table with a snap.

Death.

Her deck showed the classic image of a hooded, skeletal figure on a pale horse. The Death figure had a black flag with a white rose in one hand, and the traditional scythe in the other. People—a king and a peasant—fell down in front of the galloping horse. The sun set in the distance.

Behind me, Thompson sucked in a breath. I wasn't that worried myself. I mean, I knew that Death in tarot wasn't the final big ugly that people tended to think it was. In fact, *if* it was right side up, it could be read positively as change or transformation. The sun might also be rising, you see. And the white rose had a new bud on it—the sign that new growth was possible with a bit of wise pruning.

However, it was reversed.

Again, I wasn't terribly panicked because I had been asking about the hunt and vampires. There was a lot of death there.

The next card freaked me out a bit, though.

The Tower.

This image was harder to see as positive. Lightning struck a cylindrical building, and two figures fell from its walls, presumably to their deaths, in the stormy sea below. Even the stars in the background had trails and seemed to be falling.

I rarely got this card, so I would be curious to see what the reader had to say about it. I thought I remembered Bea saying something about how this one represented change in the status quo, which could be good, given that the hunt was kind of broken. I couldn't quite shake my sense of foreboding looking at it, though.

The last card was a minor one, the ace of swords. It showed a disembodied hand holding a sword. The whole scene seemed to float in the clouds, which looked gray and stormy.

Lots of storms. Great.

"You need an idea to change a stagnant situation," she intoned in a voice that was clearly trying to be mysterious. But her voice was too light to carry off the seriousness she intended.

I decided to see if she was a real practitioner or not. "I hate it when the cards just parrot back your question, don't you?"

She blinked, as if waking up from a dream, but then she smiled. "Should I have given you the coven discount?"

I nodded.

"Let's do a little digging, shall we?" she said, no longer

pretending to alter her voice. She pulled a card from the bottom of each pile and laid it on top of the three in front of me.

The first one showed the High Priestess. She sat on a throne, holding a book in her lap and an ankh held casually in her right hand. The other held a staff entwined with the Goddess's other symbol, a snake. Her crown was two crescent moons on either side of a full moon. Behind her was a veil that was partly opened to show a green verdant hill leading to a distant castle.

It could only represent one thing: Mom.

And it was lying right over the Death card.

I wasn't sure I liked that, especially after what Prince Luis had said about how the Queen of Witches of his region sacrificed herself to the hunt.

The next card was another queen, only this one, the queen of swords, came from the court cards. Like the ace, the queen held a sword aloft. Unlike the ace, she had a body attached to the hand and sat on a throne that seemed to float among swiftly moving clouds. She faced to the left, and her other hand was raised in a gesture that reminded me of giving—as if maybe she was offering a judgment from her throne.

I didn't know who she might be, but I thought she might be part of the clue I was looking for. She covered that horrible Tower and seemed, at least to me, to be offering help.

The last card was a baffler. It was a minor one, the seven of cups. It showed seven goblets. All of them were filled with strange things—rainbows, a dragon, a creepy shroud-wearing figure, jewels, a laurel crown, a snake, and another severed body part—this time a weirdly serene-looking head.

I had no idea what to make of that. "I know who this is, I think," I said, pointing to the High Priestess. "But what does it mean?"

The reader thought about it, but normally, not with any hint of spooky stuff. I wondered briefly if Thompson was disappointed. "I'm not sure," she said, with a glance at where Thompson sat by the doorway. "Can you tell me more about your question?"

"Not really," I admitted. "What does the seven mean? I don't get that one very often."

"Illusions. Dreams. Creativity," she said. "I always think it kind of looks like some kind of hallucination, you know?"

All the weird things floating in the cups did remind me of some kind of Dali painting. "This woman," I said, moving the queen of swords so that the card more fully covered the Tower. "She'll help? What kind of woman is she?"

"Smart, maybe with a sharp tongue. A bitch even, maybe, but with good common sense. The kind who tells you the truth you don't want to hear."

Bea? I wasn't sure. She hadn't been much help so far. The grimoire had been a dud, and, unless she was holding out on me, that pretty much tapped her knowledge of vampires and the hunt. "Could it be someone I haven't met yet? Does it have to be a woman?"

I was thinking maybe someone from Luis's camp might know more and that maybe I should go looking for advice there.

The reader shook her spiky head. "My experience is that court cards can be anybody, male or female, but usually they're

someone I know, even if I don't know them well—like a teacher
or something. But they're someone *important*—you know what
I mean?"

I did, though I still had no idea whom that card could represent. "You gave me a lot to think about," I said.

"Did your question get answered?"

"No," I said. "But it's a pretty big question."

She laughed, pulling out the Death and Tower cards to put
them back into her deck. "You think?"

"I guess that's obvious, huh?"

"I figured you were going to ask about a relationship." She
smiled, then gave Thompson a broad wink.

Oh! I supposed I should have. "Maybe another time," I said.

She tried to return some of Thompson's money, but he
refused. "No," he said. "That was totally cool."

Despite the brightness outside the tent flaps, I brooded on
the fortune. It bothered me that the High Priestess covered
Death. Did that mean Mom was going to do something against
the vampires or help them . . . or die trying? I didn't like any of
those options.

Then there was the mysterious queen who maybe had the
answer to the "status quo" toppling of the Tower—did she have
the solution to the hunt? I could only hope. But who was she?
And what was up with the trippy cups? Was a potion going to
be involved?

"What *did* you ask?" Thompson said, startling me from my
reverie.

"Oh, um." What was I supposed to say? I wanted to tell him

the truth, but he'd never believe me. "Just some family stuff, that's all."

"Man," he said. "I thought I had heavy family problems. Yours involve dead guys on horses and people falling out of buildings."

Dead guys? Ha! But I just shook my head. "You have no idea."

"No, I don't," he agreed, "but I'd like to."

"Oh, Thompson, it's not that I don't want to share; it's just . . . complicated."

"It's cool," he said with a shrug, though I could tell it wasn't cool—not entirely.

Having finally wandered far enough, we found the place where the food was being set up. I spotted the drink cooler. I dug through the melting ice for something good. A lot of the Outer Court members were foodies or health nuts, so there wasn't a lot in the soda pop department, though someone had brought home brew root beer in a barrel.

Thompson peered over my shoulder. "I don't even recognize this stuff. What the hell is basil seed drink?"

"It's weird," I agreed with a smile, remembering the first time someone had offered it to me. It was sort of like pop, but with tapioca "bubbles" containing basil seeds. If you weren't expecting those, it could be quite the surprise to find your drink . . . chewy. "You should try it."

Thompson saw my mischievous smile but took the can I offered anyway. He popped the top bravely and tipped his head back to take a big gulp. When his mouth filled with balls of goo, he gave me a horrified expression. I started to laugh as he grimaced and chewed.

"You are evil," he teased after swallowing the last of the mouthful.

I got myself a bottle of water. Someone had carefully stickered each bottle with a warning about BPA chemicals and a reminder to recycle. Thompson had moved over to check out the spread. He shot me a helpless look. "I'm not going to find chili and hamburgers, am I?"

I shook my head.

"Hot dogs?"

"Tofu pups, maybe," I offered. At all this talk of food, my stomach gurgled, but what I was craving couldn't be found at the picnic. I covered my stomach with my hand, but if Thompson noticed, he didn't say anything.

He took another mouthful of basil seed drink and plunked himself down on the picnic bench seat, his back to the various plastic-wrap-covered Tupperware tubs. I sat down beside him, ignoring how queasy the smell made me. I was about to tell Thompson to take heart. Bea's mom always made something really good, despite the often-unusual ingredients. Before I could open my mouth, I heard a familiar voice behind me. It was Mom.

I tucked my head into Thompson's shoulder to hide, and I strained to hear what she was saying. He responded by putting an arm around me and softly kissing the top of my head. It was a little distracting, but I could still hear snatches of what Mom was saying.

"No, Victor, the lottery is barbaric. We've discussed this. It will not be reinstated under my watch," Mom said.

Victor? She was talking to Mr. Kirov, Nikolai's dad!

Thompson's nuzzling grew a little more intense, but I tried to stay focused on listening.

"When they attack, it will be on your head too." His voice was menacing, not at all melodious like Nik's. He still had a trace of a Russian accent, and I always thought of him as a hard-as-stone man. Granted, I'd seen him only a few times, and each time I did, he was threatening either me or my friends.

"What else can we do?" asked a voice that wasn't my mother's.

"What of your experiments on the elite captain?" It was Mr. Kirov again. "The potion did not bind the vampire?"

I jerked, knocking my head into Thompson's chin. Holy crap! Had Elias been right? It sounded as though my mom *had* been slipping something into his drink. But what did "bind" mean? Was she trying to come up with some other way to enslave vampires . . . and trying it out on my sort-of ex-boyfriend?

"You okay?" Thompson murmured in my ear. His breath tickled erotically.

"Uh, you surprised me," I said stupidly, trying not to get all shivery. I couldn't let myself get carried away right now. What were they saying? Why did the band have to be so loud? Or Thompson's passionate breathing for that matter!

". . . No other option, then," Mom was saying. "Will Nikolai fall into line?"

"Do you even eat meat?" Thompson asked.

"What?" I snapped, irritated that I missed Mr. Kirov's response.

"No need to get cranky," he said, pushing away slightly. "It's not that I care. Not really. I've never dated a vegetarian before. Of course, I've never dated a witch either."

"Hush!" I said a little more intensely than I meant. His face crumpled and then contorted in a way that seemed ready for a fight or a protest. So, before he freaked out, I crooked my finger slyly behind my hand in Mom's direction. "That's my mom. I'm trying to hear what she's saying without getting noticed."

Thompson's mood shifted, and he seemed intrigued at playing spy.

He checked over his shoulder. "Which one is your mom?"

I'd forgotten he'd never met her. I whispered, "Curly hair. Professor clothes."

Looking again, Thompson nodded. I expected more questions or a comment on how frumpy my mom looked—because believe me, she did—but instead he just fell silent. I took the opportunity to eavesdrop.

"Gather the others tonight," Mom finished, and apparently sent Mr. Kirov on his way. I'd clearly missed the meat of the conversation.

At least I had a couple of nuggets to go on.

"Let's go find Bea," I suggested. I stood up and headed back to the bandstand. With any luck the music would be so loud that I could ask her about this without being overheard. I should find a way to corner Nikolai too. It sounded as though the big thing Mom and Mr. Kirov had planned wasn't something

Nikolai necessarily approved of. Maybe that meant I could recruit him to help me find a solution for the hunt. His expertise with vampire physiology could be invaluable.

I found Bea talking to Stevie, the drummer from the band. The band must have been on break. The two of them were laughing about something but hushed the instant they noticed my approach.

"Where's your new attachment?" Bea asked.

"What?" I asked.

Bea rolled her eyes, as if frustrated by my dimness. "Thompson," she said. "Where's Thompson?"

I hadn't realized he wasn't beside me. "Probably still at the picnic table near the buffet setup. We'll catch up with him. Can I talk to you for a second?" I gave Stevie an apologetic look. "Alone?"

Stevie shook her long blond hair out of her face. "Sure, no problem. I have to get ready for the next set anyway."

I tugged Bea aside, away from the milling crowd. "Last night, at the big meeting—what was Mr. Kirov's take on everything?"

Bea laughed. "You mean, Mr. Kill-Them-Kill-Them-All? You know him."

I didn't share her dark chuckle. "What's his plan? Is Nik involved?"

"Am I involved in what?"

I looked up to see Nik. A slight sheen of sweat covered his face. The heat had made his damp hair extra unruly, and it was all I could do to keep from reaching out and fixing his errant locks.

"Hi," Bea said simply, though somehow she managed to infuse a ton of flirt into that single syllable.

"Hey," he responded, sparing her a moment of his attention before turning back to me. "What were you talking about, Ana?"

"I was wondering if you were in on your dad's plan to kill all the vampires," I said.

If he was taken aback by my bold truthfulness, he didn't show it, although he did take a moment to take a sip of whatever he was drinking before saying, "I'm surprised anyone's bothering to formulate a plan. Last vamp I saw looked ready to gnaw off her own leg."

Of course, at that very moment my stomach decided to cramp.

The pain hit like a physical blow, and I doubled over. Instantly, Nikolai wrapped his arms around my shoulders. He murmured softly, clearly trying to comfort me and discover the source of my distress. I couldn't understand his words, though his lips brushed my ears. His nearness made my hunger worse. The scent of his sweat filled my nostrils, blocking out all other sensations. Mingled with the patchouli he always wore, the odor sent shivers of desire down my spine. He smelled so . . . tasty.

My jaw clicked. My fangs descended. I put my lips against his hand. My tongue tasted sweet salt mixed with the hint of the coppery ambrosia just under the surface. The sharp tip of my teeth must have grazed his skin, because suddenly there was blood in my mouth.

He started to pull away, and I couldn't let that happen.

I grabbed his wrist and sank my teeth deep into the back of his hand.

Somewhere beyond my bliss I had the impression of screaming and pushing and pulling. But all I knew was joy. Magic filled me; I became aware of power moving through me. I felt lighter, brighter—

And then it was gone. I hit the dirt hard. Something heavy hit me hard in the chest, and all the breath went out of my lungs.

The sunlight was so bright that I had to blink several times before I could tell what was going on. Bea knelt over me in a strange position. I was looking up at her armpit. She was whispering something fiercely. "Clean yourself off. Be quick"—I finally made out her words—"and snap out of it, Ana. Hurry!"

I grabbed the nearest thing, which was the edge of Bea's hoodie. I wiped my lips and then, horrified, stared at the blood smeared on the fabric.

"Bea, I . . ." I wanted to apologize, but I was so mortified that no coherent words came out.

Bea looked down at me and shrugged out of her sweatshirt. Quickly, she bundled it up. "She's fine," she was telling the crowd pressing around us. "She just fainted."

Where was Nik? Was he okay? I couldn't believe my first interaction with him since our breakup was to bite him on the hand. This was horrible. I wanted to stay hidden under Bea, but she helped me sit up. A woman with long brown hair tied into an elaborate braid encircling her head handed me a water bottle. She had at least one ring on every finger and a tattoo of a snake spiraling up her arm. "Thanks," I said.

Bea was ordering people around. "Give her room to breathe," she said, and I could feel the glamour in her words. A light magical spell tinged the air with the scent of violets and cucumbers. The crowd stepped back obediently.

I touched Bea lightly on the arm and tried to ask about Nik with my eyes.

She smiled maternally. "Everything is going to be all right," she said. "You just fainted."

The smell grew stronger. "That's not going to work here," I whispered. There were too many witches in this crowd, many of them far more powerful than either of us. I swore I could already hear the sensitives in the throng grumbling softly about a forget-me spell in the air.

"It's going to have to," Bea snapped at me, her voice straining on the edge of a whisper, "or you're going to be crucified by all these witches, vampire princess. What the hell were you thinking?"

I gave her a guilty shrug. She knew it was the hunger, but neither of us had expected such a strong reaction. "I don't know," I murmured. The weirdest part was that I felt full now. I couldn't understand it. Elias said he couldn't be satisfied with just a bite; I was completely recharged.

"Is Nik okay?" I handed the empty bottle back to snake-tattoo girl.

She seemed to think I was talking to her, so I got the "official" story. "He cut his hand on the glass bottle pretty bad. They've cancelled the rest of the show. He probably needs stitches." I must have looked as pale as I felt because she added,

"Lots of people faint at the sight of blood. It's nothing to be embarrassed about."

I cast a your-magic-is-strong glance at Bea, who shook her head slightly. The only thing I could think she might mean by that was that Nik had done some of his own magical misdirection. I really wanted to get away from everyone so I could ask Bea why Nik didn't use his psychic blade on me. I mean, I was biting him. He's trained to disengage vampires. Yet, from what I could tell, it was Bea who came between us. And thank the Goddess she had. What if I had drained him dry?

Bea helped me to my feet. She must have seen the question on my lips, because she shook her head again and whispered, "Later." Malcolm came over and patted me on the back kindly. Malcolm was tall and slender, and very proper looking. You almost expected him to have a British accent like Don Cheadle in *Ocean's Eleven*. I could see why he appealed to Bea, with his mahogany skin and closely shaved helmet of curls.

I checked around for a sign of Nikolai, but, if braided snake-tattoo lady was to be believed, he'd been taken off to the urgent care clinic for stitches. I somehow doubted that, though. He might be a powerful magician, but it would take some trick to convince a doctor that he or she wasn't sewing up bite marks.

I wondered if news of my "accident" would reach Thompson.

When I saw the crowd parting, I hoped it was him. I could really use some strong arms to support me—especially ones that wouldn't ask any awkward questions.

Unfortunately, the form I saw barreling toward me was none other than my mother.

Chapter Nine

One look at Mom's face and I knew no amount of magic could deflect her anger. I really missed Thompson's broad shoulders to hide behind. Instead, I brushed the grass stains off the butt of my jeans and waited for the storm to hit.

"What happened here?" Mom demanded, sweeping everyone, even poor mundane Malcolm, with her laser stare of doom.

"I fainted," I lied easily, because even if she wanted the truth, this was hardly the place to broadcast it. Malcolm wasn't the only norm within earshot. "Nik cut his hand."

Mom stood with her hands on her hips, considering us. We hadn't spoken since this morning, and a lot of unresolved tension hung in the air between us. Her eyes flicked and her mouth twitched. It was obvious to me that she didn't believe me; yet when her eyes fell on Malcolm, she nodded curtly. "Is Nikolai okay?"

"Yes, Dr. Parker," Bea said, and they exchanged some kind of meaningful look. Maybe they shared some kind of secret code that only the Elders knew. I couldn't fathom it, but it seemed to mollify Mom a little. I strained to sense any magical bindings or manacles being manifested, but I could only smell the remains of Bea's forget-me spell.

Mom gave me one final withering I'll-deal-with-you-later grimace, and then turned to start addressing the crowd like a police officer shooing people from the scene of a crime. She sent people to help Nik's band break down the set. Others were assigned cleanup, etc. It was impressive in its own way, especially when I felt Mom's deep, earthy magic strengthening Bea's forget-me spell. By tomorrow no one would remember seeing me bite Nik's hand.

Malcolm leaned close to me and said, "Your mom is scary."

I let out a little laugh. "Yeah, she can be."

"What do you want to do now?" Bea asked.

I wanted desperately to talk to her about what I'd overheard Mom say to Mr. Kirov and about what the hell happened when I bit Nik's hand, but I could see that Malcolm had attached himself to her side. "I lost Thompson over by the food. Maybe we should go find him."

"I'm starving anyway," Malcolm agreed.

His choice of words made me choke and laugh all at the same time. When Bea started to giggle, I lost it. We both collapsed in a fit of hysteria.

"What's so funny?" Malcolm wanted to know.

"Sorry," I said through tears. "The way you said that just reminded us of something else."

"Uh-huh. Sure," he said doubtfully, but he didn't press us for details.

After fifteen minutes of fruitless searching, I began to suspect that Thompson ditched me. We had wandered over to the man-made waterfall and duck pond close to the zoo entrance. Bea and Malcolm tossed bits of gluten-free rice bread at an unsuspecting mallard, while I sat on the park bench and dialed Thompson's number.

When he picked up, I asked, "Where are you? We've been looking all over the park."

"I'm in my truck."

It was a very strange answer, and I wasn't quite sure what to make of it. "Um, why?"

"I had a power bar in the glove compartment and decent music on the radio." There was some subtext that I clearly wasn't getting, because he sounded kind of angry or put out, even though he was the one who ditched me.

"Are you mad at me?"

"I mow your lawn. Not on a regular basis, but, yeah, your mom has hired us."

Now I really felt like I was missing something critical. I felt like I should be apologizing for something, but I had no idea for what. Instead, I just said, "Okay. Are you coming back? Should we meet you at your truck?"

"I remembered her because she didn't let us use the bathroom," he continued as if I hadn't spoken.

"My mom is a world-class jerk to everyone, Thompson. I wouldn't take it too personally. You should have seen her a minute ago. She scared Malcolm."

"Matt," he corrected. "Or, at least Matthew, okay? Why can't you ever call me by my first name?"

It was habit, really. When I went to watch our high school hockey team play, I got used to the way the announcers always called him out by his last name—Thompson for the score! It was the name emblazoned across the back of his letter jacket. "I'm sorry, Matt. Is that what you're mad about? Can we talk about this in person?"

"Forget about it," he said gruffly. "I'm just being stupid. Where are you? I'll meet you."

I explained and agreed to stay put until he got there. I clicked the End button but stared at the phone. What was that all about? I had a sinking feeling it had something to do with male pride. The morose way Thompson spoke reminded me of Elias going on about losing his place as my dad's right-hand man, only it made less sense. Vampires, I could understand; regular boys, not so much.

Malcolm and Bea laughed about something, panicking the duck, which fluttered off to the far side of the pool. Malcolm was a normal guy. Maybe he'd have some insight into Thompson's behavior. I called him over and explained the conversation to both of them.

Nodding sagely, Malcolm considered for a moment after I'd finished. "It's a class thing," he pronounced with all the seriousness of a doctor telling me I had months to live.

I suppressed my giggle because I wanted to understand. "Uh, okay. But, what can I do? I'm not even sure I know what that means to us."

"It means you're rich and he's poor," Malcolm said.

"What? We're not rich!" Mom only made a decent salary because of her dozen adjunct professor jobs. We'd inherited our Cathedral Hill mansion, but not much else.

"He thinks you are, Professor Higgins," Bea said, referencing the play Thompson and I were in last year. The reference was a little off, however, since I had played the street urchin, Liza Doolittle, whom the professor transformed into a proper English lady. "Anyway, just treat him with respect," Bea continued. "Act as though it doesn't matter."

"'Act'?" Malcolm repeated, arching a thin eyebrow at me critically. "Does it? Does it matter?"

"Of course it matters. You should see where he lives," she said.

I didn't get a chance to consider my own answer, because Thompson strolled up. His shoulders were hunched dejectedly and his hands were stuffed into his pockets, yet he smiled brightly when he saw me. I had a hard time believing things like "class" mattered in America in the twenty-first century, so I brushed it all from my mind.

"I saw that the band was packing up," Thompson said. "I thought they just started."

"Nik cut his hand," Malcolm said.

"I hope he didn't damage any muscles or has to get stitches. Depending on the hand, that could end his musical career real quick," Thompson said.

I hadn't thought about that. OMG. What if I just messed up Ingress's chance to get a record label!? Nik was never going to talk to me again. He probably wasn't planning to anyway, but that would be the end of things forever and ever and ever.

The boys huddled together to talk about the music industry and other rock stars who had lost limbs. Bea came over to join me on the park bench.

"It's just a bite mark, remember," Bea said. "He'll be okay."

I rested my head in my palms. I couldn't believe I bit Nik of all people, and in his hand!

"He still likes you, you know," Bea said slyly and quietly with a glance over at Thompson.

I peeked through my fingers. "You mean Matt? I know—I was totally relieved."

"No. Nikolai."

"What? Before or after I bit his hand?"

"During." I stared at her in utter disbelief. She continued. "He kept yelling for us not to hurt you. While you were sucking his blood! I mean, WTF, right? I was screaming at him to use his magic blade, cut you off, you know—but he wouldn't. I bet he would have let you drain him dry before he lifted a finger against you. Crazy, stupid boy."

I let my hands drop to my knees. "Really?"

"Really," she said with a touch of jealousy. Just for good measure, she added, "Oh, and if you ever go vamp on me without my permission"—she made the fingers of both hands into guns—"both barrels, sister."

I stared at the spot just over my heart where her fingers pointed. It was true that Bea had been more a frenemy than BFF since I became vampire princess, but this little violent gesture was not cool.

"Nice. Glad to know you've got my back," I said through clenched teeth.

Malcolm and Thompson wandered back over. Thompson said to me, "I've been deputized to tell you that we're tired of this party. We want to go somewhere else."

There wasn't room for four in Thompson's truck. We all agreed that the cure for what ailed us was Porky's hamburgers and onion rings. I buckled myself in and rolled down the window. I stuck my head out the window like a dog and let the wind pull at my hair.

My thoughts were as jumbled as my hair. What was my mom planning with Mr. Kirov? How did it involve Nik? Was Nik okay? Did he really tell everyone not to hurt me? Bea might have pissed me off, but I still wondered if she was right about Nik. Did that mean he still liked me—like, really liked me? And what if he did? What about Thompson?

Thompson drove with one hand on the wheel and the other resting lightly on the stick shift. The radio was on. Some band I didn't know was screaming about a crazy bitch who f—ked so good that it was all worth it or something. I didn't really care for the message, but the tune was weirdly catchy.

I snuck my phone out of my pocket and pulled up Nik's number. I decided there was no harm in asking him if he was okay, so I thumbed in the question and hit Send before Thompson could ask me about it. In fact, for good measure, I opened up another text to Bea.

My thumbs hovered over the pad, not sure where to start. "If there's a big mtg 2nite, tell me?" I sent it.

We were turning the corner in front of the Spruce Tree Centre when the phone chirped. The green shiny concrete block
building had been voted "ugliest building in St. Paul," and I
could see why. It looked like a bad Lego model of a squat, fat
pine tree—except with windows and a dead spruce tree in a
plant container near the sidewalk. Sad.

I flipped open my phone, expecting some snide remark from
Bea. It was Nik. Thompson didn't seem to notice, so I opened it.

"Just bruised. R u ok?"

I knew he was more than just bruised. I'd cut through his
skin. Just the memory made my teeth ache and my skin tingle
with energy.

I checked Thompson before replying. He was watching the
busy traffic along University Avenue. There was construction
everywhere, and he clearly needed to concentrate. The radio
now blared something equally as offensive as the last song. I
returned to the screen. "Sorry," was all I could think to reply.

"Ax-Man," Thompson said with a smile, pointing at a square
black building with a cartoonish hooded medieval executioner
helium balloon bobbing on its roof. The sign in the window
proclaimed free admission and lots of surplus. "I love that place."

My phone beeped with a message. "We need to meet."

"Uh, yeah," I said stupidly, though we were long past the
store. "We should go sometime."

"You've never been?" Thompson was delighted.

"Tonight?" I texted.

"No," I said. "Never."

"It's really weird, but kind of cool. You can find all sorts of stuff there, like chemical beakers, and they even have this huge iron lung. But they have all sorts of other remaindered things—party hats, crayon packs, stickers, gigantic rolls of felt. . . ."

I nodded, but I wasn't really listening. My eyes watched the phone. "B @ yr house @ 8."

"OK," I replied with my thumbs. My mouth said, "Sounds really cool," hoping that was the right response to whatever it was Thompson was saying. I stuffed my phone into my pocket guiltily. When I looked up, I wondered if I'd missed a memo. There were families in lawn chairs and blankets sitting on the sidewalks and boulevards. People were sipping sodas and watching traffic, as if there were something to see besides a bunch of vehicles. I glanced behind us, half expecting a float or marching band. All I saw was one of those old cars you might see in a black-and-white movie starring Cary Grant. Somewhere behind us a horn tooted out the first bars of "Dixie."

We pulled into Porky's parking lot. The restaurant was built to resemble a 1950s drive-in. A sign in the shape of a pig wearing a top hat winked a neon eye at us from the boulevard. The building proper was one story and painted in a black and white checkerboard pattern. Other people were parked under the separate metal awning. A lot of them had classic cars.

"It's Saturday night," Thompson said, whistling in appreciation as we passed a long, smooth convertible with batmobile wings. "University Avenue parade."

I had no idea what he was talking about, but there did seem to be something going on at the drive-in. A few of the cars' owners had propped up their hoods presumably to show off their engines, though it all looked like so much metal to me. People stood around the cooler cars, talking, smoking, and eating hamburgers.

We found Bea and Malcolm parked in one of the few available spots. "Not a lot of room for non-show cars," Bea told us. "We should get the food to go and park down the street."

There was a park just on the other side, so we agreed to meet there. Thompson ordered a double California, an order of fries, and onion rings. After what happened with Nik, I wasn't feeling terribly hungry, but the greasy smell of French fries made me order the same plus a chocolate shake. In a minute, we were circling Iris Park, looking for an empty parking place.

We got out and tried to find a nice spot to eat. The park was little more than a grassy area surrounding a water fountain. I thought it might be nice to sit near the spray, but it smelled a little like sewage, and people had tossed a lot of crap into the concrete pool. The park benches had been similarly mistreated. Wooden slats had been broken off or were missing entirely. What material was left had been completely covered in graffiti and gang tags.

Bea found a detritus-free spot under a pine tree and waved us over. Under the shelter of the boughs and sitting on the cushion of fragrant needles, you could almost pretend the park was nice—almost.

"Wow, this place is scary," Malcolm said. "I can't imagine hanging out in this neighborhood for long."

"My dojo is one block over," Thompson said snappishly.

Oh crap. This was one of those class things, wasn't it? I had to say something supportive, but all I really wanted to do was get out of there. I knew I should be thinking about Thompson, but I felt so guilty about what happened to Nik that I could hardly focus. This was especially so since I also needed to figure out how to get Thompson to drop me off at my house by eight. I had about one hour.

Bea nudged my elbow, making me toss my onion ring Frisbee-style onto Thompson's lap. I peeled it off his leg with an apologetic smile. To the others, I said, "Hey, did you guys know that Thom—Matt is a black belt in cooking karate?"

Bea shook her head. That wasn't the right thing to say.

"Kuk sool wan," Thompson corrected. "Brown belt."

At least Malcolm seemed sincerely impressed, especially when Thompson produced evidence in the form of an official-looking card that showed his rank and the organization's seal.

Bea pulled on my sleeve. "Could you be more of a dope?"

"My mind is elsewhering," I admitted.

"Obviously," she said sarcastically.

Since the boys seemed deep into discussion of the differences between various martial arts, I took a chance and whispered, "I texted Nik. He's coming over tonight."

Bea's squeal ended any chance of further private discussion, and now I was going to have to lie to Thompson's face.

The guys waited expectantly to be clued in on what all the excitement was about. I hoped Bea would do her usual social magic and redirect the conversation with a white lie. Uncharacteristically, she had nothing to say. Her hands covering her mouth, she just sat there looking absolutely guilty.

That left everyone staring at me. "Nik texted," I said. Bea's face paled, and she gave a little squeak as if she might faint. "Uh, I guess they got a record deal."

I really hoped that was true. I mean, it was all over the rumor mill as a possibility. Nervously, I checked their reactions. I turned to Malcolm first. He looked disappointed. He clearly expected bigger news, given Bea's reaction.

Bea was not helping either. She wasn't saying anything; she was just holding her hands up in front of her stupid mouth and nodding vigorously, as if she didn't trust herself to even go along with the lie. It was a little late to hold back, I thought.

Thompson, when I finally checked, looked . . . angry.

"I hate that guy," he said when our eyes met. "I seriously hate him."

With a hiss I let out a breath I hadn't even realized I was holding. "I know," I told him, and I wanted to tell him that he didn't have to worry. There was no hope of me and Nikolai ever being an item again. I had just bitten the local vampire slayer. Bea might have been able to make Thompson forget our little interaction, but there was no way it would work on a full witch like Nik.

Finally, Bea found her voice. She entertained us with stories of bad tryouts and cursed theater shows. I forgave her entirely when she came up with an excuse to cut out before eight.

Alone in the truck, I managed to keep up the small talk. Thompson seemed desperate to try to find things we had in common. It wasn't music; that was for sure. He was into heavy metal, and I liked alt rock and musicals. I tried favorite books, but

Thompson wasn't much of a reader, though I guessed he liked some superhero comic books. That sounded a bit like some of the graphic novels I liked, but we were pulling up to the curb by the time we finally hit on something.

Thompson drove me directly to my house. Only when he turned off the engine did I wonder how he managed it without asking for directions. Then I remembered that he mowed our lawn on occasion. I looked at our gorgeous garden spilling over the wrought-iron fence, and I had to fight the urge to tell him he'd done a good job. I knew that wouldn't go over the way I intended it.

I leaned in to kiss Thompson good-bye, when Nikolai's rusty Toyota pulled in to the spot in front of us. I choked. Thompson opened his eyes just in time to see Nik stepping out of the car.

The dashboard clock said it was only seven forty-five.

"What is he doing here?"

"I—I asked him to stop by," I said, scooting back to the door. "I needed to apologize for biting him."

That last part came out before I realized what I'd said.

Thompson started slightly and blinked as if waking up from a dream. I expected him to ask me what the hell I'd meant by that, but instead, he reached up and touched his own cheek.

Before Thompson could formulate more of a response, I pulled open the door and hopped out. "Sorry, got to go!" I shouted through the open window. "I'll call you!"

In my dreams, Thompson would just take the hint and drive off. I should have known better. Instead, I watched him unbuckle his seat belt.

Nik, meanwhile, had turned from the gate at the sound of my voice. "Ana," he said with a smile that faded the moment Thompson came around the front of the truck.

The two guys locked eyes over my head.

My mind swirled in a panic. But, despite my latent feelings for Nik, this meeting really was innocent. Worse, what I needed to talk to him about was more important than Thompson's jealousy. "I just need to talk to Nik about something," I said to Thompson. "There's nothing going on."

Thompson crossed his arms in front of his chest, somehow making the muscles on his arms seem ten times larger. "There had better not be," he said, looking directly at Nikolai.

Nikolai didn't posture in response. Instead, he smirked.

I wasn't sure that helped smooth things over with Thompson. In fact, Thompson took another step forward, threateningly. I put up my hands between them. To Thompson, I tried to be reassuring when I said, "I told you I'd tell you all about it, and I will."

He seemed to relax a bit. If nothing else, perhaps Thompson realized no good would come from this standoff right now. He made his way back to the driver's seat without taking his eyes off Nikolai.

We watched him drive away. He cranked up his heavy metal as he peeled out of the spot, barely missing Nik's car.

"New boyfriend?" Nik asked casually.

I nodded.

"Isn't he the guy from the play?"

We walked toward the house. "How's your hand?"

He showed me a tightly bandaged hand. As he waved it past me, I smelled mint. "My mother took care of it. I'm completely smeared with poultices and herbs. But she says there shouldn't be scarring."

"Can you still play?"

He turned his palm over as if inspecting it. "Not for a while, but Mom's magic is strong. I have faith."

I hoped he was right. "You should be mad at me," I told him. "Why didn't you—you know?" I pantomimed stabbing someone.

"Are you kidding?" His face drained, clearly horrified by the thought. "I couldn't do that to you."

We were almost to the steps, and I could feel the tingle of the wards. Nikolai seemed to sense them too, because he slowed.

"Paranoid about something?" he asked.

I gritted my teeth and stepped quickly onto the porch. "Mom accidentally invited someone in that she shouldn't have." I pulled open the screen door. The palm of my hand stung with the contact, as if I'd touched something hot. I jerked away instinctively. The door snapped back, almost catching my hand.

Nikolai grabbed the edge of the frame and held it open. "It's a bit much," he said, his head scanning the porch as if he could actually see the structure of the wards. "She should tone it down."

"She did," I said. When my feet were on the other side of the threshold, the buzzing stopped. "This is her low setting."

"What is she trying to keep out—an army?"

"Close. An army's prince," I said. "And two captains. Or one captain and a general, who knows? Three high-ranking vampires, at any rate."

Nikolai gave a low whistle, as though impressed. He stood on the rug in front of the door while I sat on the Parsons bench and unlaced my Converses. They'd pinched all day, and I couldn't wait to get out of them.

Nikolai had changed since the concert. He wore a pair of jeans and a T-shirt that showed off the tattoo on his bicep. Two dragons intertwined in a Celtic pattern around his arm like a blue and green cuff.

"I'd heard there was another vampire prince in town," Nikolai said. "So, what's he like?"

"Weird," I admitted, rubbing my sore toes through my stockings. "He came all the way from Mississippi to marry off his captain of the guard. Or start a war."

Wiggling out of the other shoe, I rubbed that foot. When I glanced over, Nikolai had his hands in his pockets. He was giving me a very strange look.

"What?" I asked.

"You're not . . . I mean, you're dating Thompson now, right?"

Did he think I was the one who'd be marrying Captain Creepy? Did he look upset about it? Did I want him to be? I shook my head to try to clear it of all the conflicting emotions. "I was dating him. Thompson's pretty angry right now, after seeing you here. Not the best start to our relationship. I'm not sure I'm going to get to go to the movies or dancing or any of that."

"Huh?" he asked, but at the same time he looked relieved to hear I wasn't planning on running off to marry some Southern vampire. I supposed that was good, but I kind of wished he'd be more upset at the idea of someone taking me out for real dates.

"Forget it," I said. "Do you want some lemonade or something?"

"What I really want is to know why you needed to talk to me. And, frankly, why you bit me."

I guess I did owe him an explanation. I got up and led him into the kitchen. I could hear Mom moving around upstairs, so I called up. "I'm home! Nik's here with me." I added that information in case she wasn't wearing much.

Flicking the switch, I turned on the kitchen's overhead light. It was starting to get just dark enough to need it. There were dirty dishes in the sink, the remains of whatever Mom had had for lunch.

"What happened today?" Nikolai asked again, settling himself against the counter and crossing his arms in front of his chest. He didn't have Thompson's massive body, but the muscles in his arms jumped like taut wires.

I looked away because, despite myself, I still felt that old attraction. "Uh, I *am* sorry about that, you know."

I reached into the cupboard, then handed him a glass. He started to take it with his injured hand but quickly switched. He'd been over at the house enough that he felt sufficiently comfortable to get ice from the freezer himself.

I got the lemonade pitcher and set it on the table.

"There's nothing to apologize for. I didn't think it was an intentional attack." He smiled. I'd forgotten how much I loved that smile. It was so warm, but always with a hint of mischievousness. "But why did it happen? Was it something I said?"

I shook my head. "Hunger," I said, struggling to keep a blush from rising from my collar at the memory of his warm blood flooding my mouth.

Nik poured himself a glass. "So, what's affecting them has caught you too, eh?"

I nodded mutely. I hated when it came down to conversations of "us" and "them," because I always felt I was on the wrong side. I hid my discomfort by fetching myself a glass from the cupboard.

"There have been more and more attacks on witches," Nik continued. "Papa has advised that no one go out alone at night. We're to travel in pairs. I'm surprised no one handed you the flyer at the potluck. Oh, right, you were hanging out with mundanes."

He was trying to poke at me about Thompson, but that wasn't what got to me. "They wouldn't have given it to me, anyway, Nik. I'm one of the ones you're protecting yourselves from."

"I know that, Ana. I mean, obviously." He flexed his injured hand. "But you're one of us too."

He had no idea the effect his words had on me. I'd just been feeling the divide between us, and that simple sentence eliminated the distance. I smiled at him, but he was staring, unfocused, at the table. The finger of his uninjured hand traced the pattern of the grain.

"Have you seen *your* father?" Nik asked without meeting my gaze. "I mean, it's sort of strange that he's letting this happen with your . . . um—"

As hard as it had been for him to mention my father, I could see it would be impossible for him to complete this sentence, so

I did. "My people?" His only acknowledgment was to wait for me to continue. I sighed. "My dad's lost it. Like, totally cracked. I tried to go talk to him, and I nearly got killed for my efforts."

"Seriously?" He finally looked at me, his expression shocked. "Are you okay?"

"Yeah," I said, and then everything came out in a flood of words. I told him about how I couldn't understand why my dad hadn't called a hunt, even though I was scared of what that might mean to the witches. I went on about how I was searching for a solution, but I stopped short of telling him about the grimoire. I wasn't sure it was a good idea for the vampire slayer to know about a magic book that contained the spell that enslaved vampires, even if the talisman was destroyed. That reminded me. "Did you know my mom's been trying out potions on Elias? To see if she can enslave him?"

Nikolai had been about to take a drink. He stopped and stared at the glass. He set it down without taking a sip. His reaction made me wonder whether I had been drinking the potion too.

"That would certainly solve some problems," he said thoughtfully.

"What?" I snapped.

"I didn't mean you!" he said. "I never mean you, okay?" He looked down at his bandaged hand. "Forget I said that."

I wanted to stay angry, but I found I could sort of understand the position he echoed. Mom had said it succinctly last night. It was one thing to sacrifice a human being when you got a kingdom of slaves in return, but it was quite another when they were actively resisting you. Who would volunteer to die when all they were doing, in a sense, was prolonging a war between races?

As disgusting as the idea was for me, I kind of *got* that Mom was trying to make the sacrifice worth the price by attempting to drug Elias into submission. If she could show her people that she had control of the vampires, the lottery might seem a more viable option.

But the more I thought about it, the less sense it made. Even if Mom hit on the perfect formula, how was she going to get all the vampires to drink it? It wasn't as though they'd all line up to drink that particular Kool-Aid. This was especially so since, outside of maybe not starving to death, bondage would not be a win for the vamps. In fact, I could see someone as proud as Elias preferring starvation.

So, what then? Was the plan to load up a tranquilizer gun and send Nikolai and his dad out into the woods to bag each and every member of the kingdom? I couldn't see that working very well. Some vampires, like my dad, hardly ever left the shelter of the caves, and those who did often had Igors to protect them.

I supposed it could all be part of a plan to load up the blood of whoever got chosen for the hunt, and afterward the witches could jump out of the shadows and yell, "Surprise! You're all slaves again!"

Well, now, *that* was an evil thought. Was I bad not to necessarily put it past my mom to consider it?

Where would I be in all this? What would they do about my hunger?

I shook my head. I had to find an alternative—something much more win/win for *everybody*.

It was fine and dandy that the Southern Region had worked out a system with a queen who took responsibility for the survival of vampires, but I imagined there was more to that story—especially given that Luis himself was a dhampyr. They clearly had a better relationship between races and probably negotiated some kind of treaty hundreds of years ago. We could barely keep our teeth out of one another's necks here in the Northern Region—literally.

Besides, who would start? As much as I wanted to solve this problem, I certainly didn't want Mom to volunteer to die in order to fix things. I wasn't too keen on the idea of offering myself either. Plus, even though I desperately wanted to trust that my dad would hold up his end of any treaty, there was a bad track record there. His marriage to my mom was supposed to have ended vampire/witch tension. That hadn't turned out so well.

Nik, as lost in thought as I had been, continued to admire the grain pattern in the table. His angular features, half-hidden in the tangle of curls, looked darkly pensive, and unfortunately reminded me of his father.

Mr. Kirov had immigrated from Russia, and, since every place seemed to handle this problem differently, I wondered what Russian witches did about the hunt. I was about to ask him about it, when Mom waltzed into the room.

Mom was dressed to go out. She had freshened her makeup and, although she wore casual jeans, she'd slipped into one of those Indian cotton tunics with embroidery around the collar and cuffs that were all the rage in the 1970s. Of course, Mom had no idea how dated the look was. She smiled and nodded a greeting at Nik as if she expected to find a young man sitting at our kitchen table at eight o'clock at night.

"Have you eaten?" she asked me.

I ignored the irony of the question but couldn't help a sly glance at Nikolai. He chuckled slightly. "Uh, yeah," I said.

"How about you, Nikolai? Would you like a sandwich or something?"

"That would be lovely, Dr. Parker," he said. He was such a proper gentleman, always remembering that my mom was a PhD. Still, I was always turned off by this Eddie Haskell/June Cleaver part of their relationship. My mom clearly appreciated the whole shtick; she started humming happily while she got ham and cheese out of the fridge. I found it gross and annoying.

My phone beeped. I considered ignoring it, but reading a text was preferable to the tableau of my mom's going all Dolly Domestic for Nik. When it chirped again, I realized it wasn't a text; it was an actual call—from Bea. Before I could even say hello, I could hear her sobbing. "They took my mom, Ana!"

"What?" My heart was in my throat. Nightmares of vampire swarms flashed into my mind, but then I realized true sunset was still an hour away.

"For the lottery," she sobbed. "They're going to sacrifice my mom!"

Chapter Ten

"They took my mom."

Even though Bea kept saying it between sobs, I couldn't believe it. No way.

I snuck a look at Mom. She was still humming to herself as she spread mayo on two slices of whole wheat. The sun set outside the window, and its golden rays highlighted the gray in her curls.

Did she know? Was she party to what happened to Bea's mom?

It wouldn't be the first time my mom was involved in something completely evil, but something about this rang false. Hadn't I heard her telling Mr. Kirov she'd never allow the lottery during her reign? But then she *had* asked about Nik being on board for something I hadn't heard. . . .

A kidnapping, though? I looked at Nik, who watched me with curiosity in his eyes. I made the sign language letter *B* with my hand up and thumb curled into the palm. He nodded that he understood but then turned his attention back to Mom, as if neither concerned nor hiding anything.

Okay, I was pretty sure that meant he didn't know what was going on—unless Nik was a better actor than I gave him credit for.

"Ana," Bea was saying, "you've got to help. Talk to your mom. Talk to your dad. Please. It's my mom! We can't let her die. Not like this."

Her voice was reaching such a fever pitch, I was worried my mom might actually hear. I turned my head slightly, to hide the receiver a little. "Hang on. I can't really talk here," I said in a way I hoped would allow Bea to catch my drift. "But I'm on top of it, I swear. On our friendship." I whispered the last three words. In grade school we'd made a blood oath to always help each other. She knew how seriously I took that.

"Okay, okay." She was calming down a bit. At least she was taking breaths between each word now. "But the sun is going down, Ana."

It was already twilight.

Would they do something tonight already?

"Trust me, please," I whispered, glancing over my shoulder. Mom had gone into the pantry to return the mayo to the fridge. I chanced a slightly louder, "I'll text, okay?"

"Can I come over?"

I thought about the Elder meeting that Mom supposedly had later tonight. "I'll let you know. It might not be safe."

"I have to do something."

Mom was coming back. "I know. I'll text you."

My hands shook as I slid the phone back into my pocket. Despite the humid, hot air blowing through the window screen, ice settled along my skin.

I stared at my mom, trying to read her mind. I supposed she might be just devious enough to be hanging around at home to have an alibi, as it were. She'd know I'd rush to Dad or otherwise try to stop the hunt. Maybe she planned to ensnare me this morning because she wanted to keep me from interfering tonight.

That was a deeply frightening thought.

"Who called?" she asked casually.

I shrugged, not entirely trusting myself to speak. "Nobody," I muttered.

"It was that Thompson guy—don't lie," Nikolai said, coming to my rescue, though he knew perfectly well who'd called.

Mom frowned as if trying to picture whom we were talking about. "That big fellow from the play? He was over here practicing his lines constantly. Are you dating?"

I wasn't doing very well with this charade, but I managed a nod.

"He dropped her off," Nikolai said.

Mom looked at Nik for a long time. A smile crossed her lips. "But you're in our kitchen."

"So I am," he said, gesturing expansively and giving me a broad wink. This was so weird.

"Pickles? Chips?" Mom asked.

"Both, please," he said.

She went into the pantry to fetch his request.

My phone beeped. Thinking it might be Bea with more

news, I checked. It was just Thompson, who texted an apology for his testosterone outburst, though he didn't word it that way. I quickly replied that everything was cool with us.

Nik glanced up, watching me send my response. He pulled out his own phone and typed awkwardly with the finger of his uninjured hand.

From the pantry, Mom called out, "Do you like dill or sweet?"

"Dill," he said, his finger pecking.

I knew it was Nik when my phone chirped again. He had written, "Something bad happened. I can tell."

I needed to know something before I told him. "Can I trust u?"

Mom caught us both staring anxiously at our phones, but she laughed as she set the jar of pickles down in front of Nikolai. I thought for sure we were busted, but she shook her head lightly. "You kids and your multitasking," she said. "No one ever focuses on just one thing anymore."

"That would be boring, Dr. Parker," Nikolai said as he punched Send.

The instant I thought she was on to us, I'd thumbed the ringer off. I felt the vibration and looked down. He'd written, "Only ever killed 4 u."

Last year during the whole talisman incident, Dad called the hunt on Mom because he thought she had it. Nik had helped me stop some of them with, shall we say, lethal force. The act had made him an official vampire slayer, no longer an apprentice. But I knew it had shaken him up. I'd always wondered whether he'd continued to kill. I looked over at him. He nodded as if trying to reassure me that what he'd written was the truth. His eyes were very serious.

As Mom leaned against the counter, her eyes darted back and forth between us. Nik ate his sandwich and played a game of Angry Birds on his iPhone. I texted Bea and asked how she was holding up.

Mom waited for a while, as if expecting something. I helped myself to some chips. They stuck drily in my throat. Nik and I made chitchat about the things he'd been up to. Actually, Nik did most of the talking. I could only make noises; if I talked too much, my voice shook from the effort to act normal.

We kept it up for the most excruciating six minutes of my life. Eventually, Mom couldn't contrive a reason to keep standing there. She wandered off to the living room. Nik put a finger to his lips and pointed to his phone.

I finally told him. "It's B. Coven has her mom."

When he got the message, he nearly dropped his phone. His eyes bulged. "Are you serious?" he whispered.

I nodded, although I couldn't really be one hundred percent sure it *was* the coven that had Bea's mom. But someone did, and Bea seemed pretty certain they were going to sacrifice her for the hunt. "What are we going to do?"

The basement door opened, and I jumped. Elias rubbed a hand over the short hairs on his head. His shirt hung open, unbuttoned. I could see the hard line of his chest—white, rough patches of scars on pale skin. When his eyes fell on Nikolai, they narrowed. "Hunter," he said in greeting.

"Vampire," Nikolai replied, standing up.

What was it with men, always squaring off? I motioned for Elias to join us in the kitchen. He took a moment to button a few buttons on his shirt, his eyes on Nikolai. "What can I do for you, my lady?"

"Cut out the posturing for a minute," I hissed. "We've got a real problem. Bea's mom has been taken. They're going to sacrifice her to the hunt!"

"They?" Elias's dark eyebrow arched. "Who?"

"It could be Igors, I suppose, but—," I started.

Nikolai cut me off. "It's the coven. People have been running scared. Maybe it's a group acting outside of royal approval." He jerked his head in the direction of the living room, indicating Mom. We huddled together near the sink, keeping our voices low. "But someone would have called me for backup if the kidnapping was perceived as an attack from the vampire camp. We've been on freaking high alert."

"And so it begins," Elias said softly as he finished buttoning his shirt thoughtfully. Only a vampire could wear a long-sleeve button-down in this heat. Outside the window, the crickets chirped lazily in the evening warmth.

I didn't like how resigned he sounded. "We need to focus. We've got to find out when the hunt is happening. You've been through this sort of thing before," I said to Elias. "Is there any special timing? Like at midnight or something? How much time do we have to rescue her?"

Elias lifted his head as if scenting the wind. His eyes grew distant, unfocused. Nik and I exchanged a curious look, but neither of us dared interrupt. After a half minute or less, Elias rubbed the space between his eyes and shook himself out.

"I don't know, my lady," Elias said. "I don't sense the call, but my ties have been severed for months now. I don't know if I would feel it anymore."

"You mean they could be starting now?" My voice was louder than I intended, but my heart leaped. I promised Bea I'd stop this! I started for the door, but Elias caught my shoulder. He spun me around.

Before he could take hold of my shoulders, Nikolai forcibly stepped between us. He pushed Elias's hands away. I felt his magical blade begin to rev up, like an electric current. "Hands off, vampire."

Elias's jaw twitched, but he allowed his hand to drop. He otherwise ignored Nik's defensive posture and spoke around him to me. "You mustn't go without a plan, lady. Coming between vampires and their hunt is dangerous beyond measure. Did the prince offer no aid last night?"

"Oh." I'd forgotten that Elias hadn't heard about the narrow escape and blood puking. "No. Dad's completely lost it. He's in no shape to help. In fact, he's kind of a liability."

We must have been talking in normal voices, because Mom stuck her head into the room and interrupted before I could explain more. "What's this huddle about?" Then, on seeing Elias, she smiled. "Ah, Elias, you're awake! How are you feeling?"

Nikolai's voice dripped with dark amusement. "Not feeling well, vampire?"

"I'm hungry," he snarled, and I could see the tip of his fangs. "And you, boy, smell of spilled blood."

The psychic blade in Nik's fist sizzled and snapped. Even

with the electric light of the overhead lamp, I could almost see a pinkish outline of a pointed dagger as he raised his fist to Elias's throat. The tip touched a spot just below Elias's jawline but stopped short of penetration.

"Just try it, asshole," he said, his bandaged hand trembling slightly.

Elias stayed perfectly still, but his silver gray eyes burned with molten hatred as the pupils slowly shifted to catlike slits.

I heard Mom's sharp intake of breath. The scent of freshly turned earth alerted me that she was drawing up her power and readying her own attack.

"Stand down, Nikolai," I shouted, grabbing his arm. I tried to pull it down and away from Elias's throat, but he was surprisingly strong. His muscles were like rock. "Elias isn't the enemy! We have to help Bea's mom. The sun is down! They could be coming for her right now."

"What?" It was Mom. Her magic faltered in surprise, changing to the smell of roses. "What about Kat?"

I always forgot that Bea's mom was named Katherine and that all her friends called her Kat. "Bea called," I explained, since Mom clearly didn't know. "Her mom's been taken."

I was unprepared for the force with which she unleashed her power. She raised her hand, palm out, like one of Thompson's superheroes, and slam! Elias was thrown back against the kitchen wall, pinioned. He grunted as the air rushed from his lungs. I could see him struggling as if against invisible bonds, but he was held hard against the plaster wall where our family calendar hung.

"If one hair on Kat's head is harmed, your people will pay," Mom said, striding forward, her finger jabbing him in the chest accusingly.

"No," I said. "The vampires didn't take her. The coven did!"

Beside me, I felt Nik drop his blade. "It's true, Dr. Parker. It wasn't them. It was us."

"What?" All the color drained from my mother's face, but she still held Elias against the wall with her outstretched hand. "It was my direct order: no lottery. Who dares disobey the queen?"

She sounded as crazy as my dad, except in an *Alice in Wonderland* Queen of Hearts kind of way. Next she was going to start shouting, "Off with their heads!"

Nikolai folded his arms in front of his chest and turned his head away as if looking out the darkened window at something. "It's not my father. He'd rather attack outright or let them starve before giving the vampires one of our own."

"If you're looking for a traitor, go to the source. The prince would know with whom he negotiates," Elias managed to croak.

"True," Mom said, acknowledging Elias briefly, as though he were nothing more than a distraction. "Ramses would happily foment dissention in my ranks. I will deal with him next."

Before I could ask what she meant by "next," Mom made her hand into a fist. Elias cried out in pain.

"Mom! No!" I shouted.

"You need to learn your place, vampire. Never threaten anyone under my roof again," she told him. She opened her hand. He fell to his knees on the kitchen floor, clutching his stomach and gasping for breath. She turned her back on him. Pulling her cell out of her pocket, she started dialing numbers. "I'm going to find out who's responsible for this."

I ran over to where Elias knelt. Dropping down beside him, I gently placed my arms around his shoulders. "Are you okay?"

He gritted his teeth as he answered. "I will be."

Mom had gotten whomever she'd called on the phone and was demanding to know what was going on. She grabbed her keys from the peg in the hallway as she headed for the front door. I heard her shout, "I'm calling the meeting now, damn it," as the door slammed behind her. "This is not on."

Nikolai stood in the middle of the kitchen, not looking at us, his arms still wrapped around his chest.

I started to help Elias to his feet, but he jerked away from my touch and pulled himself up. His eyes were still catlike slits, and they watched Nikolai warily, as if expecting another attack.

This was all messed up, and I struggled to stay focused on the bigger issue. "Where would they take Bea's mom?" I asked Elias, who was making a show of brushing himself off. "I mean, where would Ramses want the sacrifice to take place?"

"We'd never agree to go all the way to the lair," Nikolai said. His face was still turned away, as if he were talking to the sink. "We'd want some safe place where we could leave her."

The muscles of Elias's jaw flexed as he tucked his shirttails into his jeans. "It sounds as though the hunter knows more than he's said."

Nikolai's head snapped to glare at Elias. "I'm being hypothetical, you know—trying to consider what the coven would want."

When Elias straightened his collar, he twinged slightly. Unconsciously, he briefly touched his hand to his stomach. My gut ached suddenly as well, as if I'd strained core muscles at yoga. I tried to catch his eye to see if he knew why we shared this sensation all of a sudden, but he was too busy trying to act unhurt and strong in front of Nikolai. His pupils remained slit, and his fangs showed clearly when he finally spoke. "I find it difficult that your expertise was never tapped, hunter. Did your coven never ask your family for advice on this contingency?"

Nikolai flushed, color darkening his cheeks. I expected him to deny it, but he said, "Of course they did."

"That's not very hypothetical then, is it?" Elias drawled sarcastically.

Nikolai shook his head. "Look, a lot of locations got tossed around, okay?"

"OMG," I said in frustration. "I can't believe you knew any—just tell us *all* of them."

Nik's posture was still closed off, his arms folded in front of his chest. His lips were pressed together, but he didn't speak.

"He won't turn traitor," Elias quietly said to me with sympathy.

Traitor? I didn't understand what Elias meant at first, but then I gaped at Nikolai. "You can't be serious! You've got to tell us. Screw the Elders and their vows of secrecy. Someone's life is at stake. Not just anyone—Bea's mom! You know as well as I do that if your dad weren't the slayer, your mom could have been taken instead."

Nikolai took in a long, slow breath. He sounded a bit

defeated when he muttered, "Swede Hollow or Hidden Falls would be my best guess."

They were both parks in St. Paul that would close at sunset. I could see the appeal of either one, because both parks were sheltered in deep, heavily forested valleys that felt secluded and secret. I started for the door. "Come on," I told the boys. "Nik, you drive."

I pulled Nik's elbow when I passed him, and he turned and followed me reluctantly.

"We can't stop the hunt if it's started," he said.

"I've done it before," I reminded him. "Besides, we can't just sit here. We have to do something."

I checked to see that Elias was coming as well, but he was nowhere in sight. I stopped at the door. "Elias?"

At the basement steps, I heard heels clicking on the wooden stairs. In a moment, Elias reappeared with the rucksack he'd brought with him when he moved in. At my expression, he said, "Your mother's . . . display has made it quite evident that I must make good on my promise to find somewhere new to stay."

I leaned in closely and brushed my hand along my stomach, feeling for the phantom pain. "Yeah, I swear I sensed the aftermath of that punch."

Elias's eyebrows jumped. "Indeed?"

I whispered, "Is it our blood bond?"

He nodded, though he seemed a little taken aback that I knew about the bond at all. "Perhaps the hunger accentuates the connection."

The strap of the army green bag over his shoulder caught my eye, and I frowned. "You're coming with me, right?"

"As you wish, my lady," he said. I noticed his eyes had finally returned to normal. His fangs, however, had not completely retracted. "Though for once I agree with the hunter, I don't know what we can do for your friend. Honestly, I may not be able to control myself if the frenzy begins."

I wondered if I could.

I didn't want to think about that right now, so I took his hand and led him to where Nikolai waited awkwardly at the door.

Nikolai stopped outside the driver's side door, key in his hand. "Bringing the vampire is a bad idea, Ana."

Pulling at the door handle, I found that Nik hadn't unlocked it yet. The metal flap sprang back with a clank. "We don't have time for an argument. What if you're wrong about where they've taken her?"

"I've seen them hungry," he said, unmoving. He stared at where Elias stood behind me on the sidewalk. "I don't want him at my back when the others attack from the front."

"Maybe, if we hurry, it won't come to that." It was all I could think to say.

Nikolai didn't look terribly sure he agreed, but he finally opened the door. I slid into the passenger side. I pulled out my phone and found Bea's number. I texted her to meet us at Hidden Falls. It was the closer of the two parks, and I told Nik so.

Then, as an afterthought, I cut and pasted the same message and sent it to Mom. She didn't want the lottery either; maybe she'd help us stop it.

Elias shuffled some of Nik's things around before settling into the backseat. The car was littered with promotional CDs, concert posters, college textbooks, and empty cans of soda. He leaned back into the shadows, the flash of the passing streetlights illuminating a grim expression. "A plan would be helpful, lady."

But I didn't have one beyond the pounding desire to find Bea's mom. We wouldn't be much of a rescue if we couldn't stop the hunt, though. I pulled on my bottom lip. "Magic," I said after a few minutes. "What about magic?"

Nikolai started the engine and pulled out onto the street. "What about it?"

Shyly, I looked at Elias, not wanting to embarrass him. "Well, Mom had no trouble, uh, earlier . . . with . . ."

I couldn't finish without turning to check on Elias. If my comment bothered him, he said nothing. He'd rolled down the window a little, and papers rustled in the backseat.

Nikolai, meanwhile, nodded a bit as if considering. He'd turned on the car's air conditioner, and musty, moist air blew into my face.

"It would take a lot of witch power, but we could probably push back and keep them at bay. But that's more of a stalemate than a check, you know?" Nikolai said. "We might be able to keep it up until sunrise, but we'd just have to do it again when the sun set the next day."

But it would solve the immediate problem. "It's a start."

No one mentioned the one serious flaw. There was only one witch in the car. I had my own sort of magic, triggered when I pitted my vampire and witch halves against each other, but I wasn't sure how effective it would be to hold back the hunt. Last time, I'd had the talisman to boost my strength.

The time before that, I only had to stop a fight between my parents and their minions—and I'd drunk Elias's blood to trigger the power. I glanced back at where Elias sat. He seemed absorbed in watching the houses go by.

It wasn't like him to be so quiet. "Are you okay?" I asked.

He ran his fingers through the short hairs on the side of his head and then let out a long breath. "No," he said. His voice was weary, but he clenched his hands into fists in his lap. "I don't understand it, but the hunger is much worse all of a sudden. Like some kind of magical rebound . . . but that makes no sense." He shook his head as if trying to keep his mind on track. "What's important is that I thought I had it under control, but I don't just feel weak, physically. I don't know how long I can hold out—mentally."

"What do you mean?"

He flicked his gaze at the back of Nikolai's head. Then he leaned forward and cupped his hand in front of his face. He whispered scratchily, "I hate him. I hate magic." In the strobe of a streetlight that we passed, I could see his eyes beginning to transform again. "I just—I want to—" His entire body clenched with the effort to keep his pupils normal. "I want to kill everything, Ana. Everything."

Great—now I had a vampire in the backseat ready to go

ballistic. Nikolai watched us furtively as he drove. I was sure he'd heard everything and was just waiting for an opportunity to say "I told you so."

The bandage on Nik's hand flashed greenish white as he turned the corner at the stoplight. It gave me an idea. I undid my seat belt so I could turn around more easily in my seat. "Don't get in an accident," I told Nik, who watched curiously.

Reaching around the seat, I offered Elias my arm. "I have witch blood," I said. "Take some."

Elias flinched back as if my touch were fire. Nikolai hit the brakes so hard, they squealed. I had to grip the seat to keep from banging into the dashboard. "I can't," Elias said, though his gaze focused hungrily on the flesh of my arm. "I'd become nosferatu."

"Ana! What the hell are you doing?" Nik demanded, swerving us into a parking spot to the sound of multiple horns.

I ignored Nik for the moment. "What about the blood bond? Doesn't that make a difference? You've taken blood from me before without dire consequences, remember?" I'd offered this before, when Elias had been injured. He'd had no problem then.

A light of hope seemed to soften Elias's face. "The bond. Of course."

Nikolai's hand was on my shoulder, trying to get me to turn and face him. "This is so not okay. I can't let him feed on you in my car!"

But it was too late. Elias sprang at catlike speed. His teeth sank deep into my forearm.

Chapter Eleven

I was vaguely aware that Nikolai shouted. The electric light of the coffee shop on the corner was a hazy blur. The only sensation that mattered was the pounding throb of blood moving through my body.

Somehow, I too tasted coppery sweetness on my own lips. Where was that coming from? I didn't have time to process the thought as my gnawing hunger was calmed with every passing second. The sensation was like seeing a chocolate cake after a week of dieting. The first bite might be all my body needed, but I couldn't stop. I wanted more.

The hammering beat began to slow. A coldness crept into my fingers and toes. My head felt separated, floating off to somewhere far away. I wanted to lie down in the calm emptiness of it all.

I heard the sound of wings fluttering.

And then there was a horrible rending snap, an electric shock of pain. I fell back into hard, clear focus.

Nikolai had gotten into the backseat, the door left open to the rush of wind and the hiss of passing cars. One of his arms was in a choke hold around Elias's throat; his psychic blade buried in Elias's leg.

Elias spat and snarled. My blood spattered his chin. His fangs were barred, but his eyes watched me warily. "Are you okay?" he asked, his voice straining against the pressure of Nik's headlock.

I looked down at my arm. It was a mess. I'd have bruises for sure, and another scar in the shape of a dotted crescent to go with all the others. But the bleeding had slowed and was already starting to congeal. My head felt like lead, but I answered, "I'll be okay."

"You nearly killed her," Nikolai said.

Elias looked a bit chagrined but spoke to me when he said, "I went too far, and I'm sorry for that, my lady. But I couldn't have killed you, not without killing a part of myself."

Nikolai removed the blade from Elias's leg with a magical pop that made my own twinge. I must have flinched, because Elias noticed it.

"The bond is much stronger now," he said, rubbing his neck when Nikolai released it as well. We sighed in relief at the same time.

Nikolai's eyes flicked between us. "Well, that's creepy."

"Perhaps," Elias said, his eyes returning to their usual gray. "But it worked. The hunger is sated."

A semitruck passed close enough to rattle the car. Nikolai seemed suddenly aware he'd left the door open. After pinning

Elias under one last I'm-watching-you glare, he got out and returned to the driver's seat.

"Why?" I asked. Nikolai started the engine, but I didn't turn to face the front yet. "Why did it work? I thought you couldn't get satisfaction from small tastes anymore."

"Witch blood is more powerful," Elias said, though he didn't sound as though he was stating a fact so much as postulating a theory. He wiped his chin on the shoulder of his shirt, leaving a dark smudge. "And perhaps the bond added something?"

"What if we offered the vampires a taste instead of a full hunt?" I asked.

"Because it doesn't work long term," Nikolai said. "And it's disgusting."

"The hunter makes one accurate point," Elias said. "During the Burning Times, there were many fewer witches, and there was talk of suspending the lottery. Offering smaller doses was tried, but the hunger rebounded, coming back harder and more violent each time. The queen was forced to offer herself, as hers was the only death strong enough to satisfy."

"So the queen's blood has special properties?" I asked. "Why? What are they?"

Even Nikolai, who'd been muttering angrily to himself, stopped and turned to see what Elias would say.

Elias shook his head; he sounded surprised when he answered, "I don't know."

Nikolai looked to me. "Are you saying you think there's something actually different, like scientifically, in witch blood?"

"Or magically," I said, since I hadn't really considered the possibility of some molecular or cell-level specialness.

I thought about all the doctors and lawyers at the coven's picnic earlier today. I could see the political advantages of making sure there were lawyers to protect us, but why were so many of our high-ranking Elders medical doctors?

There was also the book of names. It was an ancient record that traced witch marriages, births, and deaths. Everyone who was initiated was recorded in it, sort of like when Christians added names to Bibles at baptism. I'd always thought it was just another ancient tradition meant to make those of us who were uninitiated feel left out. But what if the early recorders were actually tracking something?

"*Is* our blood different?" I looked at Nikolai's bandaged hand. His mom always took care of minor scrapes for any witch in need. I tried to remember the trips I'd had to the doctor for checkups, vaccinations, and such. We always used one of the doctors in the coven. I'd assumed it was one of those things you did to support the community, but could there have been an ulterior motive?

I turned around to face the front. "Nik, have you ever been to a doctor who wasn't in the coven?"

He was checking over his shoulder for a break in the traffic so he could pull us back onto the road. "No," he said. "There's a witch in almost every specialty. We were even able to find a cardiologist in Rochester at Mayo when my dad had those chest pains last year."

"Really? Doesn't that strike you as kind of odd?" I asked.

"It's an ancient calling. It's a healer thing." Nik shrugged as if he'd decided he didn't like this theory anymore.

"Or it's a blood thing," Elias said quietly.

There was that bloodmobile at the coven gathering. Come to think of it, I saw it there every year. "What if so many of us are doctors as a kind of protection? To make sure we get the right kind of transfusions and stuff? And so that no one looks too closely under a microscope?"

Nikolai shook his head. "I don't buy it. Some mundane would have discovered us by now."

"What if the difference is really subtle? I mean, I don't know that much about the science, but if Elias can drink regular human blood as well as ours, the difference is probably almost undetectable. But it might be just the difference we need. I mean, maybe we can isolate that one bit the vampires crave and, I don't know, make a synthetic substitute."

"Now you're talking science fiction," Nikolai said. We'd come to the big brick apartment building on the corner of Highland and Fairview, and he made a right. "Where do you plan to manufacture this synth blood—in your secret laboratory?" He said the last word in a thick Dr. Frankenstein accent, with an emphasis heavy on the "bor."

I was irritated by the intrusion of reality into my scenario. "I was thinking long term," I snapped. "Of course, I wasn't planning to whip something up in the kitchen sink."

But Nik wasn't done crushing my dream. "You're the one who pointed out how many coveners are docs. Don't you think they would have considered this idea, anyway?"

"Actually, I don't," Elias said. "Science and magic have often been pitted against each other. Your medical experts might understand that witch blood is different. They may even have researched it for their own needs, but I doubt they've considered what it means to the hunt. For our part, vampires have always assumed that the critical component to the hunt is the magic of death."

"Maybe it still is," I murmured. "In which case, Bea's mom is screwed."

We passed a business center. Lights were so bright here that the sidewalks seemed bathed in artificial sunlight.

"Perhaps there is a magic in death or sacrifice that's essential to the first blood bond between witch and vampire," Elias continued. "But the truth is, there's something to Ana's theory. I was slowly unraveling before Ana's generous offer, and now . . . things are more stable. It's a profound difference. One I could not glean from normal human blood."

My arm was still tender, and I cradled it in my lap. Nik glanced over at my movement and made a face. "We need to wrap that. *Chyort voz'mi!* That looks awful."

Nik must have been really upset to swear in Russian. He once confessed to me that he felt like a peasant anytime his father's language slipped out. I looked at my arm. He was right, of course.

I heard a ripping sound from the backseat. When I turned to look, Elias had torn off a long strip from the tail of his shirt. "Give it here, my lady. It's the least I can do."

Unbuckling, I turned around again. Nik watched us warily in the rearview, his mouth set in a grim line. Elias gently and expertly wrapped the wound on my arm. "I think you may be on to something," he said, twisting the ends into a clever knot. "Perhaps there's a scientist among the coveners whom you trust?"

Thing was, I wasn't very tight with any of the Elders. They'd pretty much shut me out since the disaster that was my Initiation. "My mom knows all the university types, but I don't know if that means we can trust them or not."

"To the queen's credit, she seemed genuinely surprised by this turn of events," Elias said, checking his work. Clearly, he'd field-dressed a bite wound a time or two in his past. The rag bandage was snug, but not too tight. I flexed my fingers. I felt as if I were wearing one of those arm-length gloves, except this one started past my wrist and stopped before my elbow.

We left the lights behind when we turned down River Road. We were almost to Hidden Falls. The summer air drifting off the Mississippi smelled strongly of fish.

"I hope we're not too late," I whispered as if saying a prayer.

Nikolai added, "I hope this is the right place."

"I hope we can actually save her," Elias said.

The lot was deserted. We pulled into a spot next to a sign proclaiming the park open from sunrise to sunset. Swarms of bugs swirled around the single overhead streetlamp. I stepped out to the chorus of tree frogs and crickets. A carpet of stars spread overhead. The trimmed grass was wet with evening dew.

Nikolai locked the car with a jangle of keys and then leaned against the hood of the car. The engine clicked as it cooled.

Elias stood beside me, his head cocked slightly as if listening intently for something.

Another car came down the sloped driveway, its headlights flashing across the grass. When it got close enough, I recognized Bea's Buick. It pulled into the spot next to Nikolai's battered Toyota. I was surprised to see that it was Mr. Braithwaite driving. Bea sat beside him, her eyes red and swollen from crying.

I ran to comfort her. Before I could open the door to help her out, Mr. Braithwaite jumped out of the car. He was dressed in khaki shorts with tons of pockets, and a black tee with the words RESISTANCE IS FUTILE and some sort of formula underneath in parentheses, which I read IF LESS THAN ONE OHM. I didn't pretend to understand his humor, or the fashion sense that would also have him wearing dark socks with his sandals.

He pointed a shaky finger at Elias. Behind round Harry Potter glasses, his eyes were wild with accusation. "You brought a vampire?"

How was it that people always knew? I turned to check out Elias, wondering if I would be able to tell if I didn't know him so well. Catlike, his eyes reflected the parking lot's overhead lamp. Okay, I could see how that might freak out Mr. Braithwaite.

"Elias is my friend. I trust him," I said calmly. "He's been able to track the hunt in the past. He helped me find my mom once, when vampires were after her."

Mr. Braithwaite's mouth worked with unformed protests.

"He's been fed. In my car, no less," Nikolai said drily. "I'll make sure he behaves, Mr. B."

Elias shot Nik a dark look but said nothing.

I opened the door and helped Bea to her feet. She didn't say anything as she wrapped me in a hug. Her face was hot and wet against my shoulder, and she took in several ragged breaths.

"Have you found her?" she asked. Pulling out of our embrace, Bea scanned the area anxiously, as if hoping to spot her mom sitting safely in our car or standing nearby.

"We only just got here," I admitted regretfully.

"Why aren't you looking?" Bea pushed away from me and ran off randomly, calling out, "Mom? Mom?"

Mr. Braithwaite took off in the opposite direction toward the river's edge, shouting, "Kat? Can you hear us? Kat?"

Nik unfolded his arms and stood up. "We should check the falls." He pointed to the right. I strained to see where he indicated. I could barely make out a shadowy, gaping break in the tree line.

I waved, trying to catch Bea's attention, but Nik shook his head. "She's too freaked out right now to be much help. Let her run off some steam. You can call her phone if we actually find Mrs. B."

I didn't like the idea of leaving Bea in the state she was in, but Nik was already on the move. I ran to catch up. There were no signs indicating a walking trail or something of interest among the trees, but Nik seemed to know where he was going. Elias fell into step behind us. Our shoes left prints in the silvery dew as we walked to the edge of the mowed lawn.

A path seemed to appear out of the darkness when we reached the tree cover. The grass was longer and weedier here, but tire ruts cut a clear route into the distance. Mosquitoes swarmed thickly. They whined in my ears and bit my naked arms.

We followed a slight curve to a concrete-slab bridge. Here the route narrowed to a footpath. Round boulders were set into concrete retaining walls that formed the channel and, at varying intervals, water trickled over algae-slicked, man-made falls. The spray smelled lightly of sewage. An abandoned plastic bottle bobbed in the lowest pool, trapped in a bay of broken concrete chunks. It was too dark to see all the way to the top. The path was barely distinguishable among the tall, untrimmed grasses and ferns.

Elias paused, posture alert.

"Vampires approach," he said quietly.

A faint rustling, no louder than wind through the leaves, sent shivers down my spine. Nik's magical blade hummed to life as we scanned the branches and the bushes. Nik edged closer to me, until our shoulders touched. Elias did the same on the other side.

A voice echoed from above, bouncing strangely off the water. "My, my, not at all who we expected."

When a naked figure dropped gracefully from the branches, I would have to say I agreed.

Chapter Twelve

I'm not sure I could've imagined a more awkward moment. Prince Luis stood in front of me, completely naked. I tried not to stare anywhere in particular, but everything hung out bare and in the open.

The edges of his light brown skin glowed silver white in the moonlight. His confident, unashamed poise made him appear alien, vampiric, but the slightly doughy thickness at his waist reminded me of his humanity. He was also hairier than most vampires, and a light dusting of black curls covered his arms, chest, and legs.

"Where's Bea's mom?" I asked.

At the same moment, Luis demanded, "Where's Prince Ramses?"

Of course, his question baffled me, but I was slightly comforted by the thought that Dad was supposed to be here. Perhaps we'd come to the right place, after all.

"Here."

The voice behind me made me jump. I spun around in time to see my dad step out from the thick tangle of buckthorn to balance on the edge of the retaining wall. He'd also left his clothes at home, which, frankly, made my brain spasm.

"You trespass on kingdom business," Dad said. "This is no place for exiles, and definitely not for a hunter."

A couple more vampires appeared beside Dad, as if to let us know that we were completely outnumbered. Beside me, Nikolai straightened and took in a steadying breath. I felt his power spike in readiness for a fight.

I opened my mouth to ask about Bea's mom again, but Elias spoke up first. "What business would you have with the Southern prince, my liege?"

My dad flinched. His mouth collapsed into thin irritation.

"You intrude on an abdication ceremony," Luis informed us.

Elias took in a sharp hiss of breath. "No!"

What the hell did that mean? I looked to my dad, whose expression was tight. "What would you have me do, Elias?" His tone was soft, wounded. He had not spoken to either of us in such a kind manner since the exile. "My kingdom is shattering under the weight of starvation. The Southern witches still respect the old way."

It took me a second to parse what he meant, but then I remembered what Luis had told me when I asked about the hunt. The queen sacrificed herself, the way it was done before the secret war.

"No, my prince, I beg you," Elias said, his voice hoarse with desperation. "Don't do this! There's another way, I'm sure of it. Ana has plans."

I did? Elias must be really upset to consider my wild theories "plans." But did all this mean that Dad was also trying to avoid the hunt? He was willing to give up his title to save his people? What caused such a radical change? This was a completely different man from the raving lunatic who had made some bad pun before throwing me to the wolves yesterday.

And what about Bea's mom?

Nik and I came to the same conclusion, and our eyes met. I could almost read what he was thinking. They didn't know. The vampires didn't know that the coven was ready to sacrifice one of its own. If we could keep Dad from finding out, we could save her life.

Honestly, it seemed like a pretty neat solution. I couldn't see Elias's problem. No one—not already expecting to, anyway—would have to die, and . . .

"Please, my king," Elias begged. He jabbed a finger at Luis. "This is a mere boy. What would he do with an animus of your stature? He's not even entirely vampire."

Luis batted Elias's hand away with a growl. "Captain! Teach Constantine how we respect the crown in the South."

Captain Creepy leaped down, but before his feet even touched the ground, Elias landed an open-palm punch in the center of his chest. My eyes could barely track the move, but the next thing I knew, the captain flew into the bushes with a crash.

"I am no one's to instruct," Elias said.

Captain Creepy shook himself off and bounded to his feet

with a strangled cry. In a blur, he launched himself at Elias. Elias was ready for him. A strong undercut to the jaw knocked the captain's head back. He stumbled and collapsed with a groan.

Luis's fists clenched. "You dare?"

Vampires dropped out of the trees like pale missiles. Elias crouched slightly, as if prepared to take on Luis's army single-handedly.

"Stand down, South," my dad said. Splashes sounded behind as Dad's people dropped into the water in a line behind us. "We came to you in peace, but no one abuses our captain of the guard without a fight."

Luis laughed.

I cringed, wishing I weren't huddled next to Nikolai smack in between these two phalanxes of pissed-off vampires.

"You have no chance against us, Ramses. You—"

I had no idea what he was going to say next, because Elias took one swift step forward and coldcocked him on the chin.

Pandemonium broke loose.

A band of Luis's vampires launched themselves at Elias, only to be met by flying kicks and punches from a pack of Ramses'. There were howls and snarls reverberating through the woods.

I screamed when I felt a hand clasp around my neck. Ramses had a fistful of my tank in one hand, and Nikolai in the other. He managed to drag us back from the center of the fighting into the shallow pool. Cold wetness filled my Converses, and I slipped and slid through the pool. Dad swung his grip around and pressed us gently against the wall. He gestured with his chin to the pale hands that reached for us. "Climb the wall. Run for safety."

"But—Elias—!"

My dad's lip lifted in a wry smile. "Elias has very cleverly put an end to this abdication ceremony. I suspect he's foxy enough to evade serious injury as well."

"But why?" I asked, pushing at the attempts to lift me. "Why would you do it?"

"Because," he said, reaching out to almost touch my cheek but withdrawing his hand awkwardly, "I nearly allowed you to be killed, my child. The emotional shock of that action has temporarily cleared my head. I don't know how long it will last; that's why I came here to offer the kingdom to Luis. I—" He turned at the sound of something in the fight. "I have to go. Run!"

As I allowed myself to be pulled over the wall, I wondered what my dad was going to say. He'd never, ever expressed even the tiniest shred of affection for me before, but here he was saving not only me, but Nikolai too.

Not that Nikolai appreciated the gesture. He struck out at the nearest vampire. She sprang out of the way of the slice of his magical blade past her waist. She hissed angrily, and I had to grab his arm before he lunged at her again.

He swung at me but stopped the moment he saw my face.

"This isn't our fight," I said. Then I whispered, "We should go. Bea's mom is still out there."

With effort, he sheathed his magical blade. Vampires moved out of his way, though the female he'd tried to slash gestured to me. "Princess, let me lead you out," she said, though she kept a watch on Nikolai.

I shook my head. "Thank you, but we have to find our friends." I was thinking of Bea and her dad somewhere out in the park. I didn't want them stumbling into this chaos. The vampire watched me with a wistful expression that made plain what she needed. "I order you to rejoin the fight."

With relief plain on her face, she gave a half salute and dashed away. I twisted around to watch her go, and I caught sight of Elias. He and my dad were back to back like kung-fu street fighters, throwing off any attacks that came their way. My dad's face was paler than usual, and it seemed his punches moved slower than Elias's. I must have taken a step toward them, because Nikolai pulled me back.

"If you want to return, we can," he said firmly, "but you'll need a weapon."

I shook my head. Elias was strong and smart. He'd get them out of there if it looked as though they weren't going to win. "We've got to keep looking for Bea's mom."

"They don't know. You heard Ramses, right? They were planning on joining the Southern clan. They wouldn't do something that drastic if they were expecting a sacrifice, right?"

"Yeah," I agreed. We jogged through the woods in the general direction of the parking lot. There was no path on this side, and my feet kept catching on rotten logs and sticky burrs. I remembered Elias's shock at the suggestion that Dad would take part in the ceremony. "What's the big deal, anyway? What's involved in an abdication?"

Nikolai stopped to help me push aside a cluster of willow branches that was blocking our progress. At least this deep in the woods, we seemed to have left behind all the mosquitoes. Nik watched my face carefully as I walked under his arm. "I've only read about this, of course, but I think the sole way your dad can stop being prince is by death."

Death? "My dad was going to commit suicide?"

Nik shook his head but said, "Kind of. I think the other prince was going to kill him."

"What?" I had a hard time imagining Luis doing something like that.

We connected to a deer trail and were able to walk more quickly single file. Nikolai went first. He turned his head to the side as he talked. "I don't know for sure, but Elias used the words 'animus' and 'transfer.' There's a legend among the hunters that, under certain circumstances, vampires can absorb the demonic soul, the animus, of another of their kind. This supposedly gives the vampire superpowers. Think Dracula level. This is a bigger problem in the Old Country, where so many nosfaratu run wild in the hills. Nosfaratu will steal one another's souls and can become insanely powerful. So, I'm guessing they were going to do a civilized version of that. A transfer of power—literally."

We broke out into the open of the park proper. Bea and her dad stood next to the park building, holding hands. Their heads were bent together, as though they were praying or talking about something intently. As we approached, I caught a strong smell of freshly baked chocolate chip cookies. I felt a heat, as strong as an open oven, radiating out in a circle around them.

"Magic," I said to Nikolai. I had to stop when the heat grew too strong. I didn't need to be a fully functioning witch to guess at what they were doing. "They're trying to contact Bea's mom. I can't help, but maybe you can."

He acknowledged my observation with a short nod. He didn't try to break into their circle, however. He just moved a short distance to sit on a park bench. He clasped his hands lightly between his knees and ducked his head. I felt his support immediately. It brushed past me like a gust of warm, wet wind off the ocean. I could almost taste the sea salt.

I waited, wishing I could help. The park was eerily quiet. The tree frogs and crickets seemed to be holding their breath. I wondered if it was in deference to the magic being performed or out of fear of the predatory vampires nearby. I glanced over my shoulder at the path to the falls. You'd never know a battle raged just beyond the trees. No one cried out. Everything was as silent as the grave.

I hoped Elias was okay—Dad too.

That last thought surprised me. I hated him most days, and the rest of the time the strongest emotion I could work up was indifference. But . . . maybe the hunger had been eating away at him the longest. When he'd first showed up at my door, he'd seemed as rational as someone claiming to be a vampire prince could be. I'd thought my mom was the villain in those early days, until he showed a darker side of himself in the business over the talisman.

Perhaps, as prince, he'd shouldered the emotional toll of the hunger the most. Could it be all this crazy wasn't entirely his fault? I could see it was possible. . . .

Though maybe I was just rationalizing because he'd been nice briefly. He had called Elias "captain of the guard" again, hadn't he? Was he saying he regretted our exile? And he'd saved not just me, but Nikolai too. I really wanted to believe that he'd had some kind of literal wake-up call when he realized he'd nearly had me killed.

Still, I should be smart about this. It was very possible that Dad was still the jerk he'd always been.

He clearly had, at some point between predawn this morning and sunset tonight, decided it was better to sacrifice himself than commit infanticide. Considering he slept all day, he'd moved fast. Did he dream? Had he tossed and turned all day, plagued by the idea of what he'd nearly done?

If it were true, that would make him almost . . . decent and caring, as a real father was supposed to be.

Huh. I wasn't sure I was ready for that concept. So I returned my attention to the magic my friends worked. Bea and her dad had begun a slow circling motion. Every so often they'd stop and go the other way. The movement reminded me of the way Mom's dashboard compass spun and reoriented at every turn.

Finally, Bea opened her eyes. I felt something release, like the tension in the string of a bow. Mr. Braithwaite smiled, and Nikolai whooped. It was obvious before Bea spoke what she was going to say, but she told me anyway. "We found her!"

Chapter Thirteen

Without further discussion, Bea and her dad were in their car and off. The Buick's engine rattled as they sped up the ramp leading out of the park. Nikolai too had buckled in behind the wheel of his car. I hadn't moved. I kept glancing over my shoulder, staring into the blackness and hoping for a sign that Elias and Dad had won the fight.

Nikolai cranked down the window. "Come on!"

It was why we'd come to this park in the first place, but I wasn't sure I could leave without Elias.

"He's more than capable. Both of them," Nikolai said, astutely guessing at my hesitation. "Bea's mom is still being held captive."

Reluctantly, with one last hopeful look, I started to the car. My legs moved slowly, painfully. Every step was agonizing. My body felt like one big bruise. At first, I thought maybe I'd sprained something in our dash through the woods, but then I remembered the bond.

Elias was the one in pain.

"No," I said. "He's hurt. You go! I have to help him."

As I turned and headed back to the falls, I heard the slam of a car door and a curse. Nikolai appeared beside me. "I'll be your weapon," he muttered.

"What?"

"I told you, you can't go back into that fight without a weapon. I'll be your damn weapon."

I couldn't help but smile a little at the generosity of his offer. "But what about Bea's mom?"

"Mr. B. is an Elder, and Bea is wicked angry. I feel sorry for anyone facing their combined wrath."

That actually made me laugh a little, and the muscles in my stomach twinged as I did.

We ran back to the bridge. I expected to see the fight raging on, but the spot was deserted. Broken branches and twigs littered the ground. Dark spatters, which might have been blood, speckled the leaves and grass.

"Where did they all go?" Nikolai asked.

I closed my eyes. I couldn't do the kind of homing spell that Bea and her dad had done, but I thought I might be able to use our blood bond to get a sense of what might be going on with Elias. If I relaxed, which was hard to do, given how worried I was, I could almost catch an impression of something. I took in a deep, calming breath. My heart pounded in time to my feet. I was running.

"They're either in pursuit or retreating," I said, opening my eyes. My fists clenched with frustration. "I wish I could tell more. I have no idea where they are, or if they're in trouble."

Nikolai surveyed the scene. "We'll never catch them on foot. For that matter, they may have taken to the trees. Either way, they're far faster than we are."

"Than you," I reminded him. If I could induce my fangs to drop, I could tap into my vampire side.

He regarded me seriously. "Okay, I'll give you that, but what are you going to do when you find them? Can you fight? Are you going to carry Elias to safety if he's injured?"

When had Nik become such a downer with all these practical questions? "I don't know," I admitted. "I just—I want to help!"

"How hurt is he?"

I tried to gauge the pain I felt. If I was honest with myself, it didn't seem life-threatening. It was just hard going, but no worse than the morning after a hard workout. I didn't want to tell Nikolai that, because I knew he'd tell me not to worry.

Nik noticed my reticence. "You'd feel something serious, right?"

"I guess," I said, because I couldn't deny it.

"Let's go help Bea for now. If things get worse with Elias, I promise that, no matter what else is happening, I'll take you to him."

"You'd do that for me?" I was flabbergasted. Nikolai hated Elias, not only because he was a vampire, but because he was a rival. "Why?"

"Because I love you, Ana."

It wasn't as if I didn't have a clue that he felt that strongly about me, what with all the recorded songs and whatnot. Yet it was entirely different to hear him say it out loud, in person. I was a bit shocked and taken aback.

His amber eyes gleamed in the moonlight as he waited anxiously for my response.

"I . . ." I liked him too, but love? Love was supposed to be forever after. Love was weddings and babies and mortgages. I didn't think I was ready for love, so I didn't finish my thought.

His face fell slightly, and he dropped my gaze. "It's okay, Ana," he said softly. "You don't have to say anything. I've known for a while that it's one-sided."

"It's not one-sided," I said to his back. "It never was. It's just always been complicated."

He'd started back down the trail to the car. At least, this time, we weren't running blindly through the woods, though I almost wished we still were. We might have been fleeing a vampire skirmish then, but at least we didn't have this emotional gulf between us.

"I've missed you," I said. "Every time I hear your voice on the radio, I get all . . ." I didn't know how to explain the girlish heart swelling I felt without sounding completely cheesy, so I shrugged. "Love is just too intense."

He stopped so fast, I bumped into his back. Turning around, he gave me a sly smile. "Too intense?"

Something in his expression told me he was going to kiss me. I swallowed nervously, unable to say anything other than, "Uh."

His lips were firm against mine. Strong arms wrapped tightly around me, pulling me close against his hard chest. I tilted into his embrace, going all melty and loose limbed. If

I hadn't been so caught up in the kiss, I would have been embarrassed by the girlishness of my response. I was still waiting on the mythical spark, but this was much closer.

Nikolai always smelled faintly of patchouli. We were closer in height, so we fit well together. I didn't have to strain on tiptoes to reach his lips. They were right there, and so tasty—a familiar tang.

Like his blood.

I pulled back, breaking the kiss. Had I tasted blood in his mouth?

"How's that for intense?" he asked in a husky whisper. He leaned in to nibble on my ear. The ticklish sensation made it difficult for me to concentrate.

"Uh. Very," I stuttered in between shaky breaths. I didn't really want him to stop, but I had a nagging sense we should be doing something else. Besides, didn't I already *have* a boyfriend? "What about Bea's mom?"

He pulled back and flashed me a roguish grin again. "Right," he said, taking my hand. "We can always come back to this later."

We could? What about Thompson? I started to say something, but suddenly we were running again. The ground still tried to trip me, but we laughed and giggled all the way out to the car.

Nik was like a different person after our kiss. He opened the door for me, which made me blush. I nearly stumbled into the seat with my attempts to smile and be graciously ladylike. I felt especially awkward when I spotted Elias's rucksack in the backseat where he'd left it.

"You have no idea how much I've missed you," Nik said, putting a hand on my thigh before starting up the car. He just couldn't seem to stop smiling, as if I'd agreed to date him again or something.

I hadn't, right?

That whole thing in the woods had been kind of spontaneous. I was pretty sure I hadn't said anything in that regard other than that I'd missed him too. And that things were complicated . . . because they were—very. They were complicated by Thompson, for one, but also by all the rest. Nothing had really changed. He was still a hunter, and I was still half the thing he hunted. He was still a rock star, and I was still a dork.

Why did I get the feeling Nik couldn't care less about any of that? Thompson wasn't going to like this new development. I'd promised him that nothing was going on between Nik and me.

I'd just kissed a boy! Oh no! We'd gone on one date, and I'd already cheated on Thompson. Well, it wasn't as if we'd discussed the parameters of our relationship. Maybe Thompson would be okay with a nonexclusive thing.

Who was I kidding? I saw how jealous he was when he saw Nik pulling up to my house. He was going to go spare if he ever found out that I'd kissed Nik.

Except, I hadn't. Not really. I'd accepted a kiss, but it wasn't as if I'd started it. Though, once again, I'd be hard-pressed to say I hadn't been a full participant.

I wished my feelings were more straightforward. If only I could say with certainty that I loved one of them more than the other, but I couldn't. There were things I adored about

Thompson, and things I hated. The same was true with Nik—and with Elias, for that matter. If only I could squish all three together into one package. Now, that would have been awesome.

Too bad that wasn't going to happen any time soon.

Man, I was going to have a lot to straighten out once we finally rescued Bea's mom.

Nikolai spent the entire drive catching me up on his life. Apparently, the rumors of the record deal were true, but what people didn't know was that the pressure was tearing apart the band. Nikolai confessed that he kind of liked being part of the local scene. He thought it was better to be a big fish in a little pond. Yet his dad was big-time against his leaving the area, which was the best argument for going national as far as Nik was concerned. He and his dad were having a huge fight about his career. His dad wanted him to finish college. The label people wanted the band now, while the group was hot.

I was totally into what he was saying, but despite my best efforts, my mind was still spinning with the bigger-picture problems. Since I had no idea what I was going to do with all the boy attention I was currently juggling, my thoughts circled back to the hunt.

Even though Dad thought Elias's stunt a clever way to elude the abdication ceremony, it was really little more than a delaying tactic. For all I knew, the exertion of the fight would make the vampires that much hungrier and crazier tomorrow.

Rescuing Bea's mom didn't help either. Someone was going to have to die, unless I could figure out the mystery of witches' blood. What I really needed was a doctor.

"Your mom is the coven's main healer, right?" I asked apropos of nothing Nik was saying.

In fact, from the confused look Nik gave me, I think I cut him off midsentence. "Yeah, of course, you know that. Why?"

"She might know something to confirm our theory," I said. Nikolai's mom mostly did folk-healing sorts of remedies, but she had a lot of practical knowledge too. "If we're right about witch blood being different on some scientific level, she'd know."

Nikolai laughed lightly. "My mom plants herbs by moon phases and carries a piece of bread in her pocket for good luck. She's the last person who'd know."

I thought he might be selling his mom a bit short. "Do you think I could talk to her about it anyway?"

"Sure," he said, as if humoring me. Then his face broke into that huge smile again. "You're ready to meet the parents already? I thought this love thing was too intense."

Was he being serious? "Uh. No. Wait. I didn't mean that," I sputtered. "You know, I am already kind of dating someone else."

"I know," he said quietly. "Beefy boy with the truck. I can tell by looking at him, it isn't going to last. I'll be here when you're done fooling around with him."

I felt a little insulted on Thompson's behalf. "How do you know? We might be perfect for each other."

"Have you told him you're a dhampyr yet? Introduced Mom as the Queen of Witches?"

I shook my head.

"And you won't either. He's a norm. You're magical. Mixed marriages never work out."

I was kind of offended by that and had planned to tell him so when we pulled up to his family's house. I'd only been to Nikolai's house a long time ago, when I was quite little, but I remembered it very well. Like a lot of witches, Nikolai's folks lived in an old house. His was a tall, narrow Victorian, complete with turrets. It was painted bright pink. There was no grass—only wild bunches of herbs growing profusely everywhere, even on the boulevard. At night the bent heads of sunflowers loomed on slender stalks in the middle of the garden like sinister sleeping sentries.

"What are we doing here?" I asked. "I know I asked to see your mom, but weren't we going to rescue Bea's mom first?"

"Bea's mom is here," he said. "At my folks' place."

"I thought you said your dad would never go for something like this."

Nik nodded. "I don't get it myself, but this is where the magic pointed."

Sure enough, Bea's unmistakable Buick was parked just ahead under the streetlamp.

I got out of the car, careful not to crush the curly parsley that lined the edges of the boulevard garden. Nik led the way, up the sidewalk and past silent, curled petals of sleeping borage, chamomile, and anise hyssop. I imagined in the daylight that the garden was stunning. However, I found myself quickening my step past indistinguishable mounds and odd, spiky silhouettes that far too easily transformed themselves into dangers in my imagination.

I was a bit surprised when Nik paused to knock at the door. Then I remembered he hadn't lived at this house since going off to college last year. "Do you feel it?" he asked me, looking up at the unlit porch light.

My eyes flicked over the cobwebs between the spindle-work columns, and I wondered if he perceived some great witch war raging overhead. But, despite my usual sensitivity, I felt nothing, so I shook my head.

"Something's wrong," he said. "No wards."

Of course! His family's house was as magically protected as ours, if not more, since his dad was the resident vampire slayer.

He turned the knob, and the door opened with an ominous creek. The downstairs was dark and forbidding, but the sound of shouting could be heard upstairs. Without bothering with the lights, Nik dashed inside.

Being less familiar with the layout, I moved cautiously. The living room was much larger than ours and, even in the dark, the parquet edging on the polished wood floor gleamed dully. A large fireplace dominated one corner of the room, and all the wood trim was painted white. The walls were of a color hard to determine in the dark, but I thought I remembered deep, rich red. There were photographs of Russian Orthodox churches on the walls, and the furniture I could see looked stately and expensive.

I made my way to the open staircase. A light was on in one of the rooms on the second floor. I paused at the landing, listening for voices. Deep blue and bloodred flecks of light dotted the floor from the moonlight passing through a huge stained glass window. Curious, I glanced over my shoulder. The image was of St. Michael slaying the dragon.

Light from a passing car made the silvery sword flash, and the dragon's underbelly seemed to spurt blood. I dashed up the rest of the flight of stairs. At the top, the arguing voices became clearer.

"No, Nikolai, we will not surrender," came the heavily accented voice of Nik's mom. "All of the non-Initiates are vulnerable. You must understand this."

Peeking around the doorframe, I looked in at the scene. Nik's mom stood with her arms outstretched, her back pressed against a door. She had Nikolai's jet black hair that fell in loose curls to her waist. Other than her darker coloring, nothing about her seemed stereotypically Gypsy. She wore jeans and a plain navy T-shirt. Like Nik, she had spirals of brightly colored tattoos on her bicep that were just visible under the sleeve.

The room seemed to be some kind of spare bedroom. In the corner was a stiffly made single bed that looked like no one had ever slept in it. It had the sort of pillow arrangement that you only ever saw in the pages of catalogs. Bea stood beside an antique mirrored dresser, her fists clenched. Fresh tears streamed down her face. Her dad was positioned partially in front of her, as though having just stepped between her and Mrs. Kirov.

Nik was right inside the door a step or two in front of me,

blocking my view from the rest of the room. No one else seemed to be there. I was impressed that Mrs. Kirov had managed to hold off Bea and her dad as long as she had. Yet, on closer inspection, she seemed to be leaning hard against the door, swaying a bit on her feet.

She wiped her forehead, her eyes darting from face to face. When her eyes landed on me, she shrieked. "You must help us, Ana! Contact your father. Tell him the sacrifice is ready."

"No way," I said. "Let Bea's mom go!"

Bea took a step forward, and magic sparked in the air like lightning. I felt her dad's shield then, like a blanket tossed over a raging fire. "Bea," he hissed, "she's a norm. You can't attack her again. It's against the rules."

"Screw the rules," Bea said in a hoarse, scratchy voice.

Her dad actually turned around and blocked Bea's rising hands with his own. "Sweetheart," he said softly, "you've already tried this. Magic doesn't work on the door for some reason. You can't blast it open."

Nik looked around wildly at that and went over to a chest. He started pulling open drawers and searching frantically. "Where's the key?" he demanded of his mom.

She shook her head mutely. Her eyes stayed locked on mine. "Please," she said. "You're one of us. If we don't do this, the witches will do it for us. All of us agreed."

"Us, who?" I wanted to know.

"The uninitiated," Mrs. Kirov said. Her gaze flicked nervously as Bea struggled with her father and Nik continued to toss up the room in search of the key. "We had to strike first.

The attacks have been growing. They'd soon turn to us. We were always the first to be sacrificed."

"What if there was another way?" I asked. I hadn't moved from where I stood partially out in the hallway. "I think I might have an idea that won't involve any death—uh, at least, maybe."

Everyone stopped to look at me then.

"Another way?" Mr. Braithwaite repeated. "I thought the hunt is an unbreakable covenant between witch and vampire."

"That's not helping, Dad," Bea said with a sarcastic sigh.

"Tell them," Nik encouraged.

I cleared my throat, uncomfortable with the attention but happy with the momentary cease-fire. "It's really just a theory, but I think maybe there's something in our blood—witch blood, that maybe we can, you know, reproduce with science or something."

Bea made a disappointed noise. Her dad actually scoffed.

Okay, this wasn't going exactly how I'd hoped.

But, when I looked over at her, Mrs. Kirov was nodding thoughtfully. "Like the Ukrainian corpse walkers."

Now the attention shifted as we all stared at her. She was rubbing her arms, as if the thought of whatever these creatures were made her blood run cold.

"That doesn't sound like something you'd create in a lab," Nikolai said. "Unless you mean Dr. Frankenstein's."

"Just so," she said, and then looking at me with accusation in her eyes, added, "This is very black magic you suggest, Ana."

"Uh, I don't even know what a corpse walker is, though it sounds bad, like a zombie or something," I said.

"Worse," she said with a visible shiver. "Back in the Old Country, to avoid the lottery, in the dark days, sometimes a corpse would be offered to the vampires. Of course, they wouldn't touch dead flesh, so the body had to be reanimated."

"And that worked?" Bea asked.

"Yes," Mrs. Kirov said, "though it must be performed only on the recent dead, or the spell rebounds and the corpse walker steals the soul of the caster."

We all contemplated that horror in silence for a moment.

"I wasn't really thinking about anything that drastic," I admitted. "I was thinking that, you know, maybe we could toss them a bag of blood from the Red Cross drive."

After a beat, the room erupted in laughter.

My face reddened. "I'm half-serious," I said. "I mean, there's got to be a ton of our blood out there. That donation bus is at every big coven gathering."

That stopped them. Mr. Braithwaite had taken his glasses off to wipe tears from his eyes, and he squinted at me.

I couldn't tell what question lurked behind his eyes, but I continued. "It's clear our blood is special. Why else would there be so many witches who are medical professionals?"

Once again, Mrs. Kirov cut off the protests. "Of course, it's our Neanderthal ancestress. Her genetic markers are in our blood. But bottled blood has been tried before. Death magic is essential to their hunt."

I felt everything start to come apart, and I slumped heavily against the doorframe.

"Why does it work to offer corpses, then?" Bea asked. She

seemed to wake up during the discussion. Her face had dried, and some of the redness had faded.

"Reanimation returns the human animus to the body for long enough for the vampires to sense its departure," Mrs. Kirov said.

"What was that word you just used?" I said, standing up.

She blinked at me curiously. "Animus. Why?"

"Humans have them too?" I asked.

"Of course. It's the soul," Nikolai's mom said.

I grinned like an idiot because I finally knew the solution. "Let Bea's mom go," I said. "I know what to do."

Chapter Fourteen

Animus.

It wasn't just what vampires called their souls. If I understood Mrs. Kirov correctly, it was also what we called our own.

When Luis got all grossed out by my not having chosen sides, he'd said something about how I had two animuses. Now I think I understood what he meant: I had one witch and one vampire soul. Maybe that was how my magic worked—the friction of the two souls working against each other. Maybe that was why it always felt like the polar opposites of a magnet pushing against each other.

But if I had two souls, did that mean I had one to spare?

I thought it must. The logic seemed good; after all, wasn't that what Luis was all freaked out about? That I hadn't gotten rid of one?

If Dad could abdicate his soul in death, maybe I could use the same magic to get rid of my extra one . . . only without the dying part.

I was nodding my head as I thought through this, feeling more and more positive it would work.

Despite my confidence in my plan, Mrs. Kirov didn't instantly move to release Bea's mom. Her eyes narrowed. "What's your plan, then?"

"I've got an extra animus," I explained. "I'll abdicate it or whatever. That can be the death magic."

Nikolai sat back against the dresser he'd been raiding and rubbed his head as if I'd given him an instant headache. "Didn't you hear my mom? Your animus is your soul, Ana."

"I know," I said, "but vampire souls are different. I have two souls. I know I can live without one of them, because I'm pretty sure that's what the vampire Initiation deal does—kills the witch soul."

Mr. Braithwaite nodded. "I believe you're right about that, but that's because, in its own way, the vampire Initiation is a little like what happens when you bring a vampire over from beyond the Veil. You remove the human soul and replace it with the vampire."

Wow. Dad never told me that part of the deal when he showed up at my door and said I should run off with him and become a princess.

Bea frowned deeply, considering. "So Ana has been carrying around a potential vampire since she was born? How does that work? I thought they all came from the Other Side."

"Maybe we do too, in our own way," Mr. Braithwaite said. "Who knows where the human soul comes from?"

This conversation was getting really deep, but I thought I

understood what Mr. Braithwaite might be implying. Maybe dhampyrs were like those eggs you sometimes come across, with two yolks—a twin, only on a soul level.

"Let Kat go, Mom," Nikolai said. "Dad has no idea you have her locked in the attic, does he?"

His mom shook her head, sending curls cascading around narrow shoulders. That seemed to me like the sort of thing that might cause a divorce, especially considering how hardheaded Mr. Kirov could be. She sighed. Her shoulders dropped as if she had let go of a huge weight. "My sewing circle is going to be royally pissed off at me if your plan backfires," Mrs. Kirov said to me.

I tried to look hurt that she'd lack such confidence in me, but I couldn't blame her. I might have come up with a possible solution for the "death magic" part of the hunt problem, but I still didn't know what we were going to do about the blood requirement.

Maybe if I could fake death with the sacrifice of my animus, I could offer my own. It seemed the responsible thing to do as the princess, but the idea scared me to death, no pun intended. There were a lot of vampires. Even if all of them took only a small bite, wouldn't I be drained in no time? I guess it depended on which part of the hunt was more important. Was it the blood or the "eating of the soul," as it were?

Maybe Dad knew. I had to talk to him soon, anyway. I couldn't have Dad killing himself before I had a chance to explain my theory to him.

Meanwhile, Mrs. Kirov had gotten a bucket of hot soapy water from their upstairs bathroom. She was proceeding to wash the attic door. Bea and I exchanged a curious look. "Witch magic was defeated by dirt?" I asked.

"No," Nikolai said quietly. "By a hex."

I didn't think Mrs. Kirov had Real Magic. How had she been able to infuse a hex with the kind of power that the combined forces of Bea and her dad couldn't penetrate?

Nik must have read my confusion on my face, because he said, "Mom's people have always had protections against Real Magic. No one knows why it works."

I nodded, leaning heavily against the doorframe. Mrs. Kirov removed a key from her pocket and unlocked the attic door. Bea and her dad pushed past her and rushed up the set of steep stairs. I heard happy noises above. Since I knew that Bea's mom was going to be okay, my lack of sleep suddenly caught up with me and I felt ready to collapse.

I rubbed my eyes. I still had things to do. As Nik spoke softly to his mom, I pulled my cell out of my pocket. There were a number of messages on it. Most of them were from Thompson. I must have been so caught up in all the excitement that I never even felt them buzz.

Scrolling through them, I looked for anything from Mom. I didn't find anything, so I typed, "Found B's mom. Everything OK," and I hit Send.

I was just stuffing the cell back into my pocket when it buzzed. It was Mom calling, so I answered.

"Where was she?" Mom asked without preamble.

Nik's head was close to his mom's. You could really see the family resemblance. They had the same nose and hair. Even though kidnapping Bea's mom was pretty evil, I didn't really want to get Mrs. Kirov in trouble with the coven, especially since Mr. Kirov didn't know anything about the "sewing circle's" ambush.

"She's okay," I said, as if Mom had asked a different question. "I'm glad you called, actually, because I think I have a solution to the hunt. You guys can call off all your lotteries and double-crossing, okay? I'm going to take care of it."

"You are?"

"Yeah, I'm going to give up my second soul," I said.

There was silence on the other end. "How is that going to work?"

I probably should have been angry that Mom didn't even ask what I meant when I implied I had an extra soul. She knew about this whole double-animus thing the whole time. As I thought about it, it made sense. She'd never told me why, but she was super against my going through the vampire Initiation. I suppose she must have known I'd lose my human soul. "Do you know about vampire abdication?"

"I've heard about it," she admitted. "Victor has talked about the nosferatu in the Old Country, how they're crazy strong after stealing souls. But what does that have to do with the hunt?"

"Apparently, a vampire can give up his soul willingly too. Sort of like what happens at the vampire Initiation ceremony."

"They don't have an Initiation cere—" She stopped herself. She sounded horrified as she realized what I was saying. "You mean the rite of passage—for dhampyrs."

"Yes," I said. "I'm thinking I can use that same process to

mimic my death. You know, so that the murder magic can be fulfilled."

"If you do that, you'll become a full vampire," my mom said.

"But it won't kill me, right? And, if Luis is any indication, I can still walk around in the daylight."

"I don't know about this."

But I did. I'd finally found a solution that would solve this problem without anyone dying. So what if I had to become a full vampire to do it! It wouldn't solve the problem long term, but it would buy me time—a full generation, twenty years—to figure out something more permanent.

"Tell everybody we'll do it tomorrow night. I need some sleep." I held back a yawn with some effort. "Don't let anybody do anything stupid in the meantime."

"We need to talk more about this," she said.

"Thanks, Mom. Love you," I said, ignoring her. Before she could continue her protest, I hung up.

Nikolai and his mom were watching me carefully. Mrs. Kirov's face was pale.

"I didn't tell her anything about you," I said.

Just then Bea and her dad came downstairs, supporting her mom between them. She looked groggy, as if she'd been sleeping. She smiled goofily when she saw Mrs. Kirov. "Great tea," she slurred happily. "You've got to give me the recipe!"

"I can't believe you drugged her," Bea snarled in a whisper as she passed Nik's mom.

I got out of the way as they maneuvered Bea's mom out the door. She smiled at me too. "Ana, I didn't know you were part of the sewing circle. Is the party still going on? I want more tea."

"I think you've had plenty of tea," Mr. Braithwaite said, flicking on light switches as he went.

"Bill, just look at this place. It's like a presidential palace." I heard her speaking as they staggered downstairs. "It's a little somber, but it's very impressive."

"I like *our* house," Bea said. "I can't wait to get home."

The door swung open and shut. They were gone.

Nik wrapped his mom in a tight hug. I hoped there would be no fallout from the kidnapping, but I couldn't imagine Bea was going to let bygones be bygones very easily. To be fair, I'd probably be feeling pretty vengeful if someone drugged my mom with plans to sacrifice her to hungry vampires. Still, the last thing we needed on top of everything else was a war between the Initiates and non-Initiates of the coven.

When Nikolai gently kissed the top of his mom's head, I felt like an intruder. I turned to go.

I had made it only as far as the landing when Nik called out, "Where to next?"

"I should find Elias," I said. I waited as he bounded down the stairs to catch up to me. "Or my dad. I need to talk to a vampire. I have to make sure this will really work."

He nodded and fished his car keys from his pocket. "To the underground kingdom, then."

I shivered at the idea of going back there again, but I supposed that was the place to go. I put a hand on Nik's arm. It was great that he was willing to play chauffeur, but I felt guilty taking him away from his family. "Is your mom going to be okay?"

"She's really scared, Ana. I blame my dad. From what I can tell, he comes home every night with horror stories of what things will be like if the hunt doesn't happen soon. To hear him talk, it's the freaking vampire apocalypse."

I didn't much care for Mr. Kirov, but I decided to keep my opinion of Nik's dad to myself.

"I just can't believe it," Nikolai said, with a glance over his shoulder. "Mom and Kat have been friends forever."

"I can't imagine they still will be when Bea's mom sobers up," I said.

A short-haired black cat padded out from the darkened living room to twine around my legs when I stopped in front of the door. Nikolai shooed it away with a gentle nudge of his toe. "You're an indoor cat, Inky."

The cat sat back on its haunches and regarded Nikolai. "No," it seemed to meow.

"Yes, you are," Nikolai admonished with an exaggerated wag of his finger.

The cat blinked and quite deliberately turned its back on us.

Nik opened the door for me, and we slipped through. Inky turned to watch us indignantly but didn't make a break for it. Nikolai stuck his head back in for a moment before latching it, and he told the cat, "Take care of Mama, Ink. She needs some love."

I swear I heard the pad of feet as the cat went off to do Nik's bidding.

"Smart cat," I said.

"Hmm?" Nik said, as if it never occurred to him that normal cats might not follow directions so well. "I suppose."

When we stepped out onto his porch, he took my hand.

"You were really amazing in there," Nikolai said. He leaned forward and put his lips on my forehead.

I ducked back. "Nik," I said, "we can't date. I'm seeing someone else."

He looked down at our hands, which I hadn't quite had the good sense to release. "Hmm."

Lifting our hands, he kissed my knuckles. It was a very romantic gesture, so I had to pull away. He grabbed my fingers and wouldn't let them go. I tried to wriggle out of his grasp, but he just held on, smiling.

"I told you I'll wait until you're bored with your mundane," he said. He let go so quickly, I nearly stumbled backward. He turned on his heels before I could react. "We should go."

I followed him down the sidewalk, frowning at his back. Of course, he had a point. Thompson could never understand my world. I mean, I barely understood all the animuses and abdications and all that, but Nik was so dismissive of my relationship with Thompson. It wasn't fair, on so many levels, not the least of which was that it had only just started. I hardly even knew what it was going to be like to go out on a real date with Thompson, and Nikolai was already planning for when it was over.

The breeze brought with it the light scent of moonflowers. Stopping in the middle of the sidewalk, I breathed it in. I closed my eyes. I decided to let go of my frustration over Nikolai's weird, smug assumptions about my future with Thompson.

Instead, I tried to focus on my bond with Elias. Maybe I could get a sense of where he was.

A strong sense of camaraderie brought a smile to my lips. My body was warm, strong, and content. I tasted something malty.

When I opened my eyes, Nik was watching curiously over the roof of his car. Arms folded, he rested his head on his hands. The electric light of the streetlamp brought out the contrast of his pale skin and jet-black hair. The tattoos on his arm stood out darkly.

"I think Elias is at a bar," I said.

"I guess they won the fight if they're celebrating." Nikolai laughed. "Do you suppose they stopped to get dressed, or should we google nudist bars?"

My only experience with bars was the one time Bea talked me into going to an all-ages show at First Avenue. "Are there really any like that?"

"I doubt it," Nik scoffed. "Can you tell where he is?"

I had no idea if I could actually see through Elias's eyes, but I tried. Closing my own again, I concentrated on trying to get impressions of where he was. It was definitely a bar. I could smell the faint scent of stale beer and the sweat of many bodies. The music wasn't loud, and I thought I could hear a lilting tune played by fiddle and penny whistle. "Irish," I said. "Somewhere with live music."

"That doesn't narrow it down much in St. Paul," Nikolai muttered.

I tried to get a sense of place, but our bond must not have been strong enough for me to actually pinpoint his location. "Sorry," I said, opening my eyes. "That's all I've got."

Nikolai straightened. "One midnight tour of Irish pubs coming up."

Because I was underage, I waited in the car while Nik poked his head in at the Half Time Rec, a windowless, freestanding square building at the corner of an otherwise mostly residential street. The exterior seemed to be made of long planks of wood. My eyes were heavy with missed sleep. I blinked slowly.

I kept going over my plan to find any hidden flaws so I wouldn't be disappointed again when someone else pointed them out. Okay, so what I knew was that I had a soul to spare—one vampire and one witch. Luis thought it was awful that I had survived this long with both intact.

That seemed pretty straightforward.

Now on to the trickier part.

Mrs. Kirov had said that the death of an animus, even a reanimated one, had worked to satisfy the hunt in Ukraine. So, it followed that if I let one of my animuses die, the magical murder part of the hunt would be fulfilled.

Check.

Next, there should be a way to give up one of my souls.

As far as I had things figured, vampires had at least two ways of disposing of the animus. One, they could abdicate theirs to another vampire. This involved death—not cool.

The other was through this rite-of-passage thing that my dad had wanted me to do when I turned sixteen, and, by which process, apparently, Luis had become a full vampire. I liked that version better, since I wouldn't have to die. Much nicer. I would have to give up the extra-special superpower I had by staying both, but, even in my sleep-deprived state, that seemed a pretty fair deal.

Not dying, but giving up super-duper power. I could live with that—literally.

Especially since Luis seemed to have it pretty good. He didn't "suffer the allergy," which meant I could go back to school in the fall and live a normal life—or at least what passed for normal for me, anyway. From what I could tell, Luis could activate the superstrength and speed of vampires when his fangs dropped. So, maybe I'd still have those advantages too. I presumed I'd crave blood a bit more regularly, which would be kind of gross, but if it stopped the hunt for now, I could deal.

Of course, I'd have to consider majoring in biochemistry in college. For this to really pay off, I was going to have to devote the next twenty years to figuring out a long-term solution to the hunt.

Presuming a solution was out there, I thought I'd covered everything so far.

Check. Double-check.

What was I missing?

Oh, yeah, the blood. The vampires go into a feeding frenzy for the hunt. But how much blood did they actually need? The Ukrainian corpse walkers, as creepy as they were, gave me hope. If I understood Mrs. Kirov correctly, the hunt had been satisfied by a corpse, so that meant, even with a soul attached, we were talking about a body. Dead hearts didn't beat. I suppose all the blood might pool somewhere, but it might not be easy to extract, and it certainly wouldn't be "fresh."

Maybe I could bring a bag from the blood bank after all? I knew everyone laughed at me, but I'd feel better knowing they wouldn't have to get all of it from me. Because, otherwise, that was the main flaw in my plan—the possibility of me getting accidentally drained.

So I just had to contact those coveners in charge of the blood bank and contrive a reason why I needed a pint or two of witch blood. I could do that.

Satisfied, I closed my eyes for just a moment.

When I next woke up, we were parked in front of the Liffey on Seventh in downtown. My neck was stiff and my mouth dry. I wondered if I'd drooled. I sat up and looked around for Nikolai. Lights glared off the glossy black paint and gold letters of the pub, which was located on the ground floor of a Holiday Inn.

As usual, the streets were empty of pedestrians.

I yawned and stretched. How long had I been here? The engine was off, so I couldn't check the time on the dash. I undid the buckle. I was just about to get out and stretch my legs when Nikolai stumbled backward out the tavern's front door.

My dad came out a second later. I almost didn't recognize him; he was wearing clothes. He had on a pair of dark slacks and a polo shirt. What, did he think this was the eighties?

Nikolai righted himself. I suddenly recognized my dad's posture as aggressive. Wait a minute. They were fighting!

I got myself out of the car just in time to see Nikolai take a swing at my dad.

Chapter Fifteen

Was it impossible for Nikolai to have an exchange with a vampire that didn't end up getting violent? I pushed out of the car, trying to get between Nikolai and Dad. Before I could even take a step, Elias emerged from the pub.

"Stop!" he commanded.

Weirdly, everyone did—even me. For a moment, the only noise was the soft hiss of tires as cars passed on the street.

Under the white electric light, the vampires' skin glowed eerily. Elias stood next to Dad. I had never noticed how much taller Elias was. His head was several inches above Dad's. Despite the height difference, my dad still had a certain regal presence. He had a hawkish nose and intense, sharp features.

Noticing me, he asked, "Is it true? You plan to abdicate?"

I shot Nik a thanks-for-spilling-the-beans look. "I don't know," I said, feeling very put on the spot. "Maybe. Except without the dying."

"Admirable goal." My father smirked. "How do you plan to pull off this miracle?"

I frowned. I was really hoping my plan would be more obvious to a vampire. "Well, I was thinking some magic like the rite of passage or whatever you call the vampire Initiation, only timed to take place during the hunt."

"Not true abdication, then," Elias muttered.

Meanwhile, my dad brightened as if I'd just handed him a present. "Finally!" He clapped his hands together. "You will be one of us, completely."

Nik gave me a sharp look, as if it hadn't occurred to him that that would be one of the consequences of the plan. Maybe he didn't mind dating a dhampyr, but he didn't look too pleased about my becoming a full vamp.

Behind my dad's beaming face, Elias frowned, deep in thought.

"Good, good," my dad was saying, almost as if to himself. "We will make the arrangements. How soon?"

"Tomorrow night?"

He nodded. "We can be ready."

"So you do think it will work?" I asked Elias and Dad.

Dad stood on the sidewalk and rubbed his chin thoughtfully. One hand was casually stuffed into the pocket of his trousers. I hated myself for the thought, but it was a lot harder to take him seriously now that he was dressed like some kind of corporate monkey. Nakedness gave him a weird sort of gravitas.

"It's impossible to say for sure. This sort of thing has never been done in conjunction with the hunt. You're going into uncharted territory, Ana," Dad said. "I'm afraid we won't know until we try."

"But we're all agreeing to try?" I looked from Nikolai to Dad to Elias in turn.

"I think, in principle, your idea is sound, Ana, but I'm not thrilled about the risks involved."

"Me either," muttered Nikolai. He'd found an old-fashioned lamppost to lean against. His arms were crossed in front of his chest.

"Do we have a lot of viable alternatives?" I asked.

"No, Ana, but you've never seen a true hunt," Dad said. "We can be . . . fierce."

"More like animals," Nikolai sneered.

"But you can call it off if things get really hairy, right?" I asked Dad, ignoring Nikolai.

"Of course," he said, straightening up a bit, as if trying to assert his power with his body language.

"Then no harm, no foul," I said.

I could tell no one really wanted to agree. I mean, I understood there could still be problems. No one mentioned, for instance, that my dad could get caught up in the feeding frenzy himself and be unable to stop the hunt. But, I told myself, if the emotional shock of only ordering an attack on me was too much for my dad, he'd never let things get that far.

I also still needed to arrange for some extra blood, but since no one asked about that, I didn't say anything. That was the only other potential hiccup I could really foresee. But I was smart enough to know that things could still go wrong. Things always did.

I couldn't let that stop me, however. Doing nothing wasn't an option. Either some other covener would have to die, or all hell was going to break loose in the vampire kingdom. I'd lose my dad to madness or he'd kill himself with an abdication. If we didn't do that, the vampires would either starve to death or become nosferatu and terrorize the witches.

This plan of mine *could* work, and it was a risk I was willing to take.

I think my dad saw my determination in my eyes, because he asked, "Is your mother aware of this?"

"Yeah," I said. "She's not terribly happy about it, though."

"I imagine not," Elias said with a little chuckle. He caught my eye, and we shared a smile about my mom.

"All right," my dad said finally, "but I want to be certain of this. We will go over every scenario."

I had to stifle a yawn. My eyes were scratchy, and I blinked slowly, trying to stay awake.

When I focused, Dad stared at me with a sympathetic look. "Tomorrow," he said kindly. "The kingdom can wait until the princess has rested."

"I'm not tired," but even as I said it, I knew how childish I sounded.

Dad smiled. It was weird, but dressed as he was, he actually sort of looked like a dad. "It's all right," he said. "We can survive one more night. You can save the world tomorrow."

I let out the yawn I'd been holding back. "Okay, good."

I barely remembered the drive home. Evidently, given that I woke up in them, somehow I got into pajamas and snuggled under the cotton sheets.

A blue jay's squawk sounded from the pine tree just outside my window. I rolled over and stuffed the pillow over my head and ears. I squeezed my eyes shut but couldn't get back to sleep.

I'd been dreaming about being chased by rabid wolves through an American Girl birthday party at the Mall of America. That last part was just the weirdness of dreams, but I knew the other images had everything to do with my plan to solve the hunt.

Pulling the pillow off my head, I blinked into the bright sun. Would it seem even brighter when I became a full vampire? I also wondered if there would come a time, if I lived long enough, when I couldn't stand the sight of it anymore.

At least I was becoming a vampire in a time of twenty-four-hour service. If I really wanted to, I could still go to a McDonald's at two a.m. The world was still different at night, but thanks to online services, I could still order books or check my bank account or shop for shoes in the middle of the night. It had not been like that when Elias was brought over; the world mostly shut down after dark back then.

It wouldn't be so bad for me.

Besides, it would be something like the year 2300 by the time I couldn't stand any sun. Who knew what things would be like then? Maybe we'd be living on Mars. And, anyway, maybe with global warming, I could just move to Finland or the Arctic Circle where it's dark for half the year and still have a "normal" life.

What I needed to do today, however, was make sure I didn't die tonight. I had a few things to do, so I wiped the sleep from my eyes and pulled myself out of bed.

First, I took a long bath and made a big breakfast. Mom shuffled into the kitchen in her fuzzy slippers and terry cloth robe. Her hair stood up in all directions. She sat down in the bright yellow chair next to the table and blinked blearily at me. "You're cooking," she remarked.

Indeed, I was. I'd gotten down the heavy cast iron skillet and was frying bacon. I had eggs beaten in a bowl ready to be scrambled. "Breakfast is the most important part of your day," I said.

She gave an unimpressed snort and pulled herself up with a groan to grab a mug from the cabinet. This one had the classic Wiccan bumper sticker phrase ANKH IF YOU LOVE ISIS printed in bright red, friendly letters on it. She poured herself a cup of the coffee I'd brewed.

I cooked the scrambled eggs and divided them and the bacon between two plates. Mom's mouth hung open even farther when I handed her a fork. "Dig in," I suggested.

"Did you talk to your dad last night?" she asked.

The bacon was crisp and salty. I nodded as I chewed.

"What did he say about this crazy plan of yours?"

First on my to-do list: convince Mom to go along with the plan—or at least not to get in the way of it.

"Look, I know you're against this," I started.

"Damn right I am," she snapped, interrupting me brusquely. She slammed her cup down so hard on the table that it clanked. Coffee splashed onto the wood, like spatters of blood. "I have never wanted you to become a vampire. It's an ugly, awful existence. You've seen them! I thought you understood. When you decided not to join them last year, I figured you'd made your choice."

"I did," I said quietly. "I like being the way I am."

"Then why do this?"

"Because somebody has to sacrifice something, Mom, and I can do it without dying—without anybody having to die."

Her frown deepened at my words, and she chewed at her bottom lip. Absently, she used the cuff of her sleeve to daub at the beads of coffee on the table. She didn't look at me for a long time; then, finally, she spoke. "When did you become such a goddamn altruist?" She snorted. "Sometimes I don't think you're related to either Ramses or me."

I took that as a compliment, despite her tone.

My mom shook her head, obviously still struggling to concede my point. "You're still not going to solve the problem, not forever. What are you going to do when the hunger comes back in just over a decade, huh? You're not going to have an extra soul to sacrifice, then, and it's going to be the same crisis all over again."

I poked at my eggs with my fork. "I'm thinking about studying biochemistry."

Mom laughed, and not at all kindly. "You think science is the answer?"

"Magic hasn't been much help," I shot back. "And, you know, things have changed since the Stone Age. We understand a lot more about blood and how it works."

"But no one has ever understood the soul," she said quietly.

"Maybe I will," I said.

She took a long sip of her coffee and watched me over the rim. "I can see you're serious about this, but I don't think the cost is worth it."

"How can you still say that? After everything that happened last night with Bea's mom?" I decided the smart way to talk to Mom about this was to focus on what the hunt did to the witch community. She might have a hard heart when it came to vampires, but she was the Queen of Witches. I knew she felt responsibility there. "If we don't solve the hunt soon, the coven is going to splinter. It already has. Someone acted on their own because they didn't trust the Elders not to sell them out."

"Who was that exactly?" Mom, curious, said sharply.

"I don't know exactly," I lied smoothly. "I just know you say you didn't orchestrate it, and Nik says his dad didn't, so unless the Elders are making decisions without you . . ."

I let that last bit hang there. It was probably mean of me, because I knew there was always tension between Mom and the council. Her eyes narrowed, and I could almost see the list of names she considered as possible traitors flash through her unfocused gaze.

"You're sure this plan of yours is perfectly safe?"

"I'm sure my life is in no danger," I said, because, well, there were risks, of course. Nothing involving vampires was "perfectly safe."

Mom seemed to sense my attempt to deflect the intent of her question, but she let it go. "I want to be there, as extra protection. If something does go wrong, I want a witch there who can hold back those monsters, if necessary."

I didn't like the way she put it, but I could appreciate the sentiment. "All right," I agreed.

"What's the plan for tonight?" she asked.

"We're going to gather tonight," I said. I realized I didn't know where or when; I knew only that my dad and Elias were working out some of the details.

She sensed my hesitation over the details. "You should do it at the covenstead," Mom suggested. "It's private, and it's far enough out of town that it will take the vampires some time to reach it. Plus, there are lots of wards already in place—things we could trigger quickly if need be."

I chewed a bit of egg slowly and swallowed it, watching Mom intently with suspicion. When I considered trying to bring her around to my plan, I didn't expect this kind of endorsement or support. What was she playing at? Was she seriously just thinking about my safety or did she have some ulterior motive? "Um, okay," I said finally, unable to figure out what she might be thinking. "That seems like a good idea. I'll get the word to Dad."

"You do that." She pushed herself away from the table, leaving her plate barely touched.

"Where are you going?"

"You reminded me that there are some people I need to talk to about what happened last night. If my authority is being undermined . . ." She pursed her lips. "Well, I should go."

It was nine o'clock in the morning. I wondered whose door she was going to pound on this early. With Mom in the mood she was in, I didn't envy her lucky target, whoever it was. "Okay, have fun," I said jokingly.

She just scowled at me and headed out the door.

I was glad to have the house to myself, frankly, so I could riffle through my mother's things. Specifically, I was looking for a phone number. I could have asked Nik, but I didn't want to worry him unnecessarily. I found Mom's old address book in the desk drawer under a stack of bank statements. Most of her newer contacts would be in her phone or on her BlackBerry, but I was hopeful that what I was looking for would be in this old, forgotten flowered booklet.

At first I thought I'd struck out. Then I found Victor's name under *K*, for Kirov. I only hoped the number listed was for the landline, because I really wanted Nik's mom and she didn't have a separate listing.

I dialed the numbers and waited. Nik's family lived on a stipend from the coven, so neither of his parents had to work, but I knew Mr. Kirov slept during the day. When I heard Nik's mom answer, I nearly breathed a sigh of relief. "It's Ana," I told her. "You owe me a favor."

Then, without waiting for her reaction, I explained what I wanted her to do. I would continue to keep her secret safe from Mom, who, I was sure to remind her, was on a rampage this morning trying to root out traitors in the coven. In exchange, she would get me several pints of witch blood from the contacts I was sure she must have in the coven's medical community. It had to be witch blood. I stressed this repeatedly.

"What is this for?" she asked.

"I'm going to stop the hunt," I said. "Remember what we talked about last night?"

"Yes, the animus. You have a way to separate it from your body?"

"I think so," I said.

"And you need the blood to feed them?"

"Think of it as a supplement," I said.

"You're crazy," she said. "A few pints of blood will never be enough to satisfy them. They'll tear you to pieces, and you will lose both your souls and your life."

I hated the way her accent came out when she said things like that. It felt as if I were receiving a fortune. "Yeah, well, let me worry about that. Just get me the blood."

"You will keep my secret?"

"Totally."

"Meet me at the Hmongtown Marketplace at three o'clock."

That was a totally strange place to pick, but I had to admire her quick thinking. It wasn't as if we were likely to run into any coveners there. The Hmong in St. Paul had their own magic workers who rarely intersected with ours. "Deal."

I killed time listening to my iPod and reading a book. At some point, Mom came back. We didn't talk; she went directly upstairs for a shower. The humidity was pretty low today, and the cool breeze lulled me into a nap. I woke up to the sound of the doorbell.

Mom answered the door before I could rouse myself. I heard her giggle. Then she called out, "Ana, a young gentleman to see you."

Okay, color me curious.

Thompson stood on the other side of the screen door with a bouquet of flowers. They were gorgeous and exactly the kind of artsy arrangement I loved to window-shop at the St. Paul Farmers' Market: a riotous combination of bright zinnias, sunflowers, and lilies.

"Hey, Matt," I said, remembering at the last minute not to call him Thompson.

He smiled.

Mom raised her eyebrows and cleared her throat.

I got the hint. "Uh, Mom, this is Matthew Thompson."

Mom opened the door and held out a hand for him to shake. He gave it a good, solid pump. "Mrs. Parker," he said.

I winced, but, for once in her life she didn't correct "Mrs." to "Dr."

"Nice to meet you," Mom said. "Won't you come in?"

I could see Mom checking Thompson over. He was in his landscaping uniform: grass-stained jeans and a green T-shirt with *Thompson's Lawn Care* embroidered in white thread over his heart. "I have only a few minutes," he said to me as he handed me the bouquet. "I'm on my lunch break."

"These are gorgeous," I told him. It was such a sweet, mundane gesture that I felt tears prickle behind my eyes. I wanted to tell him about tonight, all my fears that it wouldn't work or that something would go wrong; I wanted to cling to his strong neck and make him tell me everything was going to be okay.

But he wouldn't understand.

So I turned away and headed to the kitchen to find a vase. Behind me, I heard Mom ask him to leave his shoes by the door. I hoped he didn't take it personally. Mom made everyone do that. You'd think wood floors would be easy to keep clean, but any stray piece of dirt attracted dust bunnies like nobody's business.

Thompson shuffled into the kitchen behind me. When I'd put the flowers in water, I saw that he had the same sort of expression I had at Bea's house, as if he were afraid to sit in case he left some sort of grease spot.

I smiled at him to try to ease the awkwardness. Mom, however, her curiosity evident, didn't help by hanging in the archway. "So, how do you know Ana?" Mom asked.

"You recognize Thompson, don't you? He was Professor Higgins."

"Oh!" Mom brightened. "I remember now. You had that smart suit coat and a beautiful singing voice."

As heat flushed Thompson's cheeks, I tried to catch Mom's eye to give her the go-away-you're-embarrassing-us glare.

When she stopped beaming at us, Mom seemed to get the hint. Though she had to say, "Well, I'll leave you kids to it" in that dorky parental way. At least she hadn't made me promise to behave.

"I tried to call ahead," Thompson said.

I frowned and dug my phone out of its usual spot. It was dark, the battery completely dead. "I forgot to charge it. It's been a crazy couple of days."

"Oh? What have you been doing?"

"You know, just Festival tryouts and stuff. You were there." Uh! Even I didn't believe that lame lie. But what was I supposed to say? Reconciling with my insane vampire dad while hatching a plan to give up one of my dual souls? That sounded even crazier.

He just looked at me, and I knew he didn't buy it either.

"Do you want a Coke or something?" I offered, hoping to deflect the conversation with hospitality.

"My lunch is in my truck," Thompson said. He crossed his arms in front of his chest and leaned against the kitchen counter. He stared at me for a long time, squinty-eyed, as if trying to see me clearly. "There's something going on with you. Something to do with your life as a witch, right?"

I sighed in relief. He was more perceptive than I gave him credit for. "Yes, exactly."

"I hate that you can't talk to me about it."

"Me too," I agreed sincerely.

Impulsively, I ran over and wrapped my arms around his neck. He seemed surprised at my outburst, but he opened his arms and took me in. I laid my head against his chest. I could hear his heart beating underneath the cotton of his shirt.

He seemed to understand what I needed and rested his cheek against the top of my head. His grip tightened, and I felt held, protected.

Tears leaked from my eyes. In the safety of Thompson's arms, I let myself weep.

Amazingly, he said nothing. He asked no questions, only softly stroking my hair.

After I'd pulled myself together with a very unprincesslike snuffle, he kissed my forehead and used his thumb to brush away the tear tracks on my face. "Can I take you out to dinner tonight?"

A real date? But tonight? I started to say no, that I had bigger plans, but stopped. Why shouldn't I try to have a bit of normalcy too? "Yeah, as long as it's before sunset."

He grimaced, and I could almost see him biting his tongue. He shook his head with a light smile, and said, instead, "It's not as romantic as midnight, but I can get Cinderella home before the sun sets."

"Thank you," I said, and I meant for everything.

He seemed to understand. He let me go regretfully. "I've got to get back to work."

"Okay," I said, really wishing he didn't have to go.

I was not at all disappointed when he leaned down to give me a long, lingering kiss. I responded enthusiastically. Nikolai was wrong about him. Thompson might be a mundane, but this could work.

Of course, if things went pearshaped tonight, this moment would be the sum total of our relationship. So I kissed a bit harder with all the passion I had.

Thompson made a happy sort of growling noise in the back of his throat. Breaking our kiss to give me a rakish smile, he said, "Are you trying to keep me here?"

"A little," I admitted.

"It's working," he said, but then sighed. "But I'm already up shit creek with my dad. He's totally pissed off about Ren Fest."

"You got in?" I wondered if I'd missed a call thanks to my dead battery.

"No," he said. "The jousters took me. So, I'll see you out there?"

I showed him my dead phone again and shrugged. "I hope so."

We said our good-byes with a few more brief kisses, and then I walked him to the door. We started to kiss, but Mom was sitting on the porch swing reading some Goddess textbook. Instead, we embraced quickly, and he waved good-bye as he trotted down the sidewalk to his truck.

I tried to get back into the house before Mom could comment, but she'd already set her book down. "Do I need to change the wards to keep out horny mundane boyfriends now?"

"Mom! Don't be gross!"

"Are you dating him?"

"Yes, I told you that already. Remember, when Nik was over?" I asked, resigning myself to the interrogation.

She blinked, as if surprised she'd forgotten such an important detail. "When did this happen?"

"Yesterday at Festival tryouts."

"So it's really recent then?"

"That's what 'yesterday' means last time I checked," I said. "Can I go? I need to plug in my phone."

"We should talk about tonight."

"He's just taking me to dinner."

"Oh? Well, I guess that's all right." Her eyes followed Thompson's truck as he pulled out from the curb and drove down the street with the rattle of a loose muffler. She turned back to me. "I meant the hunt. I've been thinking about this, and I still think it's too risky."

Duh.

But I'd made up my mind about this. "We've been over this, Mom. There really isn't another way. And I think it's worth it."

She nodded seriously to let me know she understood the gravity of the situation, but then she said, "I don't want you getting hurt."

"Well, that makes two of us. You're going to have to trust me. I've got this one, Mom."

I could tell she didn't like the idea of that at all. She continued to stare in the direction Thompson had gone. "Everything is going to change when you become a vampire."

"I don't think so," I said. "I'm still going to be me. I can still go out in the sun. I . . ."

"You're not going to be you," Mom said, catching me in an intense gaze. "You don't know anything about the vampire whose soul attached itself to you. You do know how vampires are made, don't you? They destroy the person whose body they take over. Elias is not the man whose body he inhabits. None of them are."

I shook my head, unwilling to believe what she was saying. I sputtered, "But—but it's different with me, isn't it? I'm not like them in this way. As you said, this extra soul has been with me since birth. It's part of who I am."

"Part," she repeated, "but is it the part I love?"

Those last words were like a punch to the gut, and I could hardly formulate a coherent response. I couldn't believe my mom could look me in the eye and say something so utterly heartless. Did she really mean to tell me there were parts of me she didn't—wouldn't love? "I guess we're going to have to find out," I said. Turning, I ran back into the house and up the stairs to my room.

I shut the door and hung out the Do Not Disturb sign that Bea and I had "liberated" from the hotel room we'd shared at Paganicon, the local pagan convention we attended last year.

I sat on my bed with my feet tucked up close and my arms around my knees. I was so angry and hurt by what Mom had said, but my mind kept returning to the same thoughts: What if she was right? What if the soul that I released tonight was the essence of who I was? What if, by letting it die, I allowed something else, something alien, to take me over?

Wasn't that what happened when a vampire crossed over?

I wished more than ever that vampires had cell phones. I desperately wanted to talk to Luis. He was the only one who knew if there was any truth to what Mom suggested. I got up and went over to the alcove where I kept my computer. I looked out the window into the big pine tree Elias used to sit in when he courted me. Somewhere out there, very likely, an Igor lurked, watching the house and protecting me during daylight hours. Maybe I could send an Igor to Luis with my question.

First, though, speaking of cells, I had to plug mine in. I'd be completely cut off without it, and the Igor would be there all day.

I found the cord and plugged in my phone. As soon as it had power, it started beeping insistently. The cord stretched so that I could just rest my butt on the edge of the mattress. Perching like that, I scrolled through the messages. Bea had apparently spent much of last night composing a series of 140-character mini-rants. From skimming them, I gathered she was ready to call a coup on Mrs. Kirov—not that I blamed her entirely.

I flipped ahead and saw that, at least, Bea's mom seemed to be recovering from being drugged. She'd had a bad case of the munchies, which necessitated a drive to the convenience store for Doritos and Raisinets. That whole thing sounded kind of hilarious, honestly; though, judging from Bea's sparse, irritated, and expletive-laden texts, Bea clearly failed to see the humor value.

Thompson had told me he was thinking of me a couple of times.

So did Nik.

I opened one of Nik's. It read, "Remembering ur kiss. Can't wait for the next."

What was I going to do about him?

Thompson had been amazing a moment ago, and I really felt as if we'd been in sync on some deep level ever since that first kiss at tryouts yesterday. There was nothing I wanted more right now than someone like that—strong, dependable and . . . normal.

Nik had never taken me out to eat, at least, not without his whole band, the crew, and a few groupies in tow. Except the night we broke up. He'd taken me to a malt shop that night and basically told me he thought vampire Igors were freaks. Okay, we kind of agreed on that score, but talk about star-crossed. He was a vampire hunter, for Goddess' sake!

There really shouldn't have been any contest.

But, you know, brains and romance didn't always agree. Despite my better judgment, my heart did a little flip-flop when I thought back to Nik's kiss. Under the moonlight, it had felt special and just a touch illicit. He knew I was dating someone else, but he'd made his move anyway. That kind of arrogance should probably be a turnoff, but how could I not be flattered?

Plus, Nik could have his pick of any girl, but he'd doggedly pursued me. He wrote songs for me.

The phone beeped again. Thompson wrote, "Hope u r feeling better. See u at 6."

My thumbs flicked over the keypad to tell him how much I was looking forward to it, and I felt a wave of guilt. I shouldn't even be thinking about Nik that way.

After sending my reply, I went through and deleted everything from Nik—even messages I'd saved from last year when we were dating.

That made me feel momentarily more righteous, but my

mind would not stay on Thompson, no matter how much more he might deserve it.

I set the phone on my bookshelf and lay back on the bed. Staring up at the plaster ceiling, I counted the cracks.

One of the reasons Nikolai and I had broken up before was that he was always so quick to pull out his psychic knife. How many times last night had he been ready to use it on Elias?

A squirrel chattered on the pine branch right outside my window. It occupied the very spot Elias favored. I wondered where Elias was sleeping tonight. I suspected it wasn't with the Southern prince's troops, given the smack-down he'd given his erstwhile fiancée last night.

The squirrel scampered off, chasing away a couple of chicka-dees that had been hopping around in the needles.

I rubbed my face. None of this was going to matter much if I came back from tonight's ceremony a different person.

My phone rang. I thought it was probably Bea, but I checked the caller ID. It was an unknown number. I didn't get a lot of wrong numbers, but I let it go into voice mail anyway. I thought for sure the caller would hang up on hearing the wrong name, so I was surprised when, a minute later, the bell buzzed with a recorded message. Curious, I listened.

I let out a whoop—I'd gotten into Renaissance Festival! They'd hired me as a street performer.

That was the first bit of good news I'd had in a while.

Feeling buoyed by the news, I left my phone charging and snuck downstairs. Through the open screen door, I could see my mom still reading on the front porch swing. I grabbed a pair of flip-flops from the basement stairs and headed out the back. It was nice enough today that I wore a pair of cutoff jeans with the hems cuffed, and, ironically, my "Vampire Hunter D" T-shirt. What can I say? I related to a character who was half vampire, even if he did have a demon living in one hand.

I scouted through the alley for the Igor. I found a likely suspect at the bus stop on the other side of the block. Problem was, he was just kind of a greasy kid. Could I be sure he was an Igor? What if he just had unfortunate hygiene?

"Uh, excuse me," I ventured.

The kid looked startled, which could be a sign either way. Igors were used to being mostly ignored by vampires and even kind of mistreated by royalty, but, then again, this was Minnesota, so he might just be shocked by my boldness. It was not as though people made a habit of talking to strangers here.

"Yes, Your Highness?"

Okay, score. "I need to ask a favor."

He looked positively tickled. "Anything! Anything I can do to serve you!"

His enthusiasm kind of squicked me, but I needed him, so I rolled with it. "There's a prince in Hudson, Luis Montezuma. I need to ask him an important question about his rite of passage. Ask him—how should I put this exactly? Ask him what it was like. Ask him if anything changed. Is he somebody new?"

The Igor was actually writing my words down on the back of his hand with a ballpoint pen. "Anything else, Princess?"

I wanted to tell the kid to take a shower and change his

clothes, but I didn't want to be rude. I shook my head. "Just hurry back," I said. "I need to know before six o'clock tonight."

Since I was already at the stop and it was nearly time for me to meet with Mrs. Kirov, I hopped onto the first bus that pulled up. I always carried my pass, but I felt a little naked knowing that my phone was still charging at home on the dresser. I also never told my mom where I was going, but it would serve her right to worry a little. Maybe then she'd realize how much she'd miss the irritating parts of me too.

That probably wasn't fair.

She was afraid the ritual would change me into someone completely new, and now I was too. I leaned my head against the window. It was closed to keep out the heat, and the air-conditioning chilled the interior almost too much. Because this was Sunday, the bus was nearly empty. The only passengers were me and a mom with her kid in a stroller up near the front. She had bags of groceries stuffed into a two-wheeler beside her. The kid had fallen asleep, and she looked ready to join him.

The breaks hissed at every stop as we jerked along. What if I did lose me tonight? Would it be like dying, completely winking out of existence, or would I know I'd lost a part of me? Would I care? What if the new me wasn't interested in trying to fix the hunt permanently?

If that last concept was true, it sort of defeated the whole purpose of tonight's plan. I mean, yes, we needed an immediate solution, but the bigger problem would not be solved if the new me swanned off to live naked in some cave with the rest of her kin.

Still, unlike my mom, I had a harder time imagining that the vampire soul I'd possessed all this time was truly a complete stranger. Didn't I become "her" when my fangs dropped? Presumably "she" had been with me since the moment I drew my first breath. When I licked Thompson, I awoke as her on my sixteenth birthday. I did feel a little strange, maybe even different, those times when I activated my superpowers, but not so much that I wasn't myself. I always remembered who I was, what I was doing, *why* I was doing it. I never felt possessed by someone else with a completely different personality or agenda.

Maybe I had nothing to worry about.

Someone should tell my fingernails the news. I'd chewed them down to stubs by the time I made it to the stop on Rice Street closest to the Hmongtown Marketplace, a collection of warehouses surrounded by a gate. There was a big red sign with gold lettering out front, but it still had an air of privacy, a subliminal warning for strangers to stay out. I went through anyway, making my way over to where I thought Mrs. Kirov would most likely be—near the open stalls of the farmers' market. Underneath semipermanent tin roofs, sellers laid out boxes of vegetables: tomatoes, peppers, watermelons, green onions, as well as some bundles of interesting-looking greens I wasn't entirely sure I recognized. I hung out near the wall of warehouse number two, from which vantage point I could scan most of the doors to the other enclosures and much of the open-air market.

There were a ton of people there; we'd have good cover for

the exchange. Most were of Asian descent, but I was by no means the only white person, and I saw other families of various hues here and there. One of the sellers had set up a large-screen TV and was blasting an action film in a foreign language. I got so caught up watching the kung fu–style action that I never saw Mrs. Kirov approach.

"Ana," she said softly, but I jumped anyway. She held a bag in her hand. It was one of those big square plastic bags with a handle, such as you might carry clothes in. It was plaid, and when I took it, it was so heavy, I nearly dropped it.

"Ice," she explained. "You'll want to keep it cool until you need it."

Did blood spoil? I wasn't sure that anything that would mistake a Ukrainian death walker for a living person would care all that much, but I nodded. "How much were you able to get?"

"Four pints," she said. She had her hands on her hips and was shaking her head at me, as if she still thought this was the stupidest plan ever.

Any more criticism and my confidence would completely erode, so I thanked her, promised to keep her secret, and took off.

I hid the bag of blood in the carriage house. Then I went inside and dodged questions about where I'd been with the classic "out" that implied it was my business. Mom grumbled that I'd missed lunch, but otherwise she left me to my own devices. I managed to go the rest of the remaining hours without fretting

too much over the upcoming ritual. By five thirty, the biggest
thing on my mind was what to wear. Thompson had texted earlier that I should dress up, though not super formally. I'd tried
to get him to give over more details, but he was determined to
surprise me. I got the feeling he really just wanted to see me in
an actual dress. At school, I tended to go for Goth casual—lots
of black, comfortable clothes.

I owned a few sundresses, and I pulled them out of my
armoire to inspect them now. One was pink. I had no idea
where I'd gotten anything that hideous and determined it must
have been a gift from some distant relative. I had no memory of
ever wearing it.

The other two were pretty standard, though when I put the
whitish one on, the girl in the mirror looked young and foolish.
The darker one fit me in all the right places and had a more
sophisticated vibe—at least as much as a sundress could. I
fluffed out my hair and decided that with some work, I could
look all right.

With luck, Thompson wasn't hoping for anything fancier
than this. I didn't really have too many other options.

I was weirdly excited about this date. As I made myself pret-
tier, I hummed happily along with the radio I'd switched on. I'd
tuned it to the country station because the last thing I needed
was some commentary about Ingress or that stupid song about
me to come on the radio and ruin this moment. I was going to
focus on Thompson, dang it.

When the doorbell rang, I actually squealed a little. I tried
to compose myself in a more dignified manner, but I took the

stairs two at a time hurrying to answer it. Mom was already there, giving Thompson the talk about when I was supposed to be home and how she expected him to treat me with respect.

"Mom!" I could feel her magic swirling in the dust of the foyer. "He already knows better than to piss off a witch."

"True enough," Thompson agreed. He'd been zapped by Bea in the past.

I smiled at the effort he'd made for our date. He looked really handsome in a button-down shirt and tie. I noticed he still wore jeans, at least, so I wasn't terribly underdressed. He had flowers in his hands. This time he offered them to Mom. "For you."

If I kept dating him, our house was going to turn into one gigantic floral arrangement. But Mom was flattered. She'd looked pretty shocked that I'd talked openly about magic, but her face softened at Thompson's offering. "Oh, they're lovely."

Taking advantage of her distraction, I scooped my hand under Thompson's elbow. "See you." I waved.

"Don't forget to be back—"

"Before sundown," Thompson and I said in unison. He added, "I'll remember, Mrs. Parker."

When we'd gotten to the truck, I said, "It's *Dr.* Parker, actually. My mom is a college professor, PhD."

"I have to call your mom 'Dr. Parker'?" Thompson said as he held the door open for me.

"You don't have to," I said. "Nik used to call her Amelia."

Thompson seemed to consider this option very seriously. "I don't think I can do that. It seems disrespectful."

I shrugged as I buckled in. "It always seemed creepy to me. As if they were friends."

Thompson chuckled and shut my door. Through the windows, I watched him come around to his side and slide in.

"Where are we going?" I asked excitedly, no longer able to keep the huge grin from my face.

"It depends on how adventurous you feel," he said with a sly smile. "I was thinking Kurdish food."

I had no idea what that even was, but it sounded cool. "I'm up for it."

"Or we could do the Mongolian Grill in Roseville. Depends whether you want quiet or exciting."

I'd have my fill of exciting later. "Quiet sounds perfect tonight."

"Babani's it is," he said, and started up the engine.

I had no idea if that meant we'd settled on Mongolian or Kurdish, but I didn't much care. The sun was still fairly high in the sky. It wouldn't set until nine o'clock. I had three hours to enjoy dinner.

I looked over at Thompson, suddenly wondering what we were going to talk about for three hours. Thanks to my vampire princess lifestyle, most of my conversations tended to center around dealing with major disasters. What did normal people talk about?

"So, how was work?" I asked lamely.

"It was fine," he said.

Hmm, not off to the best start. I'd better try again. "Is that what you want to be? A landscaper?"

Thompson gave me a look that said I should know better. "I want to be an actor. My *dad* wants me to be a landscaper."

I realized I had no idea what my mom wanted me to be. The Queen of Witches? As far as I knew, however, she had no plans to give up that title until she died. Honestly, I didn't even know how the whole magical royalty worked. Had my grandmother been the queen before Mom? Or was it an elected position?

"You look confused," Thompson noted.

I couldn't exactly explain what I'd been thinking, so I asked, "Are you going to go to the U for acting? I guess they have a program."

Mom sometimes brought home course catalogs from the various colleges at which she taught. I flipped through them in the bathroom sometimes, reading all the various offerings.

Thompson shrugged. "I haven't really thought about it."

"Haven't thought about it?" I repeated, shocked. Everyone I knew was already obsessing about where to apply to college, even though we'd only be juniors next year. But then, most of us were already in the international baccalaureate program. College was on the mind.

"My dad is really just an overpaid lawn mower, and I have two younger sisters. My best hope for college is a hockey scholarship," he said. "I'll go to wherever I'm recruited and hope they have a good theater program."

I couldn't imagine not choosing a college for its academic track, and I was kind of stunned. It was such a different approach; his answer killed conversation for a few minutes. Plus, he had two sisters? I'd had no idea.

We drove down John Ireland Boulevard. Straight ahead was the white marble of the capitol building, and the sun glinted on the golden chariot at the top of the dome.

It was Thompson's turn to make a stab at conversation. "Do you have a favorite band?"

"Not really," I admitted. I hated this question. When I dated Nik, everyone I met judged me by my taste in music. And, trust me, with a bunch of professionally minded musicians, I always fell short. "I'll listen to anything—rock, country, show tunes, whatever. I just like songs I can sing along to."

I thought for sure Thompson would be disappointed, but he seemed pleased with my answer. "Yeah, you know, the guys on the crew listen to all sorts of stuff. I've even found a Spanish-language station that's not too bad."

He switched on the radio to show me. We laughed at the sound of familiar commercials done in another language. The music made us smile too, and Thompson and I tried to sing along to a few choruses.

Okay, now I was having fun.

All too soon, we pulled up next to a meter; it was free to park on the street after four thirty p.m. The building was an old-fashioned three-story redbrick structure with awnings over the businesses on the first floor. I thought it wouldn't have looked out of place in Boston, especially since the adjacent building had fancy columns on a second-floor balcony.

The sign in the window told me we'd come to the first Kurdish restaurant in America. I wasn't even sure where a Kurd's land was, though the font they'd used reminded me of *Aladdin*.

The interior was elegant. There was exposed brick along one wall, and the windows were tall. Sunlight poured in through the glass, shining on gray tile flooring. There were booths, but they weren't like anything you'd see in a malt shop. They were more like tall-backed cushioned chairs. The tables were polished wood.

Thompson had been watching my face as I looked around. "Do you like it?"

"I do," I said.

The waitress directed us to one of the fancy booths and gave us each a menu. I studied all the interesting-sounding dishes. Thompson had been there before and had some recommendations. There was an explanation about where Kurds were from on the back of the menu. Apparently there was once a Kurdistan, but it now included parts of Iraq, Syria, and Turkey.

There weren't a lot of other people at dinner yet, so the restaurant had a cozy, intimate feeling. I found myself looking less at the menu and more at Thompson. Could I really date a guy who was so clean-cut? I mean, look at that square jaw! It was like something out of a men's health magazine.

So normal . . .

Not like Nikolai, the slayer, or Elias, the vampire.

Nik still haunted me. That kiss! The whole romantic gesture of "I'll wait for you" and writing love songs about us. Of course, I'd already tried dating Nik. Even though I was still obviously attracted to him, our relationship had been disastrous. There was the whole slayer/vampire thing, and also the rock star/nerd problem.

I ran my fingers on the wood of the table, thinking how nice it was to be on an actual date.

Elias had totally ruled when it came to romance. I loved being courted by him. He was attentive and protective and . . . he could only come out after dark. That made traditional dating more difficult. I'm sure we could still have done it if we'd put our minds to it, but now he was headed off to possibly get into this weird loveless political alliance with the Southern captain.

Thompson came with his own set of problems too. We didn't have that much in common, outside of theater, and I couldn't talk to him about the most important stuff in my life. But, man, he was fine to look at, and he was revealing a new . . . kinder side of him I'd never known.

And he could be so sweet. Flowers! Dates! I could get used to this treatment.

He caught me staring and smiled. "What are you thinking?"

I blushed and changed the subject. "Did I tell you I got into Festival?"

"No, that's awesome!"

My diversion worked. We talked about Renaissance Festival until the waitress came to take our orders. I chose something based on its cool sound—"sheik babani." Thompson picked something I couldn't pronounce, but the waitress nodded as though she thought he'd made a good choice.

"This is so fun," I told him. "I've never done anything like this before."

He gaped at me, as if momentarily stunned. Then he asked,

"Seriously?" When I nodded, he continued. "What did you do with Nikolai?"

"Mostly I went to his concerts," I said, conveniently leaving out all the bits where we practiced magic or chased after ancient vampire artifacts.

"Dude never took you out?" He still seemed flabbergasted. I shook my head. "Well, we'll have to fix that."

I liked the sound of that more than I could say.

We passed the rest of the evening in pleasant companionship. The food was good, even if Thompson's dish looked like he was eating eight-inch-long meat-filled torpedoes. Mine turned out to be eggplant, which was not on my top-ten favorites list, but it tasted awesome. Only once or twice did our conversation lag. I found out that Thompson and I both liked weird, old horror films like *Halloween*, and secretly enjoyed the Harry Potter series.

When the bill came, I didn't know what to do. If this had been an outing with my regular theater pals, I'd have offered to split the bill, but I had no idea what the etiquette was on an actual date. Did Thompson expect me to go Dutch?

Thompson, however, clearly had a plan. His wallet was out. When he saw the worry in my expression, he said, "It's on me." He shook his head. "I can't believe no one has ever treated you right before."

Treated me right? "What, like a princess?"

"Yeah." He smiled. "Like a princess."

———

I was really sad when the time came to say good-bye. We lingered in his truck, holding hands. We'd been silent for a long time, savoring the moment.

The sun began to dip below the trees. Thompson squeezed my hand lightly. "Are you going to be okay tonight?"

"I don't know," I said honestly. "We're doing brand-new magic. It could be risky."

"Risky? How?"

I looked him in the eye. I didn't want to lie to him, not after tonight. "I could come back different."

He seemed to think about this for a moment, and then a deep frown etched his face. "How?"

I looked into his face for a long time, trying to decide what I could say. I never heard back from the Igor, so I didn't know if losing my witch soul would change me. What if the vampire-me dumped Thompson without any explanation? Would that be fair? I supposed the new me wouldn't care, but the old me, the person I was right now, found that it mattered a lot. Thompson was a decent guy. I always assumed he couldn't handle the truth about me, but what if I was wrong about that too?

Tonight seemed the time to try. After all, I might not be myself for much longer. If he freaked out and left—well, maybe it was meant to be. Perhaps I'd even be sparing him something worse from wicked vampire-me. I was sworn to secrecy about witch stuff, but I was sure there were contingencies in place for when the magic affected someone else—someone important.

In this perfect moment, with our hands clasped together and our bodies leaning close to each other's, Thompson was important enough for me to say, "I could lose my soul."

"Isn't that dying?"

I had to laugh. "Luckily, I have two."

"Two what?"

"Two souls," I explained.

"I think you lost me," Thompson said.

I smiled at him. I had to give him credit for having gotten this far in the conversation, though I could see his brow beginning to furrow. "Never mind," I said. "How about a kiss for luck?"

Our first kiss had been nice, but not earth-shattering. This one started out warm and grew hotter. By the time our lips parted, I was breathing hard and tingly in all the right places.

It was hard to let go, but the sky was turning pink. I saw my mom coming out to the porch to look for us. I looked deep into the soft denim of Thompson's eyes and thought maybe sparks came with time, after careful tending of the embers.

"I'm sorry," I told him. "I have to go."

"Don't be sorry," he said, with another light kiss on my lips. "I had a great time. I'm looking forward to doing this again, so you'd better stay safe."

Mom waited as I made my way slowly up the sidewalk to where she sat on the front porch swing. I sat down next to her. Together we waved good-bye to Thompson.

"Are you sure about this?" she asked.

Thompson had put me in an honest mood, so I said, "Not really. And I'm going to be super pissed off if this doesn't work and we end up having to do something else."

"Well," Mom said gently, putting a hand on my shoulder, "it's hard to know what will happen. I'll tell you one thing, though. No matter what, I'll be damned if I'll let your father hurt you."

"What makes you think he would?" Dad had been acting so nice lately that I was actually surprised by her accusation.

"I found your jeans in the garbage. I nearly had a heart attack until I realized there was no way the blood could be yours."

"Oh, yeah," I said. A shiver raced down my spine at the memory of the ghastly, barfing vampire. "I managed to forget about that."

"Were you ever planning on telling me about what happened?"

I shook my head. Heck, I didn't like thinking about it now. "No."

Mom stared at me with her mouth open for a moment, and then laughed. "I guess that's honest."

"If it's any consolation, Dad seems to regret giving that order." As soon as it was out of my mouth, I knew I shouldn't have said anything more about it—especially not something light and flip.

Mom's eyebrows knitted into a tight frown. All traces of the easy smile she'd worn a moment ago vanished. She shook her head. The words she spoke came out between thinly pressed lips. "I'm going to kill that man."

The light of the sun had faded to gray. In the grass, crickets started their nightly chorus. I wondered how long Mom planned to sit here, fuming about Dad.

Nikolai's Toyota came rattling down the street, and Mom stood up. Clearly, some arrangements had been made while I was out. I followed her to the boulevard. Nikolai leaned across the seats and rolled down the window. "Are you ready?"

"I guess," I said. I looked at Mom, but she opened the door and gestured for me to get in.

"I'll meet you there," she said.

"Okay," I replied, and impulsively gave her a great big hug. She seemed surprised, but she returned the hug and added a motherly kiss to the cheek when we parted. She waited until I was seated with my buckle on before shutting the door.

"See you soon," she said to me, and then admonished Nikolai, "Drive safe."

It was strange, almost as if we knew what we were doing. After we pulled away, I turned to Nikolai. "We need to swing around to the back. I have to pick something up."

He shot me a suspicious look. "What?"

"Extra insurance," I said. "Oh, and do you have duct tape?"

"Don't look," I told Nikolai as I pulled my dress off in the backseat. He'd found a roll of grimy duct tape in the trunk. The pints of blood were cold and awkward to handle as I strapped them over my chest like a suit of armor. I could tell he was having a hard time not checking the rearview as I struggled with the slippery bags and sticky tape. Getting my sundress back over the lumpy mess was pretty entertaining, but I thought the bags would hold.

Still, I had two extra bags I hadn't found a place for.

Nikolai, who had clearly been watching despite my protests, smiled and said, "You could stick them to your butt."

I ran my hand down the twin bumps over my breasts. "I guess I'd finally have curves, huh?"

"Oh, you have plenty now."

I whacked him playfully on the top of his head with one of the extra bags. "You're a dirty old man. I told you not to look."

"You were duct taping blood bags to your body. How was I supposed to ignore that?"

Grabbing what was left of the roll of tape, I carefully crawled into the front passenger seat. My sundress hung funny now, but it covered me well enough. "I feel kind of stupid," I admitted, poking at the bags again.

Nikolai did laugh a little, but he said, "I think it's actually kind of smart. I just hope they go for it, when there's plenty of warm, exposed skin to choose from." He ran a finger lightly along my bare arms, causing goose pimples to rise.

My heart jumped. "What if they don't go for it?"

Nik turned his attention to the empty alley and considered. "They're repulsed by magic. We can put a spell on your skin."

"Like vampire bug spray? Does that even exist?"

He shrugged. "I'm sure your mom knows something."

I hoped he was right.

———

The drive out to the covenstead was a long one. At some point in the 1960s, our coven bought land about an hour or so out of the Cities. What had been completely undeveloped then had become an outer-ring suburb over the intervening years. Our property was now a conspicuous clump of woods surrounded on all sides by developed farmland.

I hadn't been back to the covenstead since my failed Initiation, even though I'd learned to swim in the swampy pond at the edge of the land and had spent most summers of my youth playing in the ferns, wildflowers, and pine trees.

We passed neatly planted rows of corn. The phrase "knee high by the Fourth of July" flitted through my mind as I looked out at the tall stalks. The moon cast the broad leaves in ghostly silver light.

I turned to look at Nikolai. He hadn't said much since we'd left my house. Shortly after we merged onto the highway, he'd switched on the radio to fill the silence.

I broke it now. "Is your dad coming?"

He coughed a surprised laugh. "Are you kidding me?"

I guessed not. "What about Bea? Or her family?"

"It's going to be just us, baby," he said with a sad shake of his head. "You, me, your mom, and a whole shitload of crazy-hungry vampires; it should be awesome."

I understood his sarcasm, but Nik had never called me any kind of pet name before. Since when was I his "baby"? I gave him a sidelong glance. Was he still under the impression that

our relationship was back on? I'd told him I was dating someone else after our kiss.

I opened my mouth to clarify the situation with Thompson
for him, but then I shrugged. If I lived through the next few
hours, I'd let him down gently. If not . . . well, he and Thompson
could fight it out with the new me. Maybe she'd be the sort to
more successfully string several boys along. I seemed to be
doing it now—just not very well.

I didn't want to think about that, so I turned my attention to
the problem at hand. "I wish I knew more about the Initiation
ritual," I said mostly to myself.

"Me too," Nikolai said. We had gotten to a Stop sign in the
middle of nowhere. Nikolai came to a complete stop and took
the opportunity to turn and look directly into my face. "You
realize we're going to have to trust your dad completely. Your
life, well, your soul, anyway, is literally going to be in his hands.
Are you sure about this? About him?"

Given our history, even, say, twenty-four hours ago, I shouldn't
be. I nodded anyway. I couldn't explain it in a way that would
ever satisfy Nikolai, but I believed my dad when he said that
nearly allowing me to be killed had shocked some sense into him.

Nik started back down the road. He shook his head. "I'm not
sure I trust *my* dad that much."

I kept my opinion of his dad to myself.

It would be easy to drive past the entrance to the covenstead if
you didn't know what to look for. There was little more than a

mailbox and a tire track trail leading deep into the woods. Nikolai slowed as we bumped along the uneven road. I kept my eyes out for critters. Last time I'd been here, a deer had bounded out of the underbrush. Probably because it was the last natural wooded spot for miles, the place was overrun with rabbits, squirrels, and even the occasional coyote and red-tailed fox.

We made it to the empty field used as a parking lot for big events without crushing any major wildlife. Nikolai parked his car beside the recycling and trash cans next to the cabin's back door.

There were no outside electric lights, and I stepped out into a deep velvety darkness. The vast sky above shone with an infinite number of stars. I could even see the silky trails of the Milky Way.

Inside the shelter of the woods, the air felt cooler and smelled of pine needles and rotting leaves.

Nikolai was already at the back door, rattling keys. He held each one up to the light of his cell phone, trying to find the one that fit. Finally, I heard the latch click, and he swung the door open. He flicked on the interior light. Soft yellow illuminated squares of mosquito-filled grass. Brown bats swooped overhead as I made my way into the mudroom. Automatically, I slipped out of my shoes and stowed them under the bench that lined the wall.

In the great room, Nikolai knelt beside the stone fireplace and stared at the empty grate as if trying to decide whether to light a fire. Since the windows had been closed by the last occupant and the air was stuffy and humid, it was certainly warm enough not to, but I could understand his hesitation. It seemed there was always a fire going at the covenstead. It was a tradition.

I looked around the huge, empty room. The kind of bar that was popular in houses in the 1950s and early 1960s took up the far end. I noted a minifridge and a wine rack, a polished Formica countertop, and cracked vinyl-covered stools. When I was a kid, Bea and I loved to sit on those and spin around or play pretend-bartender with Kool-Aid.

There were no other features in the room, except the giant row of windows that looked out to a pine deck and the forest beyond. Chairs had been stacked along the paneled walls, and there was a whiteboard tucked off to the side that still had notes for someone's spell-working ritual written in purple dry-erase marker. There were two interior doors. One near the kitchenette/bar led to a bathroom. From experience, I knew that the other revealed a cramped bedroom with two single beds, a rickety end table, and a chest of drawers that contained a treasure trove of the weird things the coven members had abandoned over the decades. I hated the one time Bea's mom had made us sleep over; the room always smelled a bit musty no matter how many times spring-cleaning rituals were performed on it.

When I turned around, Nikolai stood up and dusted off his jeans. Instead of a fire, he'd conjured a tall votive in the center of the fireplace. Its fire flickered and wavered against the walls.

I knew Nikolai could do that kind of magic, but I was still surprised by the candle's sudden appearance.

When he saw the look on my face, he shrugged. "No point in holding anything back."

I nodded, wondering just how powerful a witch Nikolai could be when he put his mind to it.

The grumble of an engine announced the arrival of another car. I took in a deep, steadying breath. It would be my mom, and it meant the time had come.

When the door opened to admit my dad, I nearly fell over in shock, especially when the next person in was my mom.

Of course, it made sense. We needed my dad to teach me the right of passage ritual and to call the hunt, but I couldn't imagine my parents actually spending the hour together it would take to drive up there.

Elias was the last to walk in, and I let out the breath I hadn't realized I'd been holding. Maybe he'd driven. Weirdly, I had an easier time imagining Mom sulking in the backseat of Elias's car than her blithely picking up two vampires on the way to the covenstead.

"What is under your shirt?" Mom asked.

"Blood bags," I said, holding up the extra pair I'd brought in. "I have two more."

Nikolai pulled her aside to explain his idea about the vampire repellent, and I was left staring at my dad.

"Are you ready, Ana?" Dad asked. I noticed he was a bit shaky. He tried to act casual as he grabbed for a stack of chairs to steady himself. The hunger must be devastating him. I wondered if he'd be able to keep sane. I remembered what Elias had said about how the hunger had eaten at his mind.

I swallowed and nodded, trying to muster up more courage than I felt. "No time like the present."

As the others headed out the door, I dashed to fetch my shoes from where I'd left them in the mudroom. Elias hung back to wait for me. Standing beside the bench, he watched as I tied the laces. He seemed to be searching for the right words.

"It was my greatest pleasure to serve Your Highness," he said.

"Oh, Elias!" I blurted, though I didn't have other words for my feelings either. Standing up, I wrapped him in a hug.

His arms wound themselves around me easily, fitting comfortably, as if we were two pieces of the same thing. When I looked up into his face to ask him if I was doing the right thing after all and if he was planning to ditch the stupid political alliance/marriage thingy to the creepy Southern captain after punching him . . . he kissed me.

Elias and I had never kissed before. Not like this.

There wasn't so much a spark as the fire of unrestrained passion. Elias, usually so restrained and proper, pressed against me in a way I could describe only as sinful.

When he released me, I had to struggle for breath. He'd taken it away from me. I clung to him, panting.

"You tempt me to treason," he whispered hotly in my ear. "I would have you escape to the South with me and leave behind the kingdom I've served so faithfully. But I know you're too honorable to accept."

Was I? Actually, at that moment, Elias could have convinced me that jumping off a bridge was an excellent idea as long as he kissed me like that again.

His passion took me by surprise. We'd never kissed before, and he would have to wait until I finally had an official boyfriend to do it. God, if I didn't turn into alternate-me, I'd have a lot to confess to Thompson—although I had managed to avoid mentioning Nikolai's kiss so far.

I pushed those conflicting thoughts aside. Searching for a safe topic, my mind went to a question, which I asked him: "Have you kissed a lot of boys like that?"

Okay. It wasn't exactly a safe thing to ask. I think his passion made me stupid.

"I've never kissed anyone like that except you, my lady." His smile was wolfish. He nibbled at my ear. Each little bite raised gooseflesh on my arms.

"I mean, have you had boyfriends?"

Elias pulled back to look me in the eye. He was frowning. "Even though we use the male form of the word, an animus is a genderless thing. When a witch pulls one over into this world, she cares little if it goes into the body of a male or a female human. Let's just say I've loved a lot of souls. And, knowing this as an undeniable fact, vampires care a lot less about what body a soul inhabits."

Oh, Bea would love this answer.

"This matters at this moment because . . . ?" he asked.

It didn't, really. That was Bea's thing more than mine, anyway. What I wanted to know was the answer to a different question: "Are you seriously still going to marry that creep? You punched his lights out last night."

"We were establishing a hierarchy," he said with a slight

smirk. "My 'intended' now understands that if any pushing around gets done, it will be by me."

"Uh, gross."

"Is it?" Elias said. "I'll be going into an enemy's camp, living among them. It is important, as they say, to make a good first impression."

I was pretty sure the Southern Kingdom was already impressed with him; otherwise they wouldn't have made the political trade. "Do you have to go through with this?"

"I do if we want to avoid war. Even if the hunt is satisfied, our kingdom will need time to regroup. You saw the prince. He's barely holding on. It will take time for him to be the ruler he once was. My going south will buy time."

"Time? You're not thinking of this as forever?"

He snorted a derisive laugh. "Confarreatio is an unbreakable contract, except, of course, by death."

Whoa.

"I will always serve *my* prince," he said darkly, emphasizing the pronoun in a way to make it clear that the prince he meant was my father. Then he stepped back and took my hand in his. He kissed my knuckles lightly. Looking up from his deep bow, he added, "And my lady."

It was too intense. I broke his gaze and muttered, "Uh, we should get going."

He let my hand drop, and the heat between us evaporated so suddenly that I felt a chill. "Yes. The others are waiting," he said.

"Right," I said, finding my voice finally. I could still feel the ghost of his lips on mine as I headed for the door.

Last time I walked down the path that led to the sacred oak grove, the entire coven had had a hand in lighting tiny floating tea candles in beautiful containers and placing them along the way. It had created a lovely effect. I desperately missed even the feeble light they provided as I stumbled over tree roots and stones.

Elias steadied me when I banged my toes on a particularly stubborn moss-covered rock. When his hand cupped my elbow, I found myself straining to sense the passion he'd shown a moment ago. If it remained, it was well hidden, replaced by his customary stony efficiency.

When we reached the natural circle ringed by ancient burr oaks, I saw that Nikolai had brought a small bundle of wood and sticks from the covenstead's firewood supply. He knelt in the grass and arranged the pile in the center of a stone circle that hadn't been there the last time I'd stood in the grove. Nikolai didn't bother to produce matches. Instead, a flash of light flicked off his fingertips, and the brush caught. In a second, we had a blazing fire.

Dad stood some distance from the flame or the magic; I wasn't sure which bothered him more. He'd worn his hair loose, and it hung straight to his shoulders. In a white shirt and black jeans, he looked the part of a vampire prince. Of course, he was barefoot. I was just glad he didn't feel the need to start shucking the rest of his clothes.

I glanced around the circle.

Elias moved to stand beside his sovereign. With his military-style cropped hair, he made for an impressive enforcer in a black T-shirt that showed off his well-toned physique and muscular arms.

My mom stood next to Dad. The humidity had made her curls extra frizzy. I couldn't have looked less like her, with my father's slim features, dark hair, and pale complexion. She also looked the most like a norm, with her college professor fashion—a blazer thrown over a simple blouse. I could much more easily imagine a chalkboard behind her than the gnarled, twisted trunk of a massive oak.

Nikolai poked the fire one last time with a stick and stood up to stand by me. His hair was tied loosely at the nape of his neck. The T-shirt he wore was dark and promoted some band's concert tour. The Celtic knot tattoo was barely visible on his bicep underneath the sleeve. Maybe it was all the casual magic he'd demonstrated, but I thought he moved with a particular liquid grace that marked him as a witch to contend with.

That just left me, feeling small and stupid and way out of my league.

And, of course, everyone stared expectantly at me.

So, I cleared my throat nervously and looked to my dad for some help. "What do we do first? Call the hunt or start the rite of passage?"

He seemed to shake himself out of a dream before answering. "I will call the hunt. When you're on the brink of passing over, we'll begin the rite."

Passing over? I didn't really like the sound of that. Neither did Mom or Nikolai, from the looks on their faces. "Wait, do you mean 'dying'?"

"That's unacceptable, Ramses!" Mom said, taking a threatening step forward, which Elias matched almost unconsciously.

"Okay, so you're ruining the best part of my plan, Dad," I said. "If you're saying I have to be close to death for this thing to work, um, we need to talk more. And"—I pointed to the bumps on my chest meaningfully—"I can take these stupid things off."

Ramses stared at the lumps under my sundress. "Are those really bags of blood?"

"I didn't suddenly become a D cup." I rolled my eyes. Then, more seriously I added, "Yes, see, that's part of the whole I-don't-really-want-to-be-bled-to-death thing. I even brought extra, you know, in case we could just toss them a bag or two."

For a panicked moment I thought I left those behind in the mudroom when I set them on the bench to tie my shoes. I looked around frantically, but Elias lifted his hand to show me that he'd thought to grab them.

"You want my people to feed on prepackaged blood?" My dad sounded offended, as if he'd been expecting caviar and I'd substituted an Egg McMuffin.

"You want your people to drink me dry instead?"

"I just don't think it's going to work," my dad said. He squinted at me as if using X-ray vision. "It's not even warm."

"It's going to have to work," I said. Turning to Nikolai, I said, "What about the vamp repellent?"

He, in turn, looked to my mom. "What about an illusion,

Amelia? Couldn't we cast a desire spell on the bags? And double that up with an aversion scent on her skin?"

With effort, my mom stopped glaring at Dad. She pushed her glasses up on her nose. They caught the firelight as she considered. "That could work, if the vampires can be satisfied by bagged blood."

My dad started to open his mouth, and I could tell he was going to deny it. "They can," I interjected quickly. "Mrs. Kirov told us they can be fooled by day-old corpses."

My mom looked at my dad as if scandalized by his poor judgment. He shrugged. "News to me," he said.

"I guess it's a Ukrainian thing," I responded.

At that, everyone looked dubious, as though they figured the vampires in Ukraine must be extra shabby or stupid, but no one offered a counterargument.

"That would suffice," Dad said, "I suppose."

"If there is a question of preference, perhaps a protection spell would be in order," Elias suggested with a quiet yet firm authority.

Mom stared at him contemptuously, as if she considered him an inconvenient obstacle. How had I ever thought she liked him? Eventually, when it became clear that his suggestion was the best option, she grudgingly conceded his point. "Yes. I suppose so."

Nikolai stepped closer to Mom to confer quietly. I caught only snippets of their conversation. They seemed to be discussing the most effective choice. Mom seemed to think a binding

spell was a good idea. Nik shook his head. He didn't like anything that kept me immobilized, unable to defend myself.

"Amen to that," I muttered.

Elias laid the blood bags in front of me. He gave me a smile
as he stood up. "You'll make an excellent vampire," he said.

I grabbed at his sleeve. "Will I? How do you know?"

"Because you're brave and loyal to the kingdom already."

"But that's me," I said. "Not her."

" 'Her' who?"

"My vampire soul," I said. "How do you know she won't be
completely different? You're not the man whose body you pos-
sess. What makes you think I'll be anything like the person I
am now?"

Elias frowned deeply, and I could tell I'd offended him a
little by bringing up the whole possession thing. But it was true,
and I needed to know the answer. Behind him, Nikolai and my
mom were doing something over the blood bags. I smelled roses
and musk—an attraction spell.

"Your vampire soul crossed over a long time ago," Elias said.
"The rite of passage is not the same magic as that horrible curse
that rips us from our homeland. I've only ever seen it performed
a few times before in my entire lifetime, because dhampyrs are
rare. But I can tell you this with absolute certainty: you will be
who you've always been. Only more so. You'll finally have your
inheritance—all the power you were born with but were unable
to tap because the other animus was in the way."

"You're sure?" I asked desperately.

"You have always been part vampire, Ana. Whoever you think that other soul is, is who you've been all along."

I let go of his sleeve. "You don't think I'll change?"

"Everything you do changes you," he said philosophically. "This is a big thing we're attempting tonight. I'm sure you won't be the same afterward."

"But you know what I'm asking, right?"

"You'll have all your memories. You'll still be Ana, the sum of *all* your experiences."

He moved away when Mom and Nikolai came over to wave their hands over me. They carefully avoided the area where I'd taped the bags to my body, but otherwise their magic felt like a soft mist. I knew it worked, however, when Elias coughed and took a step farther back.

"Okay," Mom said, and with a resigned sigh she turned to Dad. "We've done what we can to try to get the vampires to take the bait. You might as well start this show."

Dad nodded. He closed his eyes and took in a long breath. I wasn't sure what I was expecting, but, a second later, he opened them. They'd gone cat-slit. A glance at Elias showed me that his had done the same. I knew without needing confirmation that the hunt had begun.

Chapter Sixteen

It was an unnerving sensation, knowing that somewhere, out in the darkness, far away, vampires were converging—their minds and bodies focused on one thing: finding and killing me.

Even though there was no way they could already be close at hand, the nerves on my back tingled expectantly. I had to grit my teeth to keep from checking the woods every time the wind rustled through the trees.

My dad watched me intensely. It wasn't a look I particularly liked. In fact, it reminded me of the way he'd been when I'd come to tell him about the Southern prince and he'd sicced his minions on me.

Elias also seemed to be having trouble not pouncing hungrily. He watched Dad studiously, his face turned away from me. But I could see that his hands had clenched into tight fists at his side.

A hoot of an owl made me jump. I must have made a little

noise, because Mom and Nik turned to look at me. I flashed an embarrassed smile. "Just a little nervous," I admitted.

"I think Elias had a good point a few minutes ago," Mom said, moving closer to me. Her voice sounded falsely casual, and her eyes never left the two vampires. "We should consider extra protection beyond the aversion spell."

"Yeah," Nikolai said. "That's a really good idea."

"Make the protection really freaking strong, okay?" I begged Nikolai. He nodded, and then he and Mom returned to conferring about various options for my protection. I shifted uncomfortably on my feet. When Dad tracked my slight shift like a panther, I couldn't contain myself any longer. "Losing my nerve over here! Could we hurry up with the spell? Feeling a bit exposed!"

Mom looked ruffled at the interruption. Nikolai, however, zeroed in on the two vampires, then tugged at her sleeve and pointed. The second Mom saw Dad's heightened posture, she gave Nikolai a brisk nod. "The second option seems the stronger," she said to Nik, apparently coming to some sort of decision.

Nikolai didn't argue. He kept his attention focused on Elias and Dad as he positioned himself between me and Elias. Mom flanked my other side. They raised their arms in unison.

The magic began almost immediately. A cool breeze shook the trees, and the usual forest sounds hushed. I recognized Nikolai's power in the musky scent in the air. My mother's magic came up through the grass like a fast-growing vine and wound its way around my legs. Instinctively, I tried to pull away, but the tendrils held fast. Meanwhile, the air caressed me, reassuringly stroking my hair and whispering in my ear that I was safe.

Dad flinched away from the magic, as if he suddenly smelled something foul. He glanced around as if trying to identify the source. After a second, his eyes narrowed, centering on Mom and Nikolai. He sneered at them, showing fangs.

If it was possible, Elias held himself more tightly, still not trusting himself to look in my direction.

Mom's magic coiled around my waist like a rope. I couldn't move my legs at all because they were so tightly bound. Even as the wind whispered its sweet nothings in my ear, I felt panic rising. What happened to my not being helpless? I'd be pinioned, unable to move, when the vampires arrived.

"Don't fight it, Ana. Please," Nikolai said out loud, his words echoing the strange noises the air made in my ear. To my mom, he added, "I told you she'd hate this."

"We've got to protect her from a pack of vampires on the hunt," Mom said, shaking her head at Nikolai sternly. When she spoke to me, she had that motherly tone she used when she wanted me to do something that might build my character or was otherwise for my own good. "The protection *is* strong, honey, but, remember, it will keep you safe."

When the curls of magic wrapped around my wrist like manacles, I spat out a curse. My own fangs dropped in response to the perceived threat.

My dad shook his head violently all of a sudden, as if someone had slapped him. Elias finally looked at me. Their fangs were retreating, and their eyes were returning to being human.

"The hunt call was severed," my dad explained, sounding dazed. He peered across the flickering fire at my face. "It's the transformation," he told Elias. "The hunt rejected her sacrifice. It's too soon. We're not cannibals."

"We have to start the rite before the call fades entirely," Elias suggested.

"We could begin it, but we'd have to stop before the rite is complete." My dad shook his head. "They won't come if she's a full vampire."

Meanwhile, I was completely imprisoned by Mom's protection spell. A finger of her magic even clung to my throat, completely immobilizing my head. I thrashed against the bonds. Despite all the reassurances, I couldn't stand the feeling of being tightly bound. The fire flashed extra bright as my eyes changed. The forest flooded with light. I pushed and strained with the extra strength the change brought.

Dad stepped into my field of vision. He put a gentle hand on my shoulder. "Ana, I need you to concentrate on the sound of my voice."

I nodded, but there were tears in my eyes. I was scared, and I didn't want to die like this, unable to even twitch.

Dad frowned and turned to Mom. His voice was a strong command. "Let her go. Or at least loosen her bonds, for Goddess' sake. You're destroying our chances."

Mom looked baffled for a second, as if she didn't know how to respond, but the tendrils unwound slightly. I took in a deep breath.

"Better?" he asked gently.

I would have preferred being completely free, but I could turn my head and wiggle my fingers. I didn't feel quite as smothered. I still felt as if I were standing stiffly at attention, but I could breathe. The claustrophobic panic subsided somewhat.

Besides, I wanted the protection. I just didn't like how it felt.

Dad took my silence for assent and motioned Elias to join him. We'd formed a tight knot. Mom and Nikolai stood on either side of me, their arms outstretched, enclosing me in their magical circle. With my vampiric eyes, their magic appeared like a greenish haze that surrounded me. Dad and Elias moved in as closely as they could without touching the enchanted mist.

He was still frowning. "The others will have to be able to get closer than this," he said.

Mom looked ready to protest.

Elias cut her off. "Or we will turn on the nearest available meal: you."

The binding spell loosened significantly. My limbs no longer felt roped in spells. Now, in their place, was the sensation of loosely wrapped blankets, like a kind of magical Snuggie. This was much nicer. Now, Nikolai's magic soothed my jagged nerves, lulling me into relaxing. My fangs retracted with a soft slide.

"The call returns," Elias said softly.

I opened my eyes to the normal darkness. Dad was nodding, but with deep concern etched into his usually haughty face. With the firelight behind him, his face was a flicker of shadow. "Yes. Better. This will work only if you're truly willing. You must have no hesitation, no regrets."

I took in a deep breath. The protection spell had relaxed me to the point of no longer feeling threatened, but was I ready for this sacrifice?

"You can ramp it back up if you need to? Quickly?" I asked Mom.

She nodded. "I swear as the Queen of Witches, I will protect you. Besides, there are other spells we can use to stop them. Hidden wards. Magical booby traps. If things get out of hand, I will protect us all."

Though by "us," it was clear Mom meant "us humans."

Okay. It was scary enough that I was going to give up one of my souls. Mom and Nik had my back. They would stop things if it went too far. Mom had just promised as a witch and a queen. She'd do it or die trying.

I closed my eyes for a moment, trying to remember why I'd agreed to do this in the first place. The hunt *had* to be stopped. Otherwise, Bea's mom and all the other non-Initiates could end up dead if I didn't try. I had an extra soul. I wouldn't die. Mom and Nikolai had been so intent on protecting me a second ago that I'd felt stifled. That was a good thing. It meant I wasn't alone in this. I just kept telling myself that they wouldn't let anyone hurt me. I would be okay.

After a long moment, I opened my eyes and said firmly, "I'm ready."

My father's face flushed with pride. He gave a nod to my mom as if to say, "You raised her right." He gave my shoulder a quick squeeze before dropping his hand. "This is a very old ceremony. The words will be unfamiliar to you, as they are in a language so old that it was ancient when I first heard it spoken. I'll talk slowly, and you can repeat the words as best you can. Don't worry. The Goddess will understand your intention if you mangle the pronunciation. All right?"

Okay, things were getting serious. Swallowing hard, I nodded.

To Elias, he asked, "You have the silver dagger ready?"

On my left, I heard Nikolai mutter in astonishment, "Silver! So, it's true."

Dad gave Nikolai the barest nod of acknowledgment. To me, he explained, "No doubt, like the hunter, you've heard the legends. Pure silver is the only material on Earth that can cut our souls from our bodies."

I didn't much care for that word "cut," but I reminded myself to stay focused and calm. If I had to bleed a little, it was okay. It would save someone's life.

"Tonight, you, Anastasija Ramses Parker, will become a full vampire. Is it your wish to join the kingdom?"

"It is," I said as formally as I could, sensing that, in some way, the ritual had begun.

"So mote it be," he said just as solemnly. He took the silver dagger Elias had produced from his back pocket and held it up in front of me. It was disappointingly tiny. Hardly bigger than a pencil and nearly as slender, it looked like a toy. But the firelight caught on the edge sharply and hieroglyphs flashed into view briefly when Dad turned and began walking around me in a circle.

"Repeat after me," he said. As he stepped, Dad intoned syllables very carefully. I stammered through them as best I could.

As I spoke, I began to feel lighter, and off balance. When I stumbled a bit, I smelled the dusty scent of sun on hay bales, and suddenly the spell that protected me swelled. It was as though arms slipped under mine, lifted me back upright, and held me close. I snuggled into the magical embrace. Even though I was standing up, I could easily drift asleep.

All my residual fear floated away with the light-headedness, spiraling away from me with each word. Hence, when I noticed the eyes reflecting in the treetops, I barely registered an emotion beyond surprise.

Dad and Elias seemed aware of the presence of the vampires. Dad stopped speaking and stepped out of the way. Pale, naked bodies dropped down from the trees. They crouched like predators at the edge of the circle of light. Their mirrorlike eyes glinted dangerously. I should have been terrified by the hunger evident in their faces. Instead, I slurred as if I were drunk, "Oh, lookie—they're here!"

If my arms hadn't felt so heavy, I would have waved a greeting.

When the first of them slid into the light, Mom noticed their approach. A hiss of breath escaped her lips, and, briefly, the protective restraints tightened around me. However, she let them go before I could even muster a sense of panic. Dad caught my eye and gave me a look that seemed half-reassuring, half-pitying. Then he made a regal sort of "come hither" gesture, and they lunged.

More vampires than I'd ever seen before leaped forward with inhuman speed. Several fell instantly on the bags of blood like a pack of wolves on a slab of meat. Even in my happy place, the sight terrified me. I would have run, but Mom's spell rooted my feet to the spot. Like dogs, they snarled with teeth bared.

A few sniffed at me, their noses wrinkled. One followed his nose to where the bags were taped to my chest, and a slow, evil smile spread across his face. Teeth bared and sank. Even though I didn't feel a thing, I screamed.

Unfortunately, that attracted everyone's attention. There wasn't enough room at my front for all the vampires to attach themselves to the bag, even though it was clear that some were content to lick the spilled blood off the ground or one another's faces. The frenzy pushed forward. Despite the repellent, I felt a few nibbles here and there on my exposed arms and back.

Nibbles became bites. Even though none of them could withstand the spell long enough to latch on, I felt my blood begin to spill.

Even the distance my dad's magical words created couldn't keep out the intensity of the pain. A scream tore from my throat.

Somewhere far away I heard my mother shouting, but I couldn't decipher the words through the haze of anguish. The protection spell constricted, and I heard the snarl of angry vampires.

I was almost angry at the interruption, because I wanted the pain to stop and I knew it would end only when they'd had their feast. My eyes were unfocused with tears and agony, but they tracked the blur of something brilliantly silver.

The slash of the knife in the air shattered something inside me. My consciousness fractured like a mirror cracking. A fissure began at the edges and began to crackle. Pieces began to drop out, and darkness took their places. The dark, a gaping emptiness, scared me. *No,* I tried to shout, *this isn't right! I'm losing something important!*

If I'd even been able to form the words, I doubted anyone would have heard me over the din of the vampires' feeding frenzy.

I tried to free myself from the protective spell with a tug, but the multiple bodies and magic held me tightly. The crack inside my mind seemed to be growing larger. I had the dizzying illusion of standing on a cliff looking over a crashing seascape, or maybe it was the turret of a tower I stood upon. An invisible force seemed desperate to push me over the edge, like a gale force wind. But I clung stubbornly to the ledge. In the distance, something rose out of the sea. I imagined it as a monster from a dream or a nightmare, a kraken of some sort, with dozens of octopuslike tentacles. But I knew it was a woman, a witch, fighting the air with her slashing limbs that cut like knives. She was the Queen of Swords. She was me—my witch soul, and she was fighting to stay. All the magic I had never been able to tap poured out of her like a beacon. She was much, much stronger than I ever imagined. She was like a queen, like a goddess.

Giant tentacle arms reached for me, but instead of swallowing me in inky darkness, they held me more firmly. Suddenly, I knew the sea and the cliff were the source of my power. The wind was the enemy.

The familiar churning sensation of my two souls pushing against each other roiled through my consciousness. Push, pull, push, pull—it began to build. Now the tower felt more like a tilt-a-whirl, spinning faster and faster.

I stood calm in the eye of the storm. In the tornado, swirls dancing around me flashed shards of mirror, like tiny flashes of light in the dark clouds of death. Tentacle arms reached out—no, it was my own arms reaching, in the Goddess position, open, palm up into the gale force winds. A mirrored splinter imbedded itself into my flesh. The pain was sharp, like a bite. But I didn't bleed. Another piece struck, followed by another. Soon my body was riddled with the broken mirror, my skin a quicksilver patchwork of countless reflections.

My souls were too entwined to separate. I would have to give up both, or none.

I would not die.

But something had to.

An explosion tore the air.

The shock wave knocked bodies everywhere. Vampires who had been clinging to me with teeth and nails suddenly flew backward as if pushed by an invisible hand. Simultaneously, the protection spell was shredded. Nikolai and Mom were thrown off balance.

Only my dad had withstood the onslaught. He held the silver knife in his hand and was making frantic gestures in the air.

Completely free of the protection spell, I found I had no strength to support myself. My knees buckled, and I dropped to the dew-and-blood-spattered grass. I tried to tell my dad how sorry I was that I'd messed up the whole thing, but, before I could move my lips, the world closed up and went dark.

The last thing I felt was a thunderclap, like the rush of air into a vacuum, and I had the impression of my father falling to the ground beside me, still as death.

Chapter Seventeen

Everything was so black when I next opened my eyes that I thought maybe I had died, after all.

Then my eyes began to adjust, and the ugly little room at the covenstead materialized out of the shadows. I was lying on my back on a lumpy mattress, my head turned toward the scratched, cheap wooden chest of drawers. A giant Mickey Mouse alarm clock stared down at me from the top, its white-gloved hands pointing at a quarter past three.

I blinked and held up my aching arms. I was covered in white bandages, like a mummy.

"Hello?" I called out to the darkness. If this wasn't some kind of weird purgatory, then someone must have carried me to this room. Ergo, I couldn't be the only one left alive.

I had to find out what had happened. Was everyone okay? Had my dad's last desperate magic, if that was what he was doing just before I passed out, worked? And what the hell had he been trying to do, anyway?

The door creaked open; electric light painfully slashing the darkened space. I raised my arms to cover my face.

"Ana?" It was Elias. He slipped into the room without switching on the light, apparently aware of my sudden sensitivity to it. Quickly, he closed the door behind him. "How are you feeling?"

I didn't really know. My entire body felt as if it had been chewed and spat out by a horde of angry pit bulls, which wasn't actually that far from the truth. However, the wellspring of power that had manifested during the ceremony remained, humming just under the surface, filling me with a reserve of energy and strength. It churned constantly, as if my souls rubbed against each other like stones in a tumbler. I felt I could run a marathon. "Okay, I guess," I said finally. "What happened?"

Elias set himself down so gently at the edge of the bed that the ancient rusted springs barely protested. "We're still trying to figure that out, honestly."

I remember the impression of my father collapsing. "Is Dad okay?"

My heart sank when Elias took in a long breath before answering. "He . . ."

"He's dead, isn't he?"

To my surprise, Elias shook his head. "Not exactly," he said. "We neglected to consider what would happen to your witch soul if we separated it from the vampire one. The magic it contained . . . well, for lack of a better word, blew up."

I'd certainly felt the monster in the sea and the explosion. What about the image of the imbedded mirror? I wished I could look at my skin. I felt certain it would be studded with reflective glass, even though that was impossible. "But I still have both animuses, don't I? Does that mean it didn't work? Is the hunt over?"

Elias's eyebrows jerked up, as if I'd said something funny. "Oh yes. Very over. Over forever."

"What do you mean?"

"The blood covenant between vampire and witch blew up when you did."

Was he implying there would never be a need for another sacred hunt? I searched his eyes for the answer. He gazed back steadily, and, as if in answer to my unasked question, he nodded.

"Yes, Your Majesty," he said again. "The vampires need never hunt to kill again. We'll need blood, but not the hunt. I suspect some will continue to hunt to kill for perverse pleasure, but the last link in the chains of our slavery has been forever broken. We need nothing more from witches. Nothing."

He smiled, and his face, which was often ever so slightly contorted by control, relaxed.

"Can you imagine? We're completely free."

His mood was infectious and I grinned back at him, but I was still very confused. "That's totally awesome. But . . . how?"

"That's the part we're all still trying to figure out, Your Majesty."

When I considered his words, the thrum of power along my nerves did feel oddly . . . communal. It was as though I could reach out and tap a whole reservoir of strength anytime.

"There's a reason dhampyrs go through the rite of passage at an early age. We chose sixteen because that's when the witches insist on their Initiation. But normally it wouldn't matter. You could have done it today, or in ten years. Except, you're not like all the others, are you, Ana?"

He smiled at me then and seemed to expect an answer, so I said feebly, "I guess not."

"No, you've found a way to use the power of both souls. No other dhampyr has ever thought to do that. In fact, most choose one path or the other. You chose to go your own way, and, on top of that, have used the souls to conjure something greater than either. We all should have remembered. You've demonstrated it often enough."

He meant those times I'd used blood and magic to freeze time or blow up the talisman—my super-duper power. "But I still don't get it. What difference does that make?"

"The more your souls work together, the more commingled they become. You don't have two souls anymore, Ana. You have two halves of one."

"Oh," I said.

The shards—the image of something shattered into a thousand pieces—returned sharply to my mind.

"But something broke," I said. "The rite broke something."

"Yes, it did. A piece of your soul shattered."

I touched my heart as if I could feel a hole there. All I felt were bandages and the sticky remains of the duct tape someone must have pried off my skin. "But I'm all still here."

He shook his head, smiling. "Yes, more miracles. Perhaps

because it was merged from two, you had a bigger soul than most."

"Huh," I said, not knowing what else to say to that. "How did that little extra bit break the hunt, then?"

"The First Witch bound her soul to the First Vampire when she brought him over to serve at her command. To control him, she had to curse her descendants with forever paying a blood price. But the magic began with two souls, combined and bound together in a single fate. You released a soul that was two-in-one in payment for the hunt. The curse was broken."

Wow.

By accident, I'd reversed the hex. "What happened to Dad?"

"We didn't know you'd broken the curse. The prince thought a death was still required. He tried to abdicate."

Dad tried to abdicate in my place. My head spun. "But—but, you said he wasn't dead."

Elias laid his hand gently on my leg.

"The hunt rejected his offering. It rebounded on him. You see, you'd already broken the curse; but even if you hadn't, it would never have worked. He's a vampire. We can't devour our own during a hunt. But we can absorb a vampire's soul during abdication . . . so his powers were dispersed. Even into you."

Elias shook his head sadly. I could tell he had more to say, so I waited for him to compose himself.

He cleared his throat of its roughness and said, "The prince hangs on to a shred of his soul. He doesn't seem able to hold on to it, though. It's leaking from him slowly. He's dying."

I sat up. "I want to see him."

"As Your Majesty wishes, of course—but, Ana, he's dying."

The worst part was, I could tell. It must have been that part of him he'd passed on to me. I could feel Dad's presence in the other room, almost as if I were the one wrapped in a blanket and huddled weakly next to the fireplace.

I struggled to swing my feet over the edge of the bed. Elias was at my side in a second, helping me stand, his shoulder under my arm. There was something more deferential than usual in the way he kept his eyes averted. I was afraid I knew the answer to this, but I had to ask anyway. "Why do you keep calling me 'Majesty'?"

His gaze flicked briefly to my face, but he dipped his head again like a bow. "Because you are my queen."

"Queen?" I repeated stupidly, grabbing for the bedpost as my knees threatened to wobble with this new revelation. "But Dad's title was prince. Even if he's . . . That is, even if I have his throne, shouldn't I still just be princess?"

Elias's strength held me steady. "Ana," he said gently, "the covenant you broke wasn't just between the kingdom and the First Witch; it was between *all* vampires and the First Witch."

Swirling clouds of countless mirrors flashed through my mind.

"Wait," I said, finding my feet enough to push him away slightly. "Are you telling me I'm the queen of all the vampires, like, not just our region, but everywhere?"

He clasped his hands in front of his body and kept his head slightly bowed as he spoke. "You will be the first vampire queen."

"What if I don't want the job?"

Looking up, Elias laughed lightly. "Then you're perfect for it, of course."

"I'm being serious," I said.

He dipped his head again, as if to apologize. "As am I," he said quietly. "Only you can decide what you do with the title, but it is yours, like it or not."

"Great," I muttered. "Just great."

Deciding I could sort out all this queen stuff later, I made my way into the great room with Elias's help. The light stabbed at my eyes, and it took a full two minutes before I could see properly. Elias explained that my new light sensitivity was probably a by-product of the failed abdication ceremony.

He helped me over to where Dad sat on the floor next to the fire, looking small and broken. His body shivered, and mine did the same in sympathy. I knelt down beside him. He glanced at me and smiled that same relieved grin Elias had. "We're free, my child. Completely free!"

"I know, Dad," I said, patting his shoulder awkwardly. My bandages didn't extend to my fingers, so I gave him a light squeeze.

I glanced up at where my mom leaned against the stone fireplace. Her arms were crossed in front of her chest, and her dark expression was hard to read. She stared hard at Dad and was either really annoyed or deeply worried, or both.

"Are you okay?" I asked him, even though I could sense the

deep hollowness inside him that was slowly draining away his life.

"I'm mortal and dying," he said, "but not today."

I nodded, feeling it to be true. I didn't know how long he had, but it was probably months rather than moments. "You're hungry." I realized the sensation rumbling through my guts actually belonged to him. "You'll feel stronger if you eat."

He looked shocked. "But the hunt is over. . . ."

"Mortal food," I explained, cutting him off. "You haven't had anything real in that atrophied mortal stomach of yours for a zillion years, Dad. Have a bagel or something. It'll do wonders."

I started to stand up to fetch him something from the pantry, but Mom was already on it with an irritated, "Oh, I'll get it."

I sat back on my heels. Wait, was she actually upset because Dad was hurt? WTF? I thought that fire had cooled sixteen years ago. I shook my head. I could cope with my dad finally acting like a decent person, but Mom too? No, that was too much.

Dad caught my expression and said, "Fussed over by two queens. I feel pretty special."

"Don't get too used to it." I laughed. Mom might be acting cool now, but I couldn't imagine it lasting once he regained some strength. "But I don't want your job, Dad. Or this piece of your soul. Can't I give it back?"

He gripped my arm and shook his head vehemently.

"I wish you could," he said. "But what's done is done. I made a mistake, and now I have to pay for it."

It was so unfair. My dad had tried to do the right thing. I felt deeply sad for him, and I wanted to take care of him. I rubbed my eyes. I wanted to go home and crawl under the covers. I looked at Dad quivering piteously under a blanket. "Where are you going to go?"

"I don't know," he said.

It was weird, but I couldn't stand the idea of him just wandering off and dying somewhere alone. "You should come live with us," I offered suddenly. "We've even got a place completely cut off from the sun because Elias needed it."

"I suppose I don't," my dad said softly, his voice light with amazement. "Not anymore."

"What? You mean you can stand the sun again? That's great. In that case," I said as Mom came back with a toasted bagel and cream cheese in her hand, "you can stay in the craft room! We can turn it into a guest bedroom. Can't we, Mom?"

Mom flashed me a horrified and angry look, but said, "Yes, I suppose we can arrange something like that."

Dad did a double-take at my mother's agreement. "You would put me up in your own home, Amelia?"

"I said we might be able to come to a suitable arrangement," she said stiffly. When I started to protest, she raised her hand. "But, seeing as you have no place to go at the moment, we could put you up temporarily."

Leaning in conspiratorially, Elias said, "I can vouch for the accommodations, but be cautious of her tea."

Mom looked affronted. "What was wrong with my tea?"

I rolled my eyes. "Only the fact that you were trying to

poison him, Mom." She looked at me blankly, so I continued. "To enslave everyone? Remember?"

"You think that was what I was doing?"

"Well, yeah," I said, and Elias backed me up with a curt nod. In case she tried to deny it, I added, "I heard Mr. Kirov ask if the potion had worked. He said something about binding the vampires."

"The vampire hunger," Mom said. "Bind the vampire's hunger. I'm surprised you could understand him at all with his thick accent and spotty command of English. Look, I was trying to come up with a potion that would cure the effects of the hunger."

I was ready to call bullshit when Elias said, "That was why it came back so strongly."

Mom looked at my surprised expression. "Didn't you notice that you hadn't been hungry until the day after we skipped our nightly tea ritual?"

My stomach had growled at breakfast that very morning.

Oh. Now I felt stupid. A deep blush colored my cheeks. I couldn't believe it. Mom had been trying to help? But what about that spell she'd cast? "You tried to zombify me again that morning. I felt your magic trying to hold me down."

"Zombify?" Mom's expression crumpled into deep hurt. "If that was what you thought, no wonder you ran away! It was protection! From the effects of the hunger. Why do you think I was so upset when I found out you'd bitten Nikolai at the picnic?"

Blurgh. Could this have been more a comedy of errors? What else could I do but apologize? "I'm sorry," I said.

"We should try to trust each other a little bit," Mom suggested.

"A good first step in vampire-witch relations," my dad muttered with a bit of a laugh.

I hadn't thought about that. If I was the queen of the vampires and Mom was the queen of the witches, what was it going to be like living in the same house? I smiled at the thought of the first time she demanded I clean my room. I could shoot back that I'd do it, but she had to give vampires a free pass to something. This could be very weird, indeed.

But, to be fair, I'd just learned that Mom had turned out to be not nearly as evil as I thought. In fact, she'd been trying to help all along. Maybe things would work out.

A sickly cough racked my dad's slender frame.

I rubbed his back. He looked up at me, his eyes watery. "I'll be okay."

I could sense his lie, but I let him keep it. "I know," I said.

He looked at his hands and flexed his fingers as if he'd never noticed the lines on them before. "So fragile," he said. "So breakable. It will be strange living as a human again."

I looked at my own pale hands. What about me? If my soul was now part of all the vampires, did I still have some of it in me? "Am I still a vampire? I mean, I must be if I'm queen, but do I still have the powers?"

"I suppose we won't know until you try," Dad said. "But I imagine you're going to be a kind of supervampire, able to tap into the power of everyone in the kingdom."

"Supervampire queen," Nikolai muttered from where he sat,

alone, at the bar, nursing a Pepsi. I hadn't even realized he was still there. "Great. My dad is going to freaking love that."

Mom offered to take me home in her car, but I explained that I had some unfinished business with Nikolai. Elias and Dad arranged to meet back at our house before sunrise. I guessed Elias was going to arrange some kind of vampire meet-up in the meantime to tell the kingdom what happened to Dad and me and everything. I almost wished I could go with them. I had no idea if the vampires would accept me as their queen. But, then again, if they didn't, that meant I could go back to a normal life. Well, at least as normal as it could be with me linked to God knows how many vampires on some weird blood/psychic level.

Sheesh. When I screwed things up, I really did it *royally*.

I settled into the passenger side gingerly, mindful of the myriad of skin abrasions all over my body. The bumpy ride down to the main drag had me gritting my teeth in order to hold back a stream of curses.

Nikolai was quiet as we drove.

I spent the first twenty minutes not knowing how to start. I kept looking at Nikolai, trying to find the words. I knew I needed to be clear, straightforward, in a way that left no doubts. I had to tell him that I was with Thompson right now, and that it was unfair to Thompson to assume things were doomed. I didn't want Nikolai waiting for me. But, every time I turned to tell him, I caught sight of his face. He looked so pensive and serious, and . . . handsome.

Then I started thinking how unfair it was that Thompson had the unfortunate timing to have asked me out a few hours before Nikolai kissed me. If he hadn't, I could be dating a rock star again.

I dithered so long that it was Nikolai who spoke first. "I can't believe you're the queen of all the vampires. Do you even know how much this sucks?"

Given the constant buzz behind my eyes and the painful way I flinched every time a headlight flashed, I had some idea. But I didn't think he meant the physical side effects. "I suppose that makes things awkward, huh?"

"A little," Nikolai said.

"Plus, I'm dating someone else."

"There is that."

"So I guess there's no 'us,' right?"

He gave me a little frustrated grimace. "Not right now. I'll never stop loving you, Ana."

I had no answer for that, so that was all we said for the rest of the drive home. Even though he sped off the instant I closed the door, I thought that had gone pretty well, considering.

Mom put in a surprising amount of effort to make the craft room nice for my dad. She and I moved some things around to make room for the foldout couch that we'd had stored in the carriage house. It wasn't much, but then, as much as I hated to think about it this way, if the remains of his soul continued to slip away, it wasn't as if he'd be staying with us that long.

At any rate, he seemed very appreciative. Elias helped Dad up the stairs. One of the stops they made must have been to some Igor's house, as Dad came fully dressed and with a grocery bag full of clothes. I brought him up a glass of iced tea. He seemed utterly fascinated by the taste of it. Likewise, he was completely mesmerized by the TV; I was almost afraid to show him Mom's iTouch. It was a little heartbreaking, though, seeing him so excited by everything.

I pulled Elias aside while Mom showed Dad how to work the DVD player. I'd noticed he hadn't brought his rucksack back. "What about you? Where are you going to stay?"

"I have places," he said.

"I know you don't get along with Mom, but you could stay in the basement a little while longer."

He gave me a patient smile. "It's a generous offer, but I don't think a married man should live in someone's mother's basement, do you?"

"Did I miss something? You didn't already do the ceremony, did you?"

"No, but it will be done soon enough."

"That guy is a creep. . . . Hey, I'm queen of Prince Luis too, right? I could just order him to forget about the whole thing." I was surprised by how much the thought of really losing Elias affected me. "I want you to stay with me. I'm going to need you now more than ever."

"You'll have your father at your side. He would make an excellent adviser to the queen."

"But you don't even like that captain guy, do you?"

"You know I don't. I know you don't like it, but your father and I discussed this. I will return," he said ominously. "And this alliance will serve as an advantage to you down the line. I will always be from the Northern Kingdom. You will always be my liege."

A tear rolled down my nose. I wanted to tell him how much I cared for him, but my feelings for Elias had always been complicated. If only I could just clearly say, "I love you," but I couldn't form the words.

Maybe he could feel my thoughts. I certainly felt the warmth of his affection as he kissed my cheek. "The captain is a minor distraction. I won't be in the South for long," he whispered in my ear. "The blood bond we share lasts forever."

It turns out vampire confarreatio ceremonies are even more boring than regular weddings, with all the ancient, flowery language and various political declarations. I don't know what Mom was talking about with the cake either. It was awful, made out of a crunchy, grainy muck someone told me was "spelt."

However, the venue was oddly lovely: an abandoned warehouse on the riverfront. Everyone had brought candles, as if for Midnight Mass, and the points of light were like hundreds of stars. I could feel the contentment and joy in the air, which helped me not be so distracted by everyone's nakedness. It was especially weird to see Elias without his clothes on. I'd gotten used to how he looked dressed. My dad, meanwhile, sat beside me in a heavy wool sweater and jeans. It was warm enough that

I wore a dress I'd bought just for the occasion; it was silver and sleeveless with a scoop down the back. Even Mom admitted I looked glamorous and queenly in it.

I swore Elias kept catching my eye as he intoned his oath to his new partner, and I felt our bond humming stronger with each word. If Captain Creepy sensed it, he would have had a strong case for an annulment—if you could get one of those for a confarreatio. Instead, I really tried to avoid seeing him sans clothes, and my stomach did a little sour twinge when I accidentally caught sight of the two of them together.

I spent a lot of my time focusing closely on Elias's face or looking around at the décor. I could see he wasn't all that into this, but he held himself with his usual grim resolve.

I hoped he'd be okay.

As stuffy and dull as the ceremony had been, the dance afterward was the opposite. Vampires always threw a kind of wild, hypnotic party and, despite my breaking heart, I lost myself in the swirl and chaos of it.

A day later, Elias was packed and gone. I wondered, despite his promise, if I'd ever see him again.

With everything I had going on and finally finishing driver's ed, I didn't really get to have a proper talk with Thompson until a rainy day out at Festival. After cast call, a lot of people went back to hide in their tents. Mom wouldn't let me stay out on the grounds, so I found my way to the Irish cottage. It was exactly what it sounded like. Out in the middle of a grassy patch some distance between the food stalls and the jousting track, sat a whitewashed, single-room cottage. A fire was blazing warmly inside, and the hostess offered me a spot next to a roaring fire. Through the glassless window, I could see only gray. Rain came down in heavy sheets, and thunder boomed overhead. What few patrons had showed up to the front gate had fled once the deluge started. I pulled off my soaking wet, mud-spattered, soft leather boots to let them dry. I almost envied the people dressed as peasants—they went barefoot, whereas I was in cold and soggy stockings.

Bea didn't get into Festival; she seemed preoccupied with everything going on at home. The snippets I heard involved her mom having a complete meltdown when she figured out the reason she'd been drugged. There was talk of divorce, and her mom was threatening to join an evangelical church. I hoped none of that was true. Of course, Bea still found a way to come out here sometimes. She'd dumped Malcolm for the pun guy, Aaron. So I sometimes saw her at after-hours parties on-site.

The door creaked open, making me jump. Thompson loomed like a huge shadow in the doorway. He must have seen me making my way to the cottage door, because he came in only a few minutes after I'd settled down and accepted the tea the hostess offered in her overly broad Irish accent.

"My lady," he said in greeting. The words reminded me so much of Elias that I felt a little twinge of heartache. Of course, everyone called me that out here, but somehow it was different coming from Thompson.

"Sir Matthew," I said, staying in character.

He didn't have on a full suit of armor, but he wore a simple green tunic over a chain mail shirt. At his side, he had buckled a massive sword I knew he'd paid through the nose to get. His dad was so not happy about that; so much for Festival making Thompson any money. Still, he looked pretty authentic, especially since he'd let his hair grow a little. It now hung over his ears.

The hostess asked if it would be all right if she went to get a Scotch egg for breakfast. We promised to look after the place in her absence and told her to take her time.

"It's nice to actually see you," I said. Thanks to Thompson's full-time summer job and the fact that our weekends were shot by a dawn-to-dusk performance here, we hadn't had much time for that dining and dancing he'd promised. Still, I had to give him credit. We talked on the phone almost every night, and he had bought tickets to that annual 1940s Commemorative Air Force hangar dance. We'd be going there next Thursday, and I was curious to see if he'd had as much fun finding World War II–era clothes as I had.

It was everything he'd promised, and I enjoyed being with someone who wasn't always embroiled in some kind of mystical crisis. Nikolai, meanwhile, had written a heartbreaking, sad song about waiting for someone who was wasting her time on someone else. The radio played it constantly.

Elias had, in a weird way, resumed courting me as well. He started sending letters—as in real pen and ink that came in the mailbox. It was a strange way to communicate, but I found it to be much more sensual than e-mail. I could smell a hint of his aftershave on the smooth paper. He even used some kind of fountain pen with rich, deep black ink.

Thompson leaned against the wall, making leather creak and chain mail clink. "Can I ask you something?"

I blinked away my thoughts. His question had a kind of seriousness that sounded as though he'd been working up to asking it. Man, I hoped to heck he wasn't breaking up with me. A little nervously, I agreed. "Sure."

He touched that one spot on his face again. I'd seen him make this unconscious gesture several times previously. I had no idea when it had started, but every once in a while I would see him looking at me with an intense sort of frown, and his fingers would go up and brush across his face, as if he were wiping something from his cheekbone.

Crossing his arms in front of his chest defensively, he said slowly, "I think you licked me once."

Oh shit. Bea's forget-me spell had finally worn off. I must have said something at some point that had triggered the ghost of a memory. Without her to reinforce it, the truth finally resurfaced.

I wanted to lie, but I couldn't do that to him. During our late-night talks, he'd shared with me about living with a mom who was a drunk, and I'd told him my dad had moved back and was slowly dying. So, I smoothed out the velvety fabric of my gown and said, "Yeah, I did. I'm part vampire."

I waited. I thought for sure this would be the end. He'd decide I was crazy and we'd break up. Instead, he just kept looking at me with that severe frown. The rain pounded on the roof, and the fire popped and sizzled.

"Right," he said finally. I couldn't quite read his tone, though I was pretty sure he was just humoring me. "A witch *and* a vampire."

"Yep," I said, holding my ground.

His eyebrow arched skeptically. "A licking vampire? Because I only remember licking. Is there something you need to tell me?"

"In all honesty, I have never bitten you."

Thompson seemed to consider this. He chewed his lip thoughtfully before simply stating, "Okay, then."

We had clearly reached the end of Thompson's ability to deal with this. That was fine by me, as long as I knew the answer to my next question. "Are you still going to take me out?"

A broad smile broke on his handsome face. "Are you kidding? Try to stop me."

That afternoon, the sun broke through the clouds, revealing a gorgeous day. As the sun set, I joined the royal court at the closing gate. Thompson stood beside me. His armor was too battered to be called shining, but, well, it was close enough.

About the Author

Tate Hallaway lives in St. Paul, Minnesota. She is also the author of the Garnet Lacey novels.

CONNECT ONLINE

www.tatehallaway.com
tatehallaway.blogspot.com